SILENT PARTNERS

Sometimes Love Is Deadly

TOM BLOMQUIST

SILENT PARTNERS

First Edition

Cover Design by Tanya Cummings
www.tanyacummings.com

Interior Layout and Design by Martha Camacho
mcdesign12@gmail.com

Author Photograph by Chuck Bowman
Chuck7711@gmail.com

Ascension ©1987 by Colleen Corah Hitchcock, Scottsdale, AZ 85254
Web Site: http://www.ScottsdaleHypnosis.com
E-mail: cchitchcock1@gmail.com Used with permission.

ISBN: 978-0692075784

www.facebook.com/SilentPartners
www.facebook.com/LindstromLegacyPublishing
LindstromLegacy@gmail.com

www.tomblomquist.com

To Ann and Katie, who gave up so much to let me take on the challenge.

ACKNOWLEDGEMENTS

After years of creating stories for the screen the transition to writing one for the page was both fun and demanding. My heartfelt appreciation goes to the merry band of friends, colleagues and family members who offered feedback and other assistance along the way: Alan Bergmann, Ann Blomquist, Ernest R. Blomquist, Chuck Bowman, Lisa Bowman, Jay Bryant, Jackie Callas, Saskia Fuckert, Babs Greyhosky, Colleen Hitchcock, Michael Kennedy, Cindy Klauss, Brennan Klein, Mike Leary, John Loprieno, Bryan Michael McGuire, Reed Moran, Marcy Vosburgh Myers, Peggy O'Neal, Dennis Palumbo, Scott Richter, Britt Blomquist Roehm, Christie Havey Smith, Andy Stahl, Mike Stevens, Lynn Steveson, Lisa Sullivan, Richard Vetere, Peter J. Wacks, Linda Walderbach and Chris Wilson.

Additionally, I want to offer special thanks to Philip Klein, MD; Warren Line, MD; and Police Inspector Larry Bloom for sharing their respective forensic, medical and law enforcement insights with me; and to writer-producer Steven L. Sears for posing a transformational "What if...?" creative question at the perfect time.

I also owe an everlasting debt to three talented women for their crucial contributions: Tanya Cummings for her stunning cover design, Martha Camacho for her elegant interior layout and design and Bonnie Blackburn for her thoughtful and expert manuscript editing.

Finally, I want to express my gratitude to actors William Sterling, Tahnee Harrison, and John Loprieno for their compelling portrayals of Zack, Nicole and Father Solano in the SILENT PARTNERS promotional YouTube video; and to Mizuki Araki, Bonnie Blackburn, Bobby Bowfinger, Chuck Bowman, Ulyana Chava, Mascha Eberhard, Ashley Boehne Ehlers, Sarah Emmons, Jason Foster, Israel Gomez, David Grzesik, Alex Iseri, Geoff Koch, Kelby McClellan, Bryan Michael McGuire, Reed Moran, Rafael Nieto, Kevin O'Brien, Peggy O'Neal, Vincent Pastor, Daylyn Paul, Raina Pratto, Dana Shockley, Andy Stahl, Donna Thomas, Brianna Werder and Robert S. Woods for their meticulous work on its production.

Zack and Nicole's story could not have been told without them all.

Prologue

A lot of people think they know what happened to Nicole Branson. After all, her untimely death sent shockwaves across the globe. That it happened in Los Angeles, where she contributed so much to the community, made her passing even more heartbreaking. Next to the Michael Jackson, Whitney Houston, and Chester Bennington tragedies it is one of the most talked-about celebrity death scandals that Southern California has ever seen.

Who could forget the devotion that the media predators on *Access Hollywood*, *Extra*, *Inside Edition*, and innumerable cable news shows demonstrated in giving us our daily ration of salacious speculation about the beautiful pop singer? Not to mention the energetic efforts of all those chatty Ken and Barbie television anchor teams across the country. There were even times when I was convinced that Harvey Levin and his obnoxious TMZ staff might have actual meltdowns on camera, they'd become so consumed by their stream of exclusive revelations about Nicole.

That's why I had to wince a little when I checked my email in the jock lounge at The Mighty K-BINGE FM. I was running late prepping my overnight oldies music show, *The Midnight Hitman*, leaving little time to spare. And now here was a fan informing me that he knew the untold story behind Nicole Branson's passing. How any detail could have been overlooked by police or the swarms of gossip hounds covering the story during the previous three weeks was never mentioned. Nor was the reason that he decided to share this little gem with me.

Needless to say, the email came from an anonymous Gmail account and it wasn't signed. Wackos rarely sign names to their junk mail, I concluded.

But halfway through my time-honored playlist, somewhere between golden musical nuggets by The Cowsills and Leslie Gore, I decided to jump ahead a few decades to play a favorite Nicole Branson track, "More Than I Should". That's when I had second thoughts about ignoring the email. Maybe it was leftover journalistic residue from my early news stints in Dayton, Rockford, and St. Louis.

Or maybe it was the cumulative effect of all the classic rock that I ingested through twenty plus years of doing Top Forty countdowns. Whatever the reason, I re-read the message and found passion in the writing, an urgency that was impossible to ignore. This wasn't a kook on the lunatic fringe, I realized. These words came from a deeper place.

And to be honest, I still had unsettled feelings about Nicole's death that I wanted to resolve.

So when the morning drive-time team staggered in at five, I called the number that my informer had provided. He'd invited me to call when my shift ended and I figured what the hell, at worst it would cost me the price of breakfast to meet the guy.

The young man waiting at Du-Par's Restaurant at the Farmers Market on Fairfax Avenue that morning introduced himself as Zack Raskin. He was in his mid-twenties and sincerity filled his intelligent eyes. The rest of his appearance was just this side of alarming, however. He looked disheveled and thin, like he'd been to hell and back. I eventually came to realize that his hell was not an abstraction. It was real.

Zack and I spent a lot of time in coffee shops over the next few weeks while he laid out his story, starting with why he chose me in the first place – he read on Twitter once that Nicole listened to my show. With that connection made, he carefully detailed the rest of his saga as if duty bound to explain why a medical student at the top of his class would turn his life upside down over a woman he'd known less than twenty-four hours.

Despite having traded my personal naiveté for dogged cynicism a long time ago, I was nothing less than astounded to hear how someone's innocence could be so quickly corrupted and his euphoria twisted into inconceivable agony.

Although the length of our conversations ran from a few minutes to an entire afternoon on one occasion, they always ended the same way: with Zack politely excusing himself to leave for another appointment. It was only in what turned out to be our final session that he divulged what those mysterious obligations of his were really all about, and with whom.

Then he vanished from my life much as he entered it: a letter arrived at the radio station simply thanking me for listening.

In an attempt to present the most accurate account possible, I've woven the essence of my interviews with Zack together with commentary from his family, friends, teachers, fellow students, and co-workers. I've included the insights of police investigators and people in Nicole's life, too, the musicians and others who knew her best. Filling in the gaps are observations of mine about the intriguing pop music world where Nicole lived and worked.

But at the center of it all is the puzzling odyssey that Zack so painstakingly disclosed to me. Some people will have difficulty believing it, as I initially did. After all, try as any of us might there are simply some things that no amount of investigation can ever verify. You'll have to judge those for yourself.

However, one fact is undeniable: *sometimes love is deadly.*

Tom B
The Midnight Hitman
Los Angeles, California

Chapter One

Everyone has a dream. Some people manage to stay realistic about theirs, setting into motion a series of goals that will hopefully take them where they want to go in life. Or at least get them close to it. Unfortunately, there are those who never quite manage to get a handle on what is attainable and what is not, and they are almost always doomed to endure resentment over illusions unfulfilled. But whether someone's dream is practical or not, there is nothing worse than a bucket of cold water being tossed on it.

Especially by someone in a position to know.

Doctor Linda Sandberg was just such an authority to the seventy-five attentive young men and women as she strode into the lecture hall one sunny April morning. Sandberg had been among the most popular teachers at the University of California Los Angeles David Geffen School Of Medicine since arriving a decade earlier. The fifty-three year-old daughter of devoted 1960's-era hippy parents, she seldom acknowledged her unconventional upbringing at a Lake Tahoe commune. In fact, almost no one knew that her given name was not Linda, but the flower-power inspired Sunshine Daydream. Sandberg wisely adopted her grandmother's name when she realized that she might want to be taken seriously as a medical professional and educator one day.

And taken seriously she was. Admired by students for her insight, dedication, and caring, she was also widely respected by her campus colleagues for holding both a medical degree and Ph.D. from Stanford University.

On this particular morning, Sandberg took an unusually long moment to study the faces of the individuals occupying the raised rows of long wooden auditorium tables in the gleaming state-of-the-art medical education facility. She skipped her customary greeting to print something in red dry marker on the white board in the well of the hall. "This is the contact information for the University Placement and Career Planning Center," she began simply. "You can either call them or walk over in person. They aren't that far away."

Students copied that down without knowing why. But everyone was used to that with Doc Sandberg. She had a way of taking the rhetorical scenic route in her presentations.

Setting her marker aside, the professor toyed with the Navajo turquoise and silver necklace that she wore every day, an unconscious indicator that her point was imminent. "I'm sorry to say that some of you are going to be needing career counseling, since so many of you are apparently under the impression that getting through medical school is easier than it was getting in."

The statement thickened the air. This was not petty admonishment. Doc Sandberg did not play games. Bodies squirmed uncomfortably, accompanied by a smattering of throats being cleared. After four years of busting your butt in college and then surviving UCLA's unforgiving 2.18 percent medical school acceptance rate, this was not what you wanted to hear about your dream of becoming a physician.

"I make that observation based on your exam performance," she concluded, clutching a fistful of test papers with tacit disapproval. "If you people had been treating human beings rather than answering exam questions, most of you would be spending your summer being deposed in malpractice suits."

She retrieved her marker and printed three large letters on the board and underlined them: A-D-R. "Adverse Drug Reaction... three of the most important words in a doctor's vocabulary," she explained firmly. "They haunt even competent professionals because two hundred thirty thousand times a year they kill patients who don't have to die. By some estimates that figure is even higher."

Sandberg ambled up the smoke-gray steps of the left side aisle, waiting for students to finish typing notes into their tablets. "I know how much you all love your precious phone apps, but believe me when I say that in private practice you won't always have Epocrates or Medscape at your disposal. In the trenches of real world medicine, you actually have to master this information. A devastating concept for some of you, I'm sure."

Her attention then focused on a sleeping ponytailed blond male in the back row wearing a Homer Simpson baseball cap and wrinkled cotton shirt on which was emblazoned the declaration: *I'm naked under this t-shirt.*

His name was Zack Raskin and Sandberg was well aware of his campus reputation. As laid back as he was tall and slender, he breezed through life with such uncommon nonchalance that student folklore had written him off as a total flake.

But that was not the case at all. Zack Raskin was simply a good-natured guy who refused to get worked up over anything. Ever. His friends often warned that he needed a more cynical and aggressive approach to life, for fear that his unwavering optimism would only lead to undeserved personal suffering.

And to the observers sitting near him that morning, suffering was personified by Doc Sandberg and she was closing in fast. Zack's roommate, Doug McKay, was the most concerned of the onlookers. Studious, stocky, neatly dressed, and barely five foot five, he was Zack's opposite in every way, so much so that he often felt more like Zack's guardian than friend. Like now, as he whispered over his shoulder, "Zack, heads up...!"

Zack's only response was an extended snore that seemed unnaturally coarse for his fragile-looking build.

Sandberg, meanwhile, continued her remarks as she drifted closer to his seat. "Furosemide diuretics for pulmonary edema that lead to collapse of the circulatory system, clots, and shock..." Her voice reverberated off the scalloped ceiling the way a seasoned actor uses the acoustics of an old theater to heightened effect. "Chloramphenicol antibiotics and fatal anemia..." she progressed before pausing beside Zack, where lots of slumberous wood was being sawed, "And renal pelvic tumors in abusers of phenacetin analgesics."

The entire class was watching now. Several women giggled and the professor silenced them with a glance before tapping Zack's arm out from under his chin. He awakened with a disoriented jolt and the sight of Doc Sandberg looming over him was a startling wake-up call, indeed.

Blinking the sleepiness away, Zack shifted his lanky frame and smiled good-naturedly. "Eh, what's up, Doc?"

Students braced themselves for what they were sure would be Sandberg's scathing oration on disappointing med students on whom she has had the displeasure of wasting energy. But she had a surprise for them as she said loudly enough for everyone to hear, "Allow me to introduce the only student to get every one of my drug questions right: Zack Raskin."

Reactions ping-ponged around the hall, ranging from uncertainty to incredulousness, though it should not have been surprising to most. Not to Doug McKay, anyway. As Zack's best friend he knew how consistently well Zack performed on exams. Frankly, Zack's effortless intelligence was one of the incongruities that made him so exceptional, and frustrating, to live with.

Sandberg handed Zack his test with straightforward curiosity. "Mister Raskin, would you please enlighten us as to why your pharmacological knowledge is so much more extensive than the rest of your colleagues?"

Zack's mind was a blank. "I dunno," he offered. "Guess I must be using the right drugs."

The portion of UCLA serving as home to its acclaimed medical complex has neither the rich historic character nor grand architectural tradition of Dickson Plaza at the center of campus. Instead, the dense cluster of huge medical structures straddling the University's perimeter and adjacent to Westwood Village are strikingly modern.

Zack and Doug rounded Tiverton Drive South on foot, passing the School of Dentistry. Like a busy city street at rush hour, the sidewalk was an international potpourri of humankind. While some of the masses were dressed in suits, crisp white lab coats, surgical scrubs, colorful religious scarves, or edgy hipster jeans, the dominant springtime campus fashion preference featured classic t-shirts, cargo shorts, and sandals. To an outsider this lively processional would have been a people-watcher's paradise, but these were familiar images to Zack and Doug, who wove their way through them without noticing.

Doug, for one, was still preoccupied with what took place in Doc Sandberg's class. "Guess I must be using the right drugs," he snipped, mimicking Zack's earlier line. "Who are you supposed to be, Jimmy Fallon?"

Zack shrugged with his usual boyish innocence. "I did okay on the test."

"And how you keep doing that I'll never know," Doug protested. But the dig lacked the zing it once carried, since he had expressed the same sentiment many times before. Zack's grades in school had been a maddening phenomenon ever since they first shared an undergraduate chemistry lab table at UC Santa Barbara, when Zack absorbed complicated formulas the way other people take to kitchen recipes. The argument between them over exam scores had long been more of a ritual than anything else. "You have to be the worst, most miserable, pathetic excuse for a student there ever was," he went on. "You don't study, you snore through class..."

"Hey, a guy's got to sleep," Zack countered, as if that explained everything.

"I'm busting my hump and what do I get? Seventy-nine percent!"

"Geez, McKay. That sucks," Zack pronounced as he turned into the shallow courtyard of the Marion Davies Children's Health Center. "I thought you studied."

"That's what drives me nuts! No matter how hard I work, no matter what I do, I never rise above average. But you, you worthless piece of scholastic crap, you don't do diddly and you cruise along like you're on vacation."

Zack's reaction was automatic. "Well, that blows!"

Doug was stunned to think that he might have actually won his point, a rare feat in their relationship, until he grasped that Zack was not reacting to him, but to the sight of a car being towed from an ABSOLUTELY NO PARKING zone. His car, the one with the counterfeit *Official University Vehicle* placard in the window.

Pieces of Zack's dilapidated red Honda Prelude clattered to the pavement as a company hired by UCLA to solve its chronic parking problems carted it away.

"They could've at least been gentle," Zack muttered. "She's not exactly showroom fresh anymore."

Doug took in the sight of his roommate on the neatly

manicured green median grass, protectively holding the rusted and pockmarked side mirror of a vehicle that only he could love. "Why don't you just break down and buy a damn parking sticker?" he finally asked.

"Who knew they'd catch me again?"

Clearly, a rational person would have gotten the hint after being towed three times in one semester and Doug told him so. Zack guiltily met his look before confessing that it had actually been twice that many. "I've tried to block the pain," he added with rising emotion. "Each time I go to the impound, the old girl's more traumatized than before."

There was a time when Doug might have assumed that Zack was putting him on, but in five years of living together in Santa Barbara and Westwood he had come to understand that the melodramatic sentiments Zack revealed in moments like this, such as gazing wistfully at the mirror in his arms, were real. Doug also knew that beneath that idiosyncratic personality was a more serious individual that he hoped to meet one day.

Reaching up to put a comforting hand on Zack's shoulder, Doug guided him along the sidewalk. "Zack," he found himself asking, "Seriously, of all the things in the world you could've gone into, all the hundreds of available career options, what possessed you to pick medicine?"

There was no hesitation in Zack's reply. "I thought it'd be cool wearing one of those neat headband deals with the little magnifying thingy on it."

Doug cocked his head in amazement. Astounding as it was, he was pretty sure that Zack was not kidding.

Westwood, California, like so many towns in sprawling urban centers, is wedged between other large municipalities. What makes Westwood unique are the other two ingredients in its real estate sandwich: Brentwood and Beverly Hills, two of the most affluent cities in America. Yet despite its upscale neighbors, Westwood is no longer quite the charming village that it was a few years ago.

Economic hard times eroded the previously immune community, as upscale pedestrian malls in Santa Monica, Old Pasadena, Glendale, Universal City, and the popular Grove in the Fairfax District stole Westwood's recreational thunder. Even its landmark movie theaters, once a favorite destination for Los Angeles couples on a Saturday night, lost much of their lure to larger Cineplex's across the city. The presence of UCLA and the medical center had become the main barrier to the further decline of the iconic Spanish and Art Deco-influenced town.

As Doug's blue Toyota Rav4 wheeled past the Bruin Theater on Broxton Avenue, Zack cradled what remained of his side mirror in one arm while scrolling through the menu on Doug's iPhone with his free hand.

Doug gave him a biting look as Zack groaned his disapproval at the music list. "Let me guess, my library doesn't do it for you," Doug began before editing himself. He knew that he had just made the mistake of challenging Zack's judgment, which was akin to pouring gasoline on hot coals.

"McKay, your taste bites the big bazzodi," Zack decreed while flipping through the menu.

"Is that a medical term?" Doug pushed back, "Or have you become an authority on everything."

Zack reacted to the titles before him with revulsion, holding the phone away from his nose as if it might be contaminated. "A Chorus Line? CATS?!"

"Those happen to be highly regarded Broadway standards," Doug bristled, grabbing the phone before Zack could continue.

"Even for you this's off-the-charts tight ass."

"You leave my ass out of this."

"No can do, old friend," Zack announced while producing a pair of surgeon's gloves from his book bag.

Doug did a double take. "I don't even want to know what those are for."

The gloves snapped loudly over Zack's hands. "Cultural therapy."

A student cyclist momentarily distracted Doug by swerving into his lane, so he did not notice Zack plugging in an iPod.

Suddenly, heavy metal power chords and manic drumming filled the car with a blaring sonic explosion that rattled the fillings in Doug's teeth. Screaming in agony, Doug yanked the player from his stereo and flung it into the street. An instant later, the sound of shattering plastic was muted by the wheels of a passing carload of teenage girls singing along with a bouncy Justin Bieber tune as it bellowed from their radio.

"You owe me an iPod, dude."

"Only if I can program it first," Doug declared.

"Okay, Iron Maiden wasn't the best choice," Zack reasoned as his mind abruptly shifted gears the way it often did. "Hey, I know...! What're you doing tomorrow night?"

"Having my hearing checked," Doug complained.

Zack manufactured a smile. It was important to humor his roommate at times like this, when he was acting like an old fart. "Come with me to a concert."

"And pay to hear that garbage? No way."

"This's different. This is... Nicole Branson." Zack paused for effect after saying the name, certain that Doug would reconsider.

"I don't care if it's the Elvis comeback," Doug answered. "Forget it."

Zack was too baffled to be hurt, which he normally would have been. Doug's inclination for anything traditional had finally crossed the line: Nicole was, as everyone knew, the amazing singer that superstars from Stevie Nicks to Celine Dion were calling the most invigorating female artist to come along in years. And that was saying something, considering the talents of women like Beyoncé, Katy Perry, Christina Aguilera, Kelly Clarkson, Carrie Underwood, Gwen Stefani, Lady Gaga, and Adele.

"We're talking about a Grammy winner," Zack rejoined.

But Doug would hear none of it. Stopping beneath the high-rise office corridor of congested Wilshire Boulevard for a long red light, he turned emphatically in his seat. "It's still rock and roll, okay? Which translated from the Latin means *excrement*."

Zack had to laugh at Doug, whom he judged had attained a new personal best in absurdity. "Then forget the music," he added. "Every hetero guy on the planet wants to meet Nicole. You are straight, aren't you?"

A trio of attractive professional women in business suits walked past the car and a realization dawned on Doug that he could not believe he had missed. "Wait a minute," he began, "is that why I'm driving you to an over-priced Beverly Hills hair salon? Because you're fantasizing about meeting that bimbo?"

"She's not a bimbo," Zack came back. "She's special."

"And you're not, okay? You're just a student and part-time EMT, in case you forgot. No bombshell like that's gonna look twice at you."

"Once is all I ask," Zack disclosed before regretting it. Doug McKay was the last person he should be discussing this with. To Doug, who did not have a romantic bone in his body, pop songs were clutter found on radio stations that had nothing else to play. And films like Casablanca were about wars, not the love-struck people caught up in them. He would never comprehend Zack's interest in a woman he had never met.

When the traffic signal changed, Zack seized it as a tactic for changing the subject. "Light's green, McKay."

But Doug was not about to budge. He was going to nail Zack for his idiosyncratic behaviors once and for all. "Speaking of bombshells," he started, "what about the time you saw Stacy Keibler? Nobody else would've even known who she was, but you followed her around the Galleria until she called security, remember?"

"I was only waiting to get an autograph," Zack claimed. "I mean, it was *Stacy*. The legs of the WWE, *The Weapon of Mass Seduction* on *Dancing with the Stars*! George Clooney was out of his mind to let her get away."

Doug stared in disbelief that Zack might actually be comfortable with that explanation. By now cars behind them were stacked up like a parade waiting to happen and people were honking their horns, but Doug was prepared to sit right where they were until he exacted an admission of psychological deficiency from his passenger.

And Zack knew it. He was trapped in the vehicle and going nowhere until he caved. Thinking fast, he mumbled, "Oh look, I'm only two miles from Rodeo Drive. Thanks for the lift."

A second later, he was out of the Rav4 and walking east on Wilshire, hoping that Doug would not follow yelling the rest of his criticisms through the open car window.

Mercifully, he did not.

NEWS ITEM:

The Hollywood Reporter, April 20

In the season's first blush with the new concert season, rock canary Nicole Branson has responded to boffo ticket sales for her upcoming stand at the Greek Theatre by extending the show for two additional nights. The singer, who is known to prefer the rapport of small houses to gargantuan stadiums, has said she's delighted to have more time to spend with her hometown fans.

Chapter Two

The Los Angeles Greek Theatre is a cultural landmark in a city that does not have many. At least, does not have many major landmarks with significance beyond its grand history of movie studios and film stars. Located in the hills of the Santa Monica Mountains above affluent residential Los Feliz on Hollywood's eastern edge, The Greek is nestled at the base of mammoth Griffith Park. It is a charming outdoor concert stage with rare audience intimacy that has been a favorite venue for artists for decades.

An hour before Nicole Branson's concert, a steady flow of fans wended through a maze of ticket scalpers, merchandise vendors, and miscellaneous hustlers outside the amphitheater compound as recorded pop music beckoned from within.

Since Nicole was a crossover artist, meaning that she appealed to fans of multiple genres, the assortment of humankind on opening night was diverse. As an eclectic blend of timeless Beatles, Beach Boys, and Eagles hits played on the sound system with new ones by Maroon 5, Pharrell Williams, and The Band Perry, aging baby boomers passed through turnstiles behind sunburned surfers, Millennials, and members of Generation X. In reviewing the evening on television one fashion critic noted, "*The smorgasbord of breast augmentations on display at the Greek was one for the Guinness Records.*"

But a rock concert is more than an excuse to show off triumphs in cosmetic surgery. And it is more than music. Over the years performances have evolved into full-blown theatrical experiences, where words and music are wrapped in elaborate packages of computer lighting and studio-quality sound, embellished with enthralling combinations of dance, costuming, video projections, and special effects. The results can transport audiences to a sensory place not accessible by other means, and Nicole Branson's concerts were renowned for being among the best transportation around.

As with any large public event, the unseen support staff at the Greek included backstage emergency medical personnel; in this case a two-man team from the Willis Ambulance Service, where Zack worked to help pay for his medical schooling. And since it was no secret to anyone at the company what it would mean for him to see his favorite entertainer, Zack's partner Angelo Giambalvo generously arranged for this plum assignment.

So while Angie, as Angelo preferred to be known, verified insurance forms in the theater manager's office, Zack whistled cheerfully and unloaded his black fiberglass paramedic case from the ambulance with the distinctive blue and gold Willis logo. Peeking at fans passing through the turnstiles, he could feel the crackle of anticipation in the air. Like him, these were not uninitiated civilians who needed convincing about Nicole's many qualities. They were devotees. *The difference was that he was one who was going to see it all from backstage! Alriiiiight!*

Now if only he could stop his heart from palpitating. After taking a quick hit of oxygen from his portable tank, Zack approached the Artists Entrance with faux indifference that belied his excitement—as if backstage passes to major concerts were routine for him.

Pausing at the security kiosk, he took no small pleasure in searching his pockets for identification. Little did the guard know, Zack privately gloated, he had not only double-checked his wallet before leaving home, but he also brought his birth certificate. No way was he taking the chance of not being admitted!

The guard issued him a security badge on a lanyard bearing Nicole Branson's recreated autograph and Zack gleefully slid it over his head as he entered the restored 1930's-era building. With his new salon-created slicked-back hairstyle, upturned collar, and carnation in his EMT shirt, the guard must have thought he looked more like someone's Las Vegas nightmare than a medical specialist.

Of course, Zack was unaware of any disapproving looks that he incurred. He was too distracted by the dynamic activity that he encountered when he reached the backstage inner-sanctum. While he had assisted at concerts in the past, this one felt unique. His attention jumped from one thing to another determined to remember every detail, from the blue cyclorama and fly lines that dangled from the loft above to the three seductive backup singers in a dim corner running through harmonies for the a cappella opening of "Love Machine", one of his favorite songs.

Panning his eyes past assorted curtains and power panels, he settled on two musicians whom he recognized from Nicole's videos, the brawny drummer with the chopped Caligula haircut and the striking blonde bass player who could hold her own in a *Sports Illustrated* Swimsuit Edition.

Zack was surprised by how relaxed everyone was, as they drank beer and smoked cigarettes. How could they not be nervous before an opening night in Los Angeles?

Then he wandered onto the stage, the main performance area of which was concealed from the audience by massive opaque scrims, and he brightened at the sight. *This was where it all happened.* He knew from attending Nicole's previous concerts and watching video clips on YouTube that the scrims would become transparent to reveal the band when the lighting came up, before vanishing in a shower of sparks and cloud of colored smoke that would cue her signature arrival. Zack was humbled by the privilege of being there.

A muscular roadie in a tattered sleeveless *Aerosmith Global Warming Tour* sweatshirt that revealed more tattoos than skin was making final adjustments to the drum kit. Zack became conscious of the wall of amplifiers, racks of keyboards, and assortment of guitars, and the complex logistics of putting on a show like this began to sink in.

As the tubby sound of a Chris Daughtry song playing for the audience drifted shapelessly towards him, he gathered that the floor monitors positioned around the stage were not being used to reproduce Daughtry's recording—meaning that without them Nicole and her band would never know what their concert sounded like. Everything they played would be reduced to the same auditory sludge that was being discharged now.

Zack grimaced at the memory of his own brief adventure as a musician, a sixth grade band concert the year he attempted to play the trumpet. He never admitted to Mr. Rogiewicz, the band director, the extent to which he had been faking his playing ability during five tedious months of rehearsals. Zack figured that he would simply pantomime the notes, thereby impressing a girl in his French class who suggested that she admired people with musical talent, but whose name he could no longer even remember.

Unfortunately, an outbreak of measles decimated his school the week of the big night. One by one, the trumpet section succumbed to the virus and the chances for pulling off his sham dwindled. He would have claimed illness, too, except that would have meant missing his first Boy Scout camping trip the following morning. As it turned out, Zack was one of only three members of the trumpet section healthy enough to appear that fateful evening and he was puzzled to discover that the other two players were even worse than him. A brusque Mr. Rogiewicz confiscated his trumpet after the show and thus ended the symphonic legacy of the Raskin clan.

Snapping out of his reminiscence, Zack noticed another crewmember checking the network of cables that had been neatly routed around the stage under protective plastic covers: he was a forty-something ox with an unfiltered cigarette dangling from his mouth and a complexion that had seen way too much sun. Zack would have bet money on the existence of pre-cancerous moles under Ox Man's unkempt mop of hair or metastatic lesions on the charred leather passing for tissue in his lungs.

So much for the glamorous world of rock and roll, he thought.

A commotion of voices out front yanked Zack's attention to a flock of press photographers busily snapping pictures and shooting video of celebrities arriving for the show. Peering around a scrim, he recognized actors Jude Law, Halle Berry, Jennifer Garner, Ashton Kutcher, Mila Kunis, and some other celebrities whose names he did not know arriving at their V.I.P. seats. It made Zack feel good that even big stars admired Nicole. He also identified Kim Kardashian in the front row with her entourage, but since he never understood why she was famous the sighting failed to resonate.

Just then, the overpowering scent of English Leather cologne announced the arrival of someone behind him. A meaty paw plopped on Zack's shoulder, confirming that his partner had arrived. A former army medic who had seen it all on the battlefield and in the years since as a paramedic, Angie Giambalvo was an imposing, barrel-chested specimen who carried himself like the athlete he once was, an All-Conference linebacker from Chicago's tough East

Leyden High School. What was formerly muscle had now partially turned to fat, but he was still in excellent shape for his age.

Angie also had a wealth of wisdom to share with anyone within earshot. And now was one of those occasions, as he looked Zack over. "Kid, how long you been riding the meat wagon?" he asked in the Chicago accent he would carry to his grave.

"Almost a year."

Angie plucked the carnation from Zack's shirt. "In all that time, you ever see me dress like that?"

Zack's morale sank. Angie's opinion was important because despite his penchant for noxious cologne and other excesses of taste, including socks that rarely matched, he was an effective mentor. "The collar doesn't work, either?" Zack speculated, already sensing the answer.

"Lemme put it this way. It was great on Ming The Merciless, but on you it's dog puke."

Zack lowered his collar, requiring no further input. The canine vomit analogy pretty much said it all.

"What's with you kids today?" Angie continued, never one to stop with an initial remark. "You're a fan of this Branson babe, right?"

"Of course I am."

"And you gotta thing for her."

Zack glanced at his feet. "Well, I wouldn't call it a thing..."

"Did you work me over for weeks to get this assignment?"

"Well, yeah."

"Then it's a thing," the master concluded.

Zack did not resist. The fact was he did feel something for Nicole—an infatuation, crush, whatever his roommate called it. But what a man like Angie would never understand was that Zack's feelings weren't anything like the torch that Angie carried for Ann-Margret in his youth. Sure, Nicole's sex appeal first attracted Zack's attention, but it was the insights of her songs that affected him in an almost spiritual way. Her music came from her soul and it avoided the mawkish sentimentality that so many contemporary singers were peddling.

And like forty million other people in the world, Zack also

followed her on social media. She was generous in sharing her views with her fans, which only solidified his attachment to her. He could not help but sense that he knew her personally.

However, Zack knew Angie very well and he would doubtless claim his own regard for Ann-Margret as spiritual. That is why Zack chose to expedite things. "You busted me, Angie, I got it bad for her."

"Then you don't want her convulsing," he asserted. "Ya gotta come across suave, ya know?" But he saw in Zack's reaction that his point was not getting across. "You know, cool. Like McQueen."

"Who?"

"What are you talkin' about, who?! You never saw a Steve McQueen movie?"

Finally, the reference clicked. "Oh, yeah, the director. *12 Years a Slave*, right?"

Angie shook his head with disgust. "Not him. The real McQueen."

Zack was lost. Then it hit him, "Oh, you mean the actor!"

"He was more than some actor, okay? Stallone's an actor. And Chuck Norris. McQueen is the coolest guy there ever was..."

"Yeah, he was pretty good in *Vampire Diaries* and *Piranha 3D*" Zack answered.

Angie stared blankly. "*Piranha 3D*?"

"Yeah. Steven McQueen."

"Okay, I don't know who the hell that is. I'm talking *about Steve McQueen. Thomas Crown Affair, Sand Pebbles, Great Escape*, you know what I mean? The chicks couldn't get enough of him and you wanna know why?"

"Sure."

"It was always the same with McQueen, that's why. Even in that dog shit *Towering Inferno*, with him he never had to say a word," Angie insisted while punctuating his commentary with his best steely McQueen look, which registered on his face like a man squinting into the sun. "You want a lady's attention," he announced, ya gotta think MCQUEEN."

Zack was hanging on every word. "... McQueen."

It was a lovely evening for an outdoor concert. The night blue sky glistened with constellations, all traces of haze having been chased away by the latest Santa Ana winds blowing in from the Mojave Desert. Underscoring the effect were the springtime fragrances of eucalyptus and wildflowers that were everywhere in the hills surrounding the Greek Theatre.

A sassy Irish girl group named Mad For Wavin served as the warm-up act playing a spirited set of contemporary rockers from their album, *Feature This*, which was a big hit in Europe. Zack could not help thinking how unsatisfying it must be to open for someone as popular as Nicole Branson, knowing that the audience really only cares about the headliner they paid a fortune to see.

And that headliner was all Zack was interested in, as well. Especially now, with her performance so close at hand. He could think of nothing else. While Angie manned their post in the wings during Mad For Wavin's show, Zack wandered the building. Angie could call by walkie-talkie if anything serious came up.

Zack's mind raced through a succession of scenarios as he imagined what it would be like to meet Nicole. Mental images of every suave mannerism he had ever seen were tried on like masks for a Halloween party, as were moments from every old Steve McQueen flick that he could recall.

At first his foray backstage was uneventful. Then, as he paused to admire a poster at a stage entrance, an adaptation of Nicole's *Best of the Best* DVD cover art, he was vividly reminded of why he was there: the long-legged woman standing on that pristine tropical beach was beyond beautiful.

In her dressing room one floor beneath the spot where Zack stood, Nicole was feeling anything but beautiful. She felt like she looked, which was tired and unhappy. Staring at her reflection in the makeup mirror, she was sickened by how often she had indulged her moods recently. There was far too much of the woe-is-me attitude that she disliked in others, especially pampered celebrities. As if existence as a pop star entitled anyone to the recipe for happiness.

Brushing her hair, she pushed away her cheerless spirits. The activity was a reassuring throwback to childhood, when time alone like this meant refuge from the suffocating consequences of her mother's mental illness. Though it was scarcely anything that she would admit, she suspected that her career would not be where it was if she had not evaded her mother's frequent bouts of anxiety by singing to herself in her room while brushing her luxurious auburn hair.

She was, of course, wearing her hair shorter now. The record company thought the new look would garner extra magazine covers and she did not resist. At age twenty-eight she knew the advantages of periodically letting executives believe their opinions mattered. The funny thing was, this time they turned out to be right. Nicole's new coiffure got more press coverage than milestones of real consequence. She sometimes feared for the welfare of the news editors and bloggers who had nothing better to do than devote valuable resources to the strands of protein growing from her scalp.

No matter. She did not care what the media thought about anything. Or music executives for that matter. There was only one opinion of consequence in her life and for him she would shave her whole damn head if he asked her to. Even now, despite the gnawing heartache of knowing it was over between them.

She caught herself glancing at her phone and pried her gaze back to the mirror. If a call came it would not be him, she knew. It would be business. Everything was business these days. Her personal life was ancient history.

Upstairs, Zack was still looking at Nicole's poster when he was stricken by a jolt of apprehension. *What if Doug was right? Only a total imbecile would come here hoping to meet her!* The word "pitiful" leapt to mind. Zack had gotten carried away with his fascination.

But it was not the first time. Even before the infamous Stacy Keibler incident at the mall, Zack had established a lousy track record with women because he tended to idealize them and then misread their intentions. Although he was not bad looking, he was not handsome. He had always been too thin to be physically impressive and he had the kind of wide-set mouth that appeared to be on the verge of smiling even when it was not. The resulting package never seemed to dazzle the opposite sex.

A wave of pessimism hit him. *What had he been thinking?! Did he honestly think the plaintive lyrics that Nicole wrote were somehow meant for him?* He wanted to die.

No, he fathomed, death would only leave him lying on the floor to be discovered by the very woman he now hoped to avoid. The ocean of anxiety he was swimming in mandated that if he wanted to keep any shred of integrity he must elude her at all cost. But he would have to act fast. Mad For Wavin could be heard playing one of their last numbers and Nicole's people were beginning to gather backstage. A crush of musicians, singers, roadies, and security staff would soon fill the area.

Zack scanned the room for any sign of her, hoping to catch a glimpse while being terrified of achieving it. He felt like an infatuated kid and he was desperate for relief. Spotting a side door, he slipped through it.

In the small staging area Zack was gratified to find few people to contend with. He felt inadequate enough without having to make small talk with disinterested strangers. Two parking attendants played cards in a corner surrounded by haphazard stacks of music stands, metal chairs, and instrument cases. Zack felt safe in his new oasis.

He crossed to a craft services table with a battered plywood top on which several sandwich platters were displayed. Judging from the condition of the remnants, the musicians and concert crew must have attacked the buffet like a pack of starving animals. Passing up the fragmented slices of deli meat and cheese that had grown stiff enough to shingle a roof, Zack gravitated to the tall commercial coffee urn. And after gratefully discovering that the dented and dull aluminum container was still plugged in, he rummaged through packages of napkins and plastic plates looking for a cup. Finding one, Zack relished his prize as only an unrepentant coffee addict could: no matter how old or bitter a brew may be, the only criterion for true fanatics is that their java be hot.

He sipped from the scalding Styrofoam and questioned how he would explain his change of attitude about Nicole to Angie. He could already hear the reaction ringing in his ears, *"Jesus H. Christ! You think you're not good enough for this chick, is that it?"* And that would be followed by one of Angie's sausage-like fingers jabbing him in the sternum. *"It's a good thing McQueen ain't here to see this."*

But Zack did not have time to dwell on the reprimand. It was time to face it head-on. Mad For Wavin could no longer be heard through the tinny backstage public address system, which meant that he was due to relieve Angie.

When he turned to leave, however, he slammed into someone who had materialized beside him. The faceless image of a woman dodging the splash of steaming liquid from his hand jerked into focus a split second later: *It was Nicole!*

In the aftermath of the collision, she and Zack chattered at once, neither hearing the other.

"Oh shit, it's you!"

"It's all right."

"Look what I did..."

"No harm done..."

"I am so... stupid... but of course you already knew that..."

"Truly, it's okay. Not a drop on me."

They went on like that for a while before floundering to a stop. Nicole was amused by the appealing guy who was apologizing so incoherently. Zack, by contrast, was aghast at finding himself in the presence of this disarmingly lovely creature, her astonishing kohl-rimmed green eyes burning holes through him.

He finally broke the awkward silence with the first thing to enter his mind. "So... did you want sugar with that?"

Nicole smiled. "No thanks. I'm trying to cut down."

He forced a grin, uneasy as he felt. He was in a transfixed state of awe where everything else in the room washed away, as if through a camera's diffused filter. There was only Nicole, light years more exceptional than he could have perceived, standing before him in a shimmering silver dress with a plunging halter neckline and spike-heeled pumps that she wore like she was born in them. She was stunning, a woman who captivated with her physical appearance while her natural charisma demanded closer inspection.

And look closer he did: her complexion was newborn smooth and her posture that of royalty. In her sumptuous round eyes Zack saw a depth of grace never conveyed through the photographs or videos he had seen. He could have dived into those emerald pools and stayed for the rest of his life.

Eventually, he managed to choke out a few more words. "I'm Zack... it's a thrill to meet you." He winced at the mindless verbiage dribbling out of him. *Did he just say 'thrill'?*

Just then the audience could be heard applauding outside. "Well, I'd better get to work," she offered sweetly. "It was nice meeting you, Zack."

Before he could think of anything clever to say, two humorless sides of beef in security windbreakers appeared at the door and Nicole was whisked away. Zack gulped the rest of his coffee in a single swig, oblivious to the scorching of his esophagus. *He met her and she talked to him! Life couldn't get any more awesome.*

As Mad For Wavin completed an encore to moderate applause, an invigorating breeze slid down the pastoral slope behind The Greek Theatre and scrubbed away the vestiges of cigarette and marijuana smoke in the air. Nicole did not believe in intermissions, maintaining that a concert should flow without hesitation. That meant keeping the show going with no reduction of momentum.

Mother Nature was cooperating nicely and now it was the staging crew's turn. Seconds after Mad For Wavin was gone so were the risers that supported their instruments in front of the scrims. The sound of synthesizer-generated wind whispered from speakers as colored fog rolled across the stage. The effect was dramatic as well as practical, providing cover for the crew's seamless transition from one act to another.

Then it was time.

A steady bass guitar line rumbled and dozens of spotlights roamed the audience as the unseen band ushered in a rocking instrumental refrain that filled the amphitheater. The pile-driving beat was infectious, urging the spectators to their feet. More instruments expeditiously layered themselves over the intro, followed by the tightly knit harmonies of the back-up singers, until everything was ready for the ultimate punctuation: *Nicole.*

Standing in the wings with other support personnel, Zack inched forward for a better view, as if in a trance. Fortunately, Angie had the presence of mind to tug on his sleeve to keep him from accidentally going on stage.

It was impossible not to be caught up in it. The music built to a pulsating climax as the fogbank engulfed the stage with pink and green smoke. Soon the scrims concealing the band were gone and sparks rained down for Nicole's entrance. Giant video screens bookending the stage captured her every move in close-ups and spotlights emphasized the sparkling sequins and seed pearls on her gown, which became contoured sorcery that mimicked quicksilver brushed on her skin. Photographers jockeyed for position when, striking a sexy pose, Nicole raised her arms and the amphitheater was transformed into a coruscating mirage. Metallic surfaces bounced florid white light from above in radically different directions, as if projected through the burnished facets of a giant diamond.

The capacity audience of 6,162 roared as she launched into the feisty hit that earned her the first of seven Grammy Awards, "Make Me", a party tune that had people dancing in the aisles before the first chorus.

Make me, make me whatever you need
I will be your fantasy, on that we're agreed
Take me, take me somewhere that it's hot
All I ask is that you give me all that you've got

As he and Angie stood watching her performance, Zack appreciated as never before how some artists are great in recordings without capturing anything close to that in a live setting. But Nicole was pure magic, feeding off the enthusiasm radiating from her fans, singing hit after hit: "Together Forever"... "Blue Lady"... "Aftershock"... "More Than I Should"... "Night Flight"... and "One More Thing" with concentrated power and versatility. In one song she was crystalline, projecting the innocence of a schoolgirl in love, followed by the soulful worldliness of a woman who had seen it all. And then in "Let Me Tell You How This's Gonna Go", the witty duet that she recorded with country music legend Brad Paisley, she was a girl who had no trouble whatsoever speaking her mind.

She was rebellious, seductive, innocent and more.

Zack soaked in every moment, awestruck. If the singer was nourished by her audience, then he was being fueled by Nicole herself. He clung to her every gesture, word, and movement as she invested herself in the show. And his attention was not dampened by the fact that each time she looked into the wings her expression confirmed that she was pleased to find him there. It was as if her smiles were intended only for him. As were some of her lyrics:

One kind of lover may not be enough
To keep some people satisfied
It might not be right to have nights
You wish you were somewhere that you're not
We all have to struggle to keep our eyes off others
Can dreaming cause you pain?
It might not be right to lose sight of a chance
To bring someone new to your life

When Angie spotted the chemistry unfolding between Nicole and Zack, he bumped up beside him chortling the way guys often do when scoping out attractive women. "Hey, kid, she's really something. No wonder you got the hots."

The reception after the show was held at the Greek's exclusive Redwood Deck area. Rambunctious rock and roll recordings reverberated as Dom Perignon flowed and V.I.P.s mingled. A sizeable cadre of celebrity hangers-on and industry wannabees conducted quests for influential connections and it would have been difficult for an uninitiated newcomer to tell one group from the other.

The instant he returned from loading the ambulance, Zack knew that he did not fit in with this crowd. He felt foolish for wanting to check out the party in the first place. This was Nicole's world, the proverbial fast lane where people reveled in knowing about the latest pretentious L.A. restaurant that had no signage to identify it for the undeserving masses. He smirked at the idea of his father sitting in his faded leather chair delighting in the irony of his son being in the fast lane when he did not even know where the on-ramp was.

But he was there and it would probably be the only time that he would attend such an event. Deciding that he would at least get something to eat for his trouble, he proceeded through the gauntlet of buffed bodies hoping to find something edible among the gluten-free, vegetarian music industry hors d'oeuvres. Fragments of conversations about record deals, videos, downloads, and chart positions percolated around him and it was surreal.

And then there were the eager guys with plastic smiles trying their damndest to hook up with one of the five cute Mad For Wavin lasses, who, judging from their revealing mini-dresses and lingerie club wear, seemed ready to accommodate them. It occurred to Zack that the band's name, which is Irish slang for 'loves sex', was well chosen.

Zack found himself starting to appreciate the vacuity of it all, guessing correctly that not a word about war atrocities or starving children would be found anywhere in the room. How different these discussions must be from those that occurred during World War Two, he discerned, when the theatre served as makeshift barracks for young soldiers preparing to risk their lives fighting oppression. He could only imagine what those courageous men would have thought of this bunch of superficial lightweights.

At least they would have liked Mad For Wavin, he concluded as he saw the girls exit with a gaggle of simpering trophy hunks. Retreating from the swarm, he reassured himself that he was nothing like those guys. He had no selfish agenda. He would leave just as soon as he located Angie.

Of course, that was a lie. Zack knew damn well that he was playing his patented game of insulating himself from disillusionment by pretending that his objective was other than what it was, which was looking for Angie as a hedge against discovering that Nicole did not remember meeting him.

Besides, he had already seen members of her band make a brief appearance at the party and leave. She probably skipped it altogether.

Zack accepted a champagne flute from a waiter and peered at the upward flow of bubbles from the glass bottom. This single serving probably cost more than an entire six-pack of the Rolling Rock beer that he usually drank, yet it bubbled much the same. With that weighty observation firmly tucked away, he turned to depart and collided with someone behind him:

Someone he immediately identified as Nicole.

This time, however, she did not jump aside fast enough. "Oh, crap," he sputtered as his glass doused her.

"Zack, we've got to stop meeting like this," she said, chuckling.

He was appalled. "I don't believe this..."

"At least we know the champagne's properly chilled," she returned softly. The hulking security man who had escorted Nicole onstage earlier came into view. Ted Gimble was a grizzled forty year-old, his stocky build and taut military manner obviously out of place in the reception's ultra-hip setting. Zack found himself intrigued by Gimble's nose hairs, which resembled thick stalks of gray and black broccoli.

Gimble frowned at Zack the way police do when pulling someone over for speeding. "Anything wrong, Miss Branson?" he asked accusingly.

"I think I'll survive, Ted," she answered before abruptly stepping back.

Zack soon detected a foul odor, though he was slow to recognize the source of the smell. At first he thought it might be rotten eggs or rancid meat. Or the sensory welcome to a diseased colon that some of his instructors perversely enjoyed unleashing on unsuspecting new medical students. Whatever it was, it was vile. When he finally traced the stench to Gimble's breath, he wanted to give him the name of a gastroenterologist he knew at UCLA.

The large man hesitated. "You sure you're okay?"

"As you can see, a medical professional is already on hand," she said politely.

Gimble looked from Nicole to Zack with suspicion, and Zack pointed to the Willis Ambulance emblem on his uniform with a wink. "You ever need a prostate exam, you know who to call."

The man lumbered off and as Zack shook off the exchange he was struck by the bizarre comprehension that he was having a conversation with Nicole Branson. "Nice guy," he joked while his mind cried out, *don't blow it... don't blow it!*

"Believe it or not, you caught him on a good night," she returned.

"Guess you caught me on a bad one," Zack admitted. "Two collisions in a row. Hang around me long enough and there's no telling what damage I might do."

She touched his arm, her hand remaining a bit longer than necessary. "Thanks for the warning."

The dressing room downstairs was an austere box reminding Zack of roadside motels that he occupied with his parents during childhood vacation trips. The apparent lack of interior design by theater management struck him as incongruous. The biggest names in entertainment passed through this room and yet it was starkly institutional-looking, with its bland office couch-and-chair set and functional carpeting. Only a few framed travel posters and a floral arrangement from Nicole's record label provided any warmth. That and the small collection of glass animals on a table, which she was known to take with her on the road.

He sat on the couch fidgeting with a decorative throw pillow, gulping a glass of wine. "Easy, Zackster... easy... there's no reason to hyperventilate," he mumbled. *Just be cool. Think McQueen.* His insecurities boiled over. "You are going to totally humiliate yourself!" he berated himself. *What kind of moron would think that a woman like Nicole, a star who can have any man she wants, would break ranks with the rest of her gender and choose an eccentric goofball?*

Zack's feet had already taken him halfway to the door when he stopped. *How could he leave?! He'd already sent Angie home!* Still holding the pillow, he turned, torn with indecision. *Okay, they had a pleasant conversation at the party. And apparently she'd invited him to join her for a drink, though he couldn't actually remember any of that. All he knew was that he was here.*

But to be alone with her in such close quarters was more than he had hoped for. Besides, he assured himself, if she threw him out he could use Uber for a ride home.

Just then, Nicole cracked the door to an adjoining space. "Sorry to make you wait, Zack. I'm on hold, but it won't be much longer."

He threw himself into what he hoped looked like a relaxed pose on the couch and quipped, "Oh, no problem."

Her face appeared at the open door. "So, how'd you like the show?"

"It was neat... well, I don't mean neat like the geeks-have-landed neat..." He cursed to himself. *Get a grip, Raskin. You're slobbering on the carpet.*

A moment later, he stopped. She was standing in the threshold now. At the party he failed to notice how hypnotic the lilac color of her dress was, but he was sure noticing it now. The effect invited him closer, almost urging him to touch it, an alarming notion that he did his best to suppress.

"I'm glad you liked it," she said, floating onto the couch beside him. "To tell you the truth, I was a little nervous about the whole thing."

Her skirt accidentally hiked up to expose one of her thighs and his metabolism accelerated. "It sure didn't seem like you were nervous."

"That's good," she added. "Sometimes I doubt how successfully I hide what I really feel."

The floral fragrance of her perfume was mesmerizing and Zack struggled to keep his act together. He knew the physiology of what was happening to him and there would be no stopping it. Not only was the vagus nerve sending tremors throughout his cardiovascular system—hence his racing pulse—but oxytocin hormones were also radiating from his ribcage and dopamine was surging to his extremities. *He had to calm down... think McQueen!*

Eventually he shifted back to the conversation. "I still can't believe I'm here talking to you," he confessed. "I mean, I've been to a bunch of your concerts and I never imagined I'd be hanging out with you."

His attention then involuntarily diverted to the slender dress strap carelessly falling from her left shoulder, accenting the supple bare skin beneath. She smiled perceptively, pulling the delicate material back into place. "That makes us even. I never thought I'd be hanging out with you, either."

He returned her smile. "Well, it took some effort, but I was glad I could work you into my busy schedule."

Nicole refilled his empty glass. "So, how many shows have you seen?"

"Six."

She looked at him with surprise. "You're kidding!"

"Denver, ... Dallas, ... Oakland and San Diego, ..." he continued until she stopped him with a genial laugh.

"That must qualify you for some sort of resilience award."

"Actually, resilience had nothing to do with it," he admitted. It was amazing how much more comfortable he felt with her now. Even his heartbeat was finding its way back to normal. "Your songs helped me through some pretty rough times."

"It means a lot hearing that, Zack. Thank you."

He met her smile with one of his own and his mouth became dry. *So what now? You don't just nail a Goddess like this with a kiss.*

"What's wrong?" she asked.

"Nothing," he answered while making a point of sipping, rather than gulping, his wine this time.

"You look like there's something on your mind."

Was there ever. He hastily picked another subject. "Can I ask you a question?"

"Of course."

"Well, there were all kinds of guys at the reception... friends of yours, music people, movie stars... you had your pick of who to hang out with."

"And...?"

"What am I doing here?"

Nicole laughed easily and took a sip from a bottle of Evian. Freshly moistened, her lips seemed more tantalizing than ever and Zack knew that he had never wanted to kiss a woman more than he did at that moment. "My best friend, Glen, is my band leader but he never stays for these things. And to be honest I only have a few other close friends, but they aren't coming until tomorrow," she explained. "Contrary to popular belief, even people on magazine covers get lonely once in a while."

Her eyes drilled a hole through him. *God, those eyes... Those phenomenal green eyes!*

"With one of those characters upstairs I still would've been, believe me," she finished. And she meant what she said. Zack was a delightful change, an authentically nice person who made her feel better. "Besides, I never trust men with perpetual tans," she added. "They're almost always shallow."

"I'll try to remember that," he answered lightly.

Nicole took another sip of water before continuing, "The truth is there's a lot that people don't know about me, and one is the solitary life that I lead."

The statement seemed absurd. *Solitary?! Nicole Branson?* He summoned the courage to inquire further. "If you don't mind my asking, how can someone like you not be in a serious relationship?"

"I never said I wasn't," she clarified. Then she changed the subject, bringing the wine label into view. "How is this wine, anyway? It was a gift, so I have no idea."

"It's really good, thanks. Aren't you having some?"

She retrieved her Evian. "I have to stay in shape for the tour," she explained. "So, now that you know I'm practically a hermit, it's your turn. What unfathomable secret are you concealing from the world?"

He looked intently into her eyes once more and any reticence that he would normally have felt began to recede. "Well..." he eventually ventured, "I'm worried about what happens after med school. But I don't know if we ought to get into that..." He wavered slightly, though not for long. There was something about her that made him want to open up even more.

She recognized it, too. "Go on, Zack. It's okay."

"Growing up I never got much approval," he continued without further hesitation. "I mean zip. My father was career military and at Camp Raskin good grades didn't matter. They were never good enough because I never measured up."

He paused again. Fragments of his life blinked by: joyless Christmas memories of opening presents with his mother and father in silence, knowing how underwhelmed they were by the gifts he had made... his father chewing him out over his errors in Little League baseball games... and being the only child at school open house whose parents did not lavish praise over his prized artwork.

But there was no point in describing all that, Zack decided. "According to my father my attitude was wrong, my friends were wrong, I even brushed my teeth wrong," he told her. "And after fifteen or sixteen years of that, I got even. I became living proof that he was right... that I'm a waste of space."

Nicole touched his arm with concern. "I'm so sorry."

"A lot of people have it worse."

"How could anyone treat their little boy like that?"

"It's all the old man knew, I guess. He couldn't help it."

"What about your mother?"

"She was a good soldier. She knew her place in the chain of command, ya know?" Nicole nodded as he went on. "The trouble is, I've been hiding behind this goofy facade so long now I don't get who I am anymore." He looked away, as if his innermost thoughts were scripted on the carpet. "I don't even know if I have what it takes to be a doctor."

Then he stopped. He could not believe that he actually said that out loud. He had never made that admission to anyone. In fact, he did not know anyone he would have dared share it with. Zack's finely honed unpredictable persona had served him well as a barrier to keep people from seeing inside. The upside of the tactic was that little was expected of him, but the downside was nobody knew him very well. And when all was said and done that made for a pretty empty existence. He marveled at how easily he shared it with her.

"What made you want to be a doctor in the first place?" she asked after waiting for him to process his disclosure.

"I always wanted to work with kids," he heard himself tell her.

"Nothing's worse than children fighting for their lives in a hospital ward. Cancer, in particular... the little guys are so helpless, ya know?"

Nicole was moved by the simplicity and purity of the revelation. "Something tells me you're going to be a terrific doctor. No matter what you might think right now."

"I wish I had your confidence," he replied, still marveling at whom he was having this conversation with. *She believed in him!*

But whatever confidence she had in Zack, she countered with an admission of her own, starting with her description of how rough things had been since she and her boyfriend broke up two months ago. She even conceded to wishing that she could roll back the clock to her early days in Youngstown, Ohio, and return to a simpler time before the trappings of fame closed in.

She also talked about people's tendency to discount attractive women before they know them, and how hurtful it is to be viewed as an object. But Zack already knew that part. He recognized the message behind one of her first hits, "Please See Me", in which she pleaded for the listener to see her only through the sincerity of her lyrics.

You noticed me in all the right ways
I can't complain, it was a flattering start
But now I want more from you, starting today
Don't look through your eyes, just once use your heart
Please see me...

When he reminded her about the song she smiled. Nothing validates an artist more than someone relating to the embedded meaning of a specific work.

Then Nicole glanced at her watch with surprise. "Oh my God! Do you know how long we've been sitting here?"

Zack had no idea. For him time had been suspended.

She did not wait for an answer. "It's almost six o'clock!"

"Holy crap..." he blurted, checking his watch. Somehow an entire night had passed. And apparently she was as absorbed by the experience as he was.

She grabbed her purse and an oversized long knitted cardigan sweater and took him by the hand. "I've got an idea."

Nicole and Zack emerged onto the silicone-coated flat roof of the Greek's hospitality and office building that surveyed the south concourse and pitched rows of empty theatre seats. The world around them was on the verge of giving way to dawn and everything in sight was shrouded in a wispy state of diffused light and desaturated color. It was neither night nor day. It was otherworldly.

Still holding his hand, she led the way to two weathered chaise lounges haphazardly positioned among rooftop vents, conduit runs, and discarded beer cans.

"I love this time of day," she enthused as she draped the sweater over her shoulders and settled into one of the sun-bleached beige cushions. "Everything's so quiet. Listen..."

And listen he did. Dropping into the other chair, he reveled in the intriguing noiselessness that accompanied the light show that was unfolding across the distant horizon. The only sound was the rustle of unseen trees in the mild puffs of brisk springtime air, which played softly in the background like the orchestral score of a romantic movie. Zack's attention was drawn ever-deeper into the elongated strands of darkened far away clouds as they awakened with giant brush strokes of brilliant red, yellow, and pink that contrasted sharply with the patches of vivid Easter egg blue sky behind them. It was every bit as beautiful and serene as it was thrilling, as if he had been cured of cerebral achromatopsia, a particularly severe type of color-blindness.

It was then that he realized that she was still holding his hand and his heart skipped. "Amazing," he affirmed, referring to a whole lot more than the sunrise.

Falling into spontaneous silence, they absorbed the daybreak and its overwhelming ethereal calm. Photographers refer to this time as "magic hour" and now Zack understood why. Of course, those poor bastards had to coin the term without the benefit of experiencing it with Nicole Branson, he realized, but he had to admit that the visuals were pretty spectacular all by themselves.

She squeezed his hand tenderly and their eyes met. Whatever it was that was taking place between them, be it his synergy with her musical soul or simply a connection between two lonely people, they found themselves being swept away by a wave of mutual desire.

"So, here we are," she said shyly.

God, he wanted to kiss her so much! "Do you happen to know if there are any security cameras up here?" he finally asked.

"I haven't seen any," she responded with a slight quiver in her voice.

"Good," he remarked as he slid onto the cushion beside her. A moment later his lips were on hers, gently at first, then with determination. She was so incredibly soft and the taste of her was like nothing he had ever experienced. As she pulled him close, the feeling of her body against his made the synapses in his brain fire so fast he was sure she could hear them.

Zack was electrified. This couldn't be real!

But it was. And as far as he was concerned their kiss was the greatest in the history of kisses. Pulling away, Nicole's face was flushed. "It's been a long time since I met anyone like you, Zack," she conceded.

"That's what the Army shrink used to say," he answered.

She grinned and reclined him in the chair. More kisses followed, before her fingernails traveled his chest and stomach, leaving a trail of quivering nerve endings in their wake. He reached into the open front of her sweater and she offered no resistance. His mind was really spinning now, having discovered that she was not wearing a bra. Zack was sent into orbit by the feel of her. She was small and firm and perfect. He reveled in touching her, in examining the details of her curves. Like a teenager fondling a girl for the first time, he was enthralled by the dramatic newness of it.

Nicole kissed him again, as lovingly as he had ever experienced. Her fingers found their way to his belt and he ached with anticipation as she unbuckled it. Making love was inevitable now and they both knew it. Everything seemed predestined and the certainty of that was wonderfully arousing. When she slipped her sweater and dress straps from her shoulders, they fell away. Her skin was so exquisitely flawless and silky that he had to remind himself to breathe.

Then as she began undoing the buttons of his shirt, Zack observed something truly odd: while he had never been modest he found himself feeling bashful! Here was the man who once streaked a Comic-Con convention wearing nothing but a Batman mask and cape—*and now he was being bashful?*

When she slid his hand into her white lace bikini panties, his uneasiness disappeared. Soon she was on top of him and the intensity of the moment grew as she reached for a condom in her purse, opened the package, and guided it onto him. Nicole was warm and trembling as she lowered herself onto him. Opening his eyes to make sure he wasn't hallucinating, Zack found her smiling. And in her smile he saw everything he that had ever wanted: love, life... *possibility*. He recognized that as much as he wanted her physically, he would have been happy to stay in her gaze forever.

But he was also inside her, an astounding fact that he still could not believe. As their gentle union gave way to craving and his thrusts accelerated to match the rolling of her hips, she arched her back in elation and the sight of her breasts rising inches from his face was as erotic as anything that he had ever seen.

Zack did not know how long they made love, because for him time no longer existed. There had been other women in his life, of course, but this was different. This was *Nicole*. Finally, when their bodies could no longer outlast the pinnacle they had reached they climaxed in a reciprocal convulsion. Their exhilaration passed slowly and the lovers remained entwined in a close embrace, the cool morning air caressing them as the sky above turned the most beautiful shade of blue he had ever seen.

Nicole pulled her sweater over them and murmured contentedly, and Zack added his concurrence. He was adrift on a sweet cloud of flowered perfume. He did not want to think about the return to existence without her.

NEWS ITEM:

Daily Variety, April 21

Only one word can describe the evening Nicole Branson gave her fans last night at the Greek Theatre: fabulous. The comely singer was in top form as she once again demonstrated that she is more than a talented artist. She's all woman and doesn't mind showing it.

Concert continues through April 26

Chapter Three

A compact disc entered the beat-up Pioneer CD player that Zack once won as a door prize and soon "Take It Like A Man", one of Nicole's most playful rockers, came on. He pranced across the spacious living room of the 1930's era apartment, singing along with the pronounced animation usually reserved for a kids' TV show.

Take it like a man
Show us that you can
You dish it out like you're one of the best
Mmmmmm, now let's see if you're up to my test
Take it like a man

To anyone witnessing the woman's voice coming from the wildly gyrating young man's face, it would have seemed weird. But then, this was Zack Raskin and the only people watching would be neighbors who were probably accustomed to the unusual.

The bedroom door with a frayed paper skeleton on it swung open and a hung-over Doug lurched forward in UCSB Gauchos boxer shorts and a pale blue surgical shirt. Through the bleariness of his Saturday morning coma he could hear a peppy male voice proclaim, "Top o'the mornin, big guy! It's study time!"

Doug knew it was Zack, but that was where his information flow ended. Nothing else was registering. "What the hell time is it?" he mumbled as he located a clock. "Seven thirty? Are you fucking nuts?!"

Zack danced past him, oblivious to his sour mood. "You know I am. Erythromycin... what's it used for?"

But Doug was not interested. "Turn that shit off and take a Valium." He headed towards his room, only to find himself blocked by Zack who was still rocking out.

"Erythromycin," he persisted.

"Have a heart, Zack."

"One clue, it's not for the heart."

Doug stared back. "This's inhumane."

Zack executed a deft Fred Astaire spin that ended at his classic Carver tube amplifier with dashing flair. "A sucko seventy-nine on Doc Sandberg's exam forfeits any right of protest," he declared. "Now either you get into this or we probe your pain tolerance."

Doug watched him reach for the volume nob and hastily raised his hands in surrender. "Okay! Okay! Jesus! Let's see... Erythromycin... it's a bacteriostatic antibiotic... effective for gram-positive organisms. Now can I get back to sleep?"

Zack continued to move, touching the volume knob in a direct threat. "Which organisms?"

"I don't know."

Zack goosed the stereo. Music thundered and picture frames shuddered. Doug yelled above the din, "You win! Streptococcus, staphylococcus, and... I'll get it... gonococcus. Who cares?!"

"Doc Sandberg cares. Clofibrate," Zack barked.

"I hate clofibrate," said Doug. "And I hate you!" With that he entered his room, slamming the door behind him. The paper skeleton jiggled briefly from the vibration.

As Doug fell onto his bed, he barely had time to hit the sheets when Zack's voice spoke from the hall. "One way or another you're going to know this stuff," he scolded. "And this mutha's got 350 watts per channel."

Doug mumbled from beneath his pillow, "I don't want to do this now."

"I don't care what you want."

"Clofibrate's an antihypertensive."

Zack paused. "Wrong-o."

Suddenly Doug's head appeared from concealment, his eyes popping at what his incorrect answer meant: more rock and roll torture.

He practically flew into the living room screaming, "It's an antihyperlipidemic!"

Then he stopped. The music was off and Zack was calmly sipping a cup of take-out coffee, beaming. "Very good, McKay! Tell him what he's won, Johnny." He continued, his voice imitating a bombastic game show announcer, "A fresh bagel, Bob. Yes, so warm and inviting, this scrumptious sesame miracle comes from the toasty ovens of Sol's coffee shop in scenic Westwood, California!"

Zack tossed him one like a Frisbee. Doug caught it, taking in his roommate with incredulity. "You know, until now I never thought much about mercy killings."

"I don't believe you," Zack objected. "You aren't even going to ask?"

"Ask what?"

"Why I'm so ebullient."

"I chalked it up to you finally going 5150."

Zack overlooked his cynical use of the code for involuntary commitment to a mental hospital. "I think I'm in love, Dougie." He gripped Doug's arm for emphasis. "I'm not kidding. This's it... the big 'L.'"

Doug glanced at the hand on his arm. "All right. We can smooch, but no tongues."

"I'm talking about Nicole, you moron." Zack explained. "I met her and we hit it off. I mean, we really, *really* hit it off. We spent the night together."

Doug stopped mid-bite, the doughy bagel filling his mouth. "Get real," he mumbled semi-coherently.

"I am."

"No, Zack," he countered while chewing. "Real is admitting your mind's gone and all those aberrant fantasies have taken over." Doug got up to leave. "Thanks for breakfast."

Zack moved with him. "I know it's hard to believe," he pleaded, "but honest to God, Nicole Branson and I were together last night."

Doug looked up, studying him squarely before swallowing. "Geez, how are you going to break this to Stacy?"

"Who?" Zack asked blankly.

"How quickly they forget..." Doug replied. "Your other true love, *The Weapon of Mass Seduction*, Stacy Keibler."

At The Greek Theatre, the second night began as a replay of the first. Except for the weather. This time a low-hanging layer of clouds and coastal moisture blocked any hope of a star-filled sky, while threatening to dump several inches of rain on the Los Angelinos below.

Once again lights roamed the fog-laden stage while Nicole expertly controlled her loving audience. And once again Zack was captivated by her every move, as if the off-center slit and spaghetti straps of her emerald green satin empire dress were designed exclusively for him.

He clutched at his concert security badge and each moment of their night together resonated with such detail that a monsoon could have struck Griffith Park along with a 9.0 earthquake and he would not have known it. His senses were teeming with experiences that he would never forget—the seductive bouquet of her perfume, the taste of her lips, the playfulness of her touch, and the incomparable feeling of their bodies joined.

But he had been nervous before the concert, too. He had sent her a dozen roses and then second-guessing the gesture with a million paranoid questions: *Would she be glad to see him? Would she want to repeat their adventure? Was sex with him even any good?*

Oh, God...

Zack had tortured himself like that throughout Mad For Wavin's set, his mind reduced to a mangled wreck of self-doubt. For him the Irish band was a blur of vague sights, sounds, and the musty backstage electrical aroma of their guitar amps. Fortunately, his insecurities were put to rest the moment that Nicole appeared in the wings. She looked gorgeous as she breezed through the door—and when her eyes found his everyone else in the room vanished, as before.

It was just the two of them as she kissed him on the cheek with such tenderness that he nearly gasped. "Thank you for the flowers," she had whispered. "I love them." But it was her emphatic squeeze of his arm that signaled what he wanted to know. So did the glances that she exchanged with him during her first few songs. They were private looks reserved for lovers only.

And so, possessed with the confidence that their time together meant something to her, Zack was free to let her show wash over him. His fantasies ran to the possibilities of what other nights with her might be like, because he now had reason to hope that there would be more.

Unfortunately, Zack's romantic daydream proved fleeting. Twenty minutes into her performance, as Nicole began her classic ballad, "Missing You", Zack's insides clenched; *something was wrong.* Members of the staging crew and security team in the wings saw it, too. She was struggling as she sang.

Sometimes life gets hard
And feelings can... be so confusing
My heart fights my mind and... says...
I cannot... be... in love
Yet... there you are... there... you are...

Zack moved to his partner with concern. "Angie, do you see that?"

Angie nodded. "I thought it was the lights or somethin'..."

"It's not," responded Zack. And Angie knew he was right.

Then she stumbled on a lyric, something she had never done in concert before.

You've been my friend and lover...
Sometimes a little more... of one than the other
Helping me up... when I needed... you...
Loving me gently as... as...

Members of her band traded anxious looks as she gestured for them to stop the song. When the instruments faded into silence, a hush fell over the amphitheater.

Nicole rubbed her arms and a chill passed through her. "I'm so sorry," she said, taking a sip of water. "I'm... not feeling very... well..." The plastic bottle slipped from her grasp, thunking to the stage floor.

For an instant her eyes found Zack and they were uncomprehending and pleading. There was something else, too. Fear. He wanted so badly to hold her in his arms, but in that interminable moment his legs were immobilized. And his stomach was in his throat.

Events unfolded after that at a trancelike pace. Two musicians assisted her to the wings on the opposite side of the stage, but before Zack or Angie could get to her an anxious backstage throng besieged her. The partners were frustrated trying to plow through all the bodies. "Paramedics... step aside!" Zack yelled as he put a shoulder to the human wall.

"Let's go. Everybody move it!" Angie added muscularly.

When people finally let them through, Zack and Angie could see Nicole disappearing through a door on the arms of her security guards, Gimble and Strauss.

Zack was furious. "What the hell are they doing?!"

Angie did not respond. Soon they were pounding down the metal stairs and Zack's head throbbed with anxiety. Under his breath, he cursed the security team for wasting valuable time. First responders refer to such delays as empty minutes and they often have tragic consequences.

The downstairs hallway was jammed with onlookers and venue staff, which Angie negotiated with skill as they pushed past them. Zack followed his thunderous, "Comin' through! Comin' through!" pronouncement and briefly noted individuals that he passed. Trepidation was etched into their faces.

Within seconds Zack was checking Nicole's airway and strapping an oxygen mask to her pallid face as she lay on the dressing room couch, slipping into unconsciousness. Angie expertly shined a penlight into her pupils and examined her with a stethoscope while Zack elevated her feet and fumbled for his phone. Noticing security man Ted Gimble watching nearby he snarled, "I can't believe you brought her all the way down here!"

Gimble shot him a contentious look. "Miss Branson didn't want to cause a scene."

Zack would have slugged the guy if there had not been more pressing issues to deal with. He turned to Angie as he had so many times before. "What do I tell 911?"

Angie need not have said anything. He was already administering chest compressions. "Tell 'em I can't find her pulse."

Zack froze as the declaration echoed. His mind floundered

in search for another interpretation of this perversion passing for reality. But that took no more than an instant. His EMT training took over as his call went through and an insulating barrier of professional reflex finally interjected itself between conscious thought and what was a brutal avalanche of emotions. Nicole was in cardiac arrest, which he knew has a survival rate of less than fifteen percent when it occurs out-of-hospital. A horrifying statistic that is magnified by the mere five minutes of oxygen deprivation patients can withstand before their brains begin to die.

"My name is Zack Raskin," he informed the dispatcher. "I'm an EMT with Willis Ambulance. We have a Code Three SCA at the Greek Theatre. 2700 North Vermont in Los Feliz."

Angie motioned his head toward Nicole. "Fire up the AED."

"Heard," Zack reported as he reflexively slid into position over her to continue the precise pattern of compressions that Angie had initiated.

Holding the diaphragm of the stethoscope to Nicole's chest once more, Angie opened the automated external defibrillator beside his medical case. "She's still with us," he reported.

Now acutely aware of his connection to her life, Zack pumped her heart like a man obsessed. "Come on, Nicole. Keep it up, keep it up..." he begged under his breath.

Angie brought two defibrillator pads into view with a procedural reminder that did not require discussion. "Underwire and jewelry check."

Zack tore open her dress and used surgical scissors to open the center of her bra to eliminate metal wire that might conduct electricity and burn her. He also removed her necklace, but did not have to look for body piercings since he already knew from personal experience that she had none. "Ready," he declared, moving out of the way.

Angie placed one pad on the right center of Nicole's exposed breast and the second below the left side of her ribcage. "Analyzing... clear!" he commanded before pressing one of the machine's buttons.

Without waiting for the read-out, Zack began the next crucial step. "Preparing the epinephrine," he confirmed to his partner that a syringe of the powerful vasopressor used to increase cardiac output was on the way.

Angie read the digital AED report as it appeared, "Don't give up, Nicole. Hang on." He noted the increasing concerned look on Zack's face, but did not divulge any reaction. "Defibbing... clear," was all he offered before pressing the shock control that he hoped would get her heart working again.

Zack resumed the regimen of chest compressions and privately questioned if waiting for the fire department ambulance to arrive was the best strategy, even if it was standard protocol to stabilize patients before transporting them. Somewhere in a separate part of his brain, he prayed, *"Please let her be all right... please let her be all right..."*

Unobserved by anyone, on a nearby table stood a crystal vase of long stem roses. The enclosure card tied to one of the branches with a piece of white ribbon said: *Looking forward to spilling something on you again soon. Zack.*

An hour later Zack was sitting in an orange plastic chair in the trauma care unit of Providence Saint Joseph's Hospital in Burbank. Harsh fluorescent light bathed the concert security badge and lanyard in his hands with antiseptic coldness matching the medicinal odors that civilians detested but he no longer even noticed. He was only distantly aware of having ridden in the ambulance beside Nicole.

In the treatment area behind a drawn curtain, a crash team reluctantly ceased their efforts to resuscitate their famous patient. They glanced at the monitors on which her vital signs were no longer exhibited and exchanged solemn looks. Nicole Branson was gone. A nurse covered her face with a sheet and the curtain was opened slowly.

Zack knew right away what it meant, but he did not want to accept it. He could not. Hours ago he was coupled in ecstasy with a woman who was so full of vitality. *And now this?! No way.* Allowing an injustice like this would be an insult.

He read the despondency on the faces of the doctors and nurses as they shuffled past and wished that somebody would wake him from his nightmare. That, of course, was never going to occur. This was a nightmare, but there would be no escape.

Angie took up the chair beside him. No matter how many times he held the dying or consoled those who were left behind, these moments were always hard. With Zack it was even worse. "Myocardial infarction, kid. I'm so sorry."

"But that's impossible!" Zack muttered. "It can't be..."

Angie put a hand on his arm. "It could've been anything. Medications and ventricular arrhythmia, diuretics, or even problems like Wolff-Parkinson-White or long QT. The medical examiner will figure it out."

Angie said more but Zack could no longer hear him. All he was conscious of were people overflowing from a lounge that the hospital had set aside for private conferences with family members. He hazily recalled seeing some at the concert and would later learn that among them were Glen Conway, Nicole's friend and keyboard player, Road Manager Dennie Seifert, and record producer Elliot Kefler.

Then he saw a doctor approach the group in surgical scrubs. He watched as the people succumbed, one by one, to tears.

Across the room, a man got up from his chair and ambled past a banner that proudly announced Providence Saint Joseph's ranking as one of the best hospitals in America. He turned toward an unoccupied alcove and calmly pressed an auto-dial number on his flip phone. It did not take long for the call to go through. "She checked out at eleven thirty-three," he said in a low, grim voice. "Congratulations."

NEWS ITEM:

The Los Angeles Times, April 22

The Los Angeles Medical Examiner has promised a full investigation into the sudden death of rock star Nicole Branson. Branson, 28, succumbed last night during a concert at the Greek Theatre in Los Feliz. Despite the efforts of emergency medical and security personnel, Branson was pronounced dead at Providence Saint Joseph's Hospital in Burbank at 11:33 pm.

This is not the first high-profile tragedy to be handled by the busy coroner's staff. In addition to the death of actor Paul Walker, the Lana Clarkson murder at the hands of record producer Phil Spector, and the Michael Jackson-Whitney Houston drug overdoses, notable celebrity cases in Los Angeles County have included Marilyn Monroe, Janis Joplin, Freddie Prinze, Natalie Wood, Robert Kennedy, John Belushi, Phil Hartman, Carrie Fisher, Chester Bennington, and Tom Petty.

Chapter Four

Zack had seen his share of death. First there were the military funerals that he had been condemned to attend as a boy, plus the passing of grandparents, aunts, and uncles. As an emergency medical technician he had witnessed even more, from traffic fatalities and gunshot victims to drownings and heart attacks. But he had learned to compartmentalize most of those. While the deaths of aging relatives were certainly sad, they were not entirely unexpected, and when patients passed away, the saving grace was that they were people he did not know. Like the cadavers he studied in Gross Anatomy class, the subjects were anonymous.

Nicole Branson, of course, meant much more to him. Zack had known her intimately, and that was something to which he assigned profound personal meaning. He had never been a hook-up kind of guy. For him their lovemaking had been the miraculous culmination of years of investing himself in her art and admiring what she stood for.

Now as he sat alone in his dreary apartment, engulfed by the smoky glow of the television fluttering on shadowy walls, he again recalled every detail of their romance. The images were fresh and excruciating, and he opened another beer in an attempt to blot them out. He lost count of how many green bottles there had been before this, nor did he care. The prospect of reliving the past descended on him as a curse. Her mouth would never again ease into that playful smile. She was gone forever.

His blurring mind was overcome with chaotic indignation. *How does anybody reconcile the unfairness of death, anyway? Why does one person survive a catastrophic plane crash while another slips and dies in a bathtub? And why did this happen to Nicole instead of a violent gangbanger or serial killer? Why?!*

As if to punctuate the question, NBC News anchor Lester Holt intruded on the moment to analyze the meaning of Nicole's death on television. "Few performers enjoy national popularity for long," he began somberly. "Especially in the music business, where careers come and go with unpredictable frequency." The narrative droned on, but Zack did not absorb it. What disbelief had failed to anaesthetize, Rolling Rock had not.

He guzzled his beer and was reaching for another when he thought he heard a woman's voice, "Zack..."

Startled, he spun in his chair to find the front door open. He headed across the room to investigate and as his legs swayed he discovered with bemused satisfaction that the alcohol was kicking in. He was hammered.

Zack checked the hall and stairs but found no one there. Content that he imagined the voice, he swung the door closed and paused to note that its previously irritating creak now seemed oddly satisfying. Funny what a little brew can do, he mused on his wobbly return trip to the couch.

Then the voice spoke more insistently, "Zack..."

His heart seemed to stop. *It sounded like Nicole!*

Hurriedly touring the room, he flipped one lamp on after another in an attempt to drive away whatever was doing this to him. And for a moment it worked, the memory was silenced. Zack smirked at the restored command of his existence, smugly feeling the empowerment that only intoxication can provide. *Nothing could touch him now.*

Or so he thought, until the lights dimmed and an eerie chill passed through him. And then he saw it: the silhouette of someone standing at the end of the darkened hall. "... Who's there?" he demanded in a hoarse whisper. There was no response, only the familiar fragrance of floral perfume. Zack tried to focus as the figure advanced. He staggered back against the couch, which kept him from going off his feet altogether, as he quickly saw that the intruder was a woman. Her sheer black designer hose and leather skirt were the first to infiltrate the light, then her open black lace cardigan blouse and embroidered bra.

Lastly, he saw her face. "Nicole..." he rasped.

Impossibly, it was her. Pausing in the threshold she looked exactly as he remembered, so astoundingly beautiful. Yet there was something different about her, too. In those initial moments Zack did not see it, but as she continued her approach he noted that the magical sparkle was gone from her eyes. Now they were filled with a haunting dimension of misery.

"Don't say anything," she asked, closing the door before embracing him.

Zack memorized the scent of her and the feeling of her body against his. He knew he was wasted but he didn't care. *For now he had her back.*

On the television a few feet away, Lester Holt was concluding his story: "... Grammy-winning singer/songwriter Nicole Branson, dead tonight at age twenty-eight from an apparent heroin overdose."

When Zack came to on the couch an hour later he was still drunk, though not nearly enough to suit him. In the moment of awakening, his dream about reuniting with Nicole seemed almost real. Then, as consciousness sluggishly returned to his thickened mind, a gnawing dose of duplicity and rejection took over.

He found what was left of a warm beer and chugged it. All he could think about was the revelation that Lester Holt made on TV about a heroin overdose. *Fucking heroin?!* He never would have imagined such a thing, either of the artist he admired or the woman he made love to. But the authorities had confirmed finding drug paraphernalia among her possessions at the Greek Theatre and lethal levels of diamorphine in her blood.

Zack had been duped.

That Nicole was probably impaired during their time together trivialized everything—the way he felt about her and the intimacies they shared. Anger, hurt, and confusion seethed inside him. Even worse, her deception ended her life when it did not have to. Had he and Angie known about her drug use they could have administered the reliable opioid antidote naloxone and the outcome might have been different.

Grabbing his jacket and car keys, he left the apartment. There had to be absolution from his desolation. *Had to be.*

Zack drove aimlessly around Westwood and Santa Monica. He started out with the nebulous notion of finding some coffee to sober up with, but he knew from serology class that coffee does not actually counteract the effects of alcohol.

Besides, he had earned the diminished mental state he was now experiencing. *Talk about a one-two punch!* To Zack it seemed that his disarray was a Purple Heart for crippling injuries received in the carnal battlefield. His Badge of Honor. And excess drinking was the bona fide rite of passage for all honorees, he assured himself. For him and all the other hapless groupies in the world who had ever been exploited by a wasted rock star. He just wanted to avoid killing somebody with his car. His own safety seemed irrelevant. *Bring it on, whatever*, he argued through the cloud of depression. *Pedestrians and fellow drivers beware.* Hopefully their interoceptive instinct, the physiological sixth sense that alerts people to danger, would not desert them as it had him when he met Nicole.

Eventually, he was on Pacific Coast Highway driving north to the exclusive Point Dume enclave where Nicole lived. He had no idea what he would do when he got there; his actions were entirely impulsive. All he knew was that this pilgrimage seemed like the natural thing to do. When he passed Malibu Bluffs Park and Paradise Cove, he recognized that he was close.

Then when PCH veered close to the ocean at Zuma Beach he saw them on the sand beneath her spacious cliffside home. Hundreds of people were gathered with lighted candles and the sight hit him hard. They were grieving fans and, like him, they had been fooled by the deceptions of a drug-addicted celebrity. Unlike him, he reasoned, most of them probably had the good judgment not to sleep with her.

He remembered his father's adamant proclamation that people are the authors of the scripts of their lives and determined that it was true after all. Nicole had no one else to blame for what happened to her and Zack should have known better than to get involved.

As he stepped from his car on Westward Beach Road the pungent sulfury stink of damp seaweed greeted him. He peered out at the ocean but could barely make it out under the thick marine layer that muted everything below. All he could see of the water was a blackened mass that made sound but did not appear to move. The sea was an enigmatic place that he found tolerable only from a distance, especially at times like this.

Following a flight of uneven concrete stairs to the sand, Zack's vision began to adjust to the darkness. He could make out rows of foamy white waves breaking offshore, as if they lacked the stamina to make it all the way to their destination. He pondered how far they must have traveled only to peter out in the end.

He wandered among the mourners for a while, peering into their stricken faces, and speculating about their emotional connections to Nicole. Her fans were of every age and most looked as if they had just lost a close member of their family. Noticing one particularly distraught woman clutching one of her CDs to her heart, Zack contemplated his own collection standing upright on his living room shelf. The one with the damaged jewel box that he had intended to replace but never did, and the one with a defective track six that illogically skipped around "Girl Talk" every time he played it. He did not know why he was thinking of those things now, only that they seemed significant.

But staying at the vigil did not. The spectacle brought him no solace. He had to keep moving. Returning to his car, he headed back to the city.

Ninety minutes later, Zack was back at the Greek Theatre, drawn there as if by an unexplained magnetic pull. He was sitting in his car thinking about what he was supposed to do next in lieu of fortifying his fading drunkenness at the nearest bar. The crew was setting up another event, so the distant pounding of hammers and whirring of tools were the only sounds. He wondered if anybody thought to bring a flask.

Wrenching himself from the car, he navigated past the place where Nicole was loaded into a Los Angeles Fire Department ambulance. Where worried onlookers had futilely pinned their hopes on the young Willis Ambulance Service EMT climbing into the vehicle beside her. As he approached the security kiosk, the night watchman let him pass without comment. Maybe the man perceived what he was going through. The level of his despair was obvious, Zack thought. Or maybe the staff got word that he was the unwitting chump who Nicole shacked up with after mainlining an after-show fix.

Zack walked through the theatre courtyard to the stage door and shivered. The night was colder than before and the ground excreted a chill through his sneakers. The breeze flowing through the canyons of Griffith Park was no longer invigorating, as it had been during their night together. Now it was invasive and bitter. And if the air still carried the fragrance of wildflowers, he was in no frame of mind to care.

The hallway leading to the dressing room appeared narrower than before, as Zack halted at the end deciding if he should proceed. The craggy cinderblock walls seemed poised to close in on any interloper who dared to challenge them.

It took everything that he had to repress his apprehensions and head through the tunnel. While his feet dragged themselves across scratched and stained cement, movement became agonizing, showcased by the stark security bulbs in the ceiling that glowered down to distort everything in sight. Zack graphically recalled his desperation as he pushed through people blocking his path the night Nicole died.

Then he stopped. On the door were handwritten letters in the black ink of a Sharpie marker that spelled her name on masking tape. A flush came over him and his fingers trembled as they touched the letters one by one. In the recesses of his mind he could hear himself bragging to Doug, *"This's it... the big L."*

Doug's voice fired back, *"Get real."*

There was more than enough reality to go around and Zack hated it. Nicole's death was traumatic enough, but the idea of being manipulated by her was eating a hole in his gut. She had been dishonest in their intimacy and then ended her own life, leaving him completely devastated. *How's that for real?!*

Gently peeling the tape off the door he folded it and put it in his pocket, bracing himself before entering. In an instant he was deluged by a barrage of conflicting images: Nicole kissing him on the roof... that alarming glassy stare after her collapse... her beguiling smile when she learned how many concerts he had attended... the color draining from her complexion as he performed CPR... and the devastating moment he awoke to remember the television news report about her drug overdose.

Zack flopped on the couch and ran his fingers across the cushion where she suffered and his emotions finally got the best of him. Tears came with a vengeance. It was the first time that he had allowed himself to cry since this all began. *If only he hadn't fallen for her. If only she hadn't demeaned everything with that fucking overdose! If only... everything.*

When he had no more crying left in him, when he reached what he hoped was his suffering plateau, Nicole's voice reverberated in the hollowness of his memory, "*What unfathomable secret are you concealing from the world?*"

"*A secret?*" he repeated angrily to himself. "*Like shooting smack?! How could I ever match that?*"

The remembrance persisted as her voice made the request again, "*What secret are you concealing?*"

Zack's wrath flared. "*Why should I tell you anything? Honesty means nothing to you.*"

The space remained still until his tantrum dissolved. He did not have enough energy to stay mad any longer. Lester Holt's voice then tumbled forward in his memory to shatter the silence. "*... pop singer/songwriter Nicole Branson, dead tonight at age twenty-eight from an apparent heroin overdose...*"

Returning to the Greek was a horrible idea and Zack knew it. He headed for the door hoping to repel the words swirling around him, "*dead tonight... heroin overdose... dead...*" As he rushed out, he could hear Nicole's voice echoing loudly from the stage, "*I'm so sorry. I'm... not feeling very... well...*"

Zack slammed the door behind him and steeled himself against the truth that those were the last words anyone would hear her speak.

Someone was asking, "Hey, are you okay?" as Zack sluggishly became aware of his surroundings. Like a person awakening in the surgical recovery room, he was standing at the sink in his bathroom though not at all sure how he got there. He had apparently sliced himself trying to shave and the inquisitive voice piercing the fog belonged to Doug McKay, whom he eventually realized was addressing him from the doorway.

Zack tried not to look rattled, but the last thing he remembered was fleeing the Greek Theatre—and now here he was with blood trickling from a slash on his chin. *Blackouts were not good. Not good at all. What the hell was happening to him?!*

He tried to stop the bleeding as Doug inched closer. "I asked if you're okay."

"How do I look?" Zack asked back.

"You look like shit."

"Well, I guess that sums it up," Zack concluded as he fumbled to apply a piece of wet tissue to his face.

Doug moved in to help. "Here, let a semi-professional do that..."

"Thanks."

Doug pressed a tissue on the cut, less as first aid than a tactic to draw Zack into conversation. "You know, you've had me a little concerned the past few days."

"I always have you concerned," Zack came back with artificial levity. In fact, he was panic-stricken over how long his blackout might have lasted. *Hours were bad enough, but DAYS?! He had to get a grip.*

"You know what I mean," Doug said understandingly. The burden he felt over not paying more attention to Zack's story about his night with Nicole was considerable.

"I need time alone, that's all," Zack told him without any idea of how alone he had already been or for how long.

"Man, this's a gusher," Doug added. "You need a Band-Aid."

"I'll be all right."

Doug rummaged through a vanity drawer. "You're hemorrhaging like a stuck pig."

"Forget it. Really..."

Locating some bandages, Doug held up the box. "Look, they even have Disney characters on them. I'll find Goofy for you."

"I said forget it!" Zack snapped, knocking the package to the floor.

Doug paused to look at the debris. Zack's defensiveness had caught him off guard. "You want to take this from the top? I started with 'Are you okay'... not 'shove it up your ass.'"

Zack was reeling inside. He did not want to be having this discussion. "Doug, look," he finally offered, "I just don't want anything on my face, okay?"

Doug pretended to consider his response but he already knew what it was going to be. That was, after all, the point of the dialogue he wanted to have with Zack. He had watched his roommate sink into this funk and he was really worried. "Maybe you ought to think about skipping the funeral," he suggested.

Zack's mind faltered. *Funeral? Is that where he was going?* He grabbed the sink for support. *Where did the time go?* "I've gotta see this through," he said without knowing why.

"Who says?"

"I do." Zack sounded resolute but inside he was writhing in grief and the lingering sting of treachery over Nicole's drug use. "It's hard to explain," he added. The fact was if her funeral was today then he had to be there.

Doug took in his despair and thought he understood what was behind it. "Listen to me, Zack," he started carefully, "you did the best you could for her."

"I know that," Zack assured him, not sure where this was heading.

"You don't act like it," Doug went on. "There's nothing to feel guilty about. Nicole did this to herself. There isn't an EMT anywhere who could've done more for her."

Zack could only stare. What Doug was thinking must have seemed so cut and dried: that his misery was solely the result of his medical attendance in her final hours. That was partly true, of course. He would have given anything to administer a lifesaving antidote. But he reminded himself that Doug did not understand the big picture. Doug could not possibly fathom why the drug disclosure had sent him into such a ferocious tailspin.

Zack considered his anxious friend. "Thanks," he said meaning it, "but I'll be fine." Then his eye glimpsed the calendar hanging in the hall. It was April 27... meaning *five days* in his life were unaccounted for. *Shit!*

He was anything but fine.

After showering, Zack stood at his dresser wrestling with the necktie that Doug loaned him. Thankfully, Doug had also gone to his clinical shift at the hospital and the solitude was nice. He was finally able to reflect on the ordeal he was being dragged through.

Gazing past the thin layer of dust on his mirror, he tried to push all negative thoughts aside and concentrate on the technique for tying the knot that his father taught him. It had been quite a while since he attempted a Full Windsor or Half Windsor, or whatever. He vaguely recalled that the military preferred one of them, but getting the ends to come out right seemed impossible.

Meanwhile, the sole sound was whatever Doug left on the TV in the living room, which passed as background noise—until a familiar voice broke through in the unaffected melody of a song:

I'm thinking about the old days
As the rain rolls off my roof tonight –

Zack's pulse skipped and his anguish and turmoil washed away. Following the sound like a beacon, he gravitated to the source. He had heard Passion and More many times but now Nicole's clear and crisp intonations were especially consoling.

I remember all the good times
We used to have when we didn't fight –

Walking along the hall, Zack passed the spot where Nicole appeared the night she died and the exotic memory of her silhouette converged with the voice that was wafting in his direction.

I think of you, distant lover
With the truth gently hazed in this light—
As I sit here in Southern California
On a lonely Tuesday night

As he rounded the kitchen table, the television came into view and images of Nicole appeared in a music video. She smiled at the camera as if to counter Zack's sullen disposition. And then he stopped. There was a special radiance in the footage, a shimmering essence, that was transformative and suddenly all of the resentment that he felt about her deceitfulness magically dissolved into a coveted aura of reconciliation and peace.

It was then that he knew: *No way could she have been an addict! The speculation about her death didn't make medical sense... where was the respiratory crisis or miosis, the constriction of her pupils, that night? There was none!*

Zack felt ashamed for letting his bruised ego obstruct his acumen since he was first blindsided by the NBC news report.

"Passion and More" was followed by Martha Quinn, one of MTV's popular original VJ's from the 1980s, appearing on camera. "Working at MTV was quite an experience back in the day and I'm so honored to be with you again for this special tribute to my friend Nicole Branson. I had the privilege of having her on my radio show many times and spending time with her socially. I know that she would be touched by your response to her passing. We continue now with an MTV exclusive, her final composition..."

Zack lowered himself into a chair, hypnotized, as Quinn continued, "This remarkable video features Nicole's recent live acoustic performance of a new song that she never had the chance to record in the studio. Here's Nicole Branson and "Silent Partners.""

Icy jolts of dejection shot through Zack as her screen image materialized. There she was, looking so young and vital, alone onstage with her guitar at a political fundraiser. Her hair shining in subtle stage lighting, she never looked more beautiful. Word by word, the song drove itself into Zack like a stake through his soul:

Baby, you've just got to believe
It was hard to conceive of life without you
But loving you just wasn't enough
To find the words to say all that I feel
Now you're gone - all I have of you are my dreams
Of your kiss, your smile, your eyes on me
Loving you

Everything that Nicole sang expressed what Zack was feeling. It was uncanny. If he could have stepped through the screen to be closer to her, he would have.

How can I be silent when I really want to shout?
How can I be happy when it's you I live without?
How can love be good, yet oh so very bad?
How can I release the man I never really had?

There were more lyrics, but he could not listen anymore. He darkened the set and tossed the remote aside, sinking into the cushion as his body trembled. His insides felt like melting wax. *What the world was saying about her was an appalling fucking lie!*

Just then, a comforting hand touched his cheek. Zack jerked around to find Nicole sitting beside him. "Jesus Christ...!" he cried out.

She contemplated him affectionately. "I didn't mean to startle you."

He could not speak or think. Searching her face for an explanation, he was lost.

He wasn't asleep and he wasn't drunk. This couldn't be!

"Zack...?"

He held his silence before suddenly standing. "What the hell's wrong with me?!"

"Nothing," she exhorted.

He laughed caustically. "No? Well, I'm not shitfaced this time,

Nicole, but here you are anyway."

On the balcony outside Zack pressed against the railing and looked down at the street, lost in a jumble of thoughts. They were not even thoughts, really, but a rupture of incongruous sentiments trying to take form. But he was not going to let that happen. What he needed was separation from this and having visions of Nicole was not helping.

He heard the sliding door open behind him and tried not to react. It was upsetting to think that what took place inside might not have been a figment of his imagination.

As always, her voice was gentle. "I was hoping you'd be glad to see me."

"You don't know how much I wish I could," he said without turning.

"But you can."

"Yeah, well we both know the truth about that, don't we."

She was beside him now, too close to ignore. "I know that I'm here with you right now." Her perfume enveloped him and the hairs on his neck tingled.

He spun to face her in frustration. "What the hell happened?!"

"I wish I knew," she answered.

Then he stopped as he realized that for a moment he actually believed she might be standing there. "Now I'm talking to myself," he swallowed as he turned away.

Nicole studied him for what seemed like an eternity before forcing herself to say the words, "I'm sorry. I won't bother you again. Take care."

He watched her walk to the door, moving as if in slow motion in the coastal gust that whispered across the balcony.

"Nicole, wait," he called out. She turned and his voice cracked, "Please stay."

"How can I if I'm not here?" she asked.

"I don't know," he told her. He had never spoken more truthfully. "The important thing is you're with me again," he added.

"Do you believe what they're saying about me?"

"Look at me," he commanded, meeting her gaze. "I know you

aren't like that."

"Everyone says I am."

"Then I'll prove them wrong." He enveloped her in her arms and the touch of her was breathtaking. Could this be real? He knew it could not be but he was not going to question it.

She accepted his kiss and paused to run her fingers through his soft blonde hair. "Being with you was more than a one-night thing for me."

"Me, too," he assured her, relieved to hear her say it.

Nicole smiled and, taking his hand in hers, led him inside. Neither of them spoke as they entered his bedroom, where she began to undress. Zack had assumed that lovemaking could never be more exciting than it was that night at the Greek, but she proved him wrong. There was something about the irrationality of their union this time, the pure danger of it, that made being with her now all the more electrifying.

NEWS ITEM:

The Associated Press, April 27

A memorial service for singer-songwriter Nicole Branson will be held at noon today in Glendale, California, at Forest Lawn Memorial Park. The popular entertainer, who died last week following a drug overdose, instructed in her will that her remains be interred with those of her parents, Lawrence and Frances Branson.

Chapter Five

Zack meandered aimlessly among the uniform rows of simple headstone markers at Forest Lawn Memorial Park. The euphoria of being with Nicole again had receded and his despondency returned. He was only vaguely aware of the statuary reflected in a nearby pond or their striking adornments of flowers.

In the distance, cheerless organ music dispensed serenity across the impeccably manicured grounds. Unfortunately, Zack's bewilderment went beyond the cosmetic effects of landscaping or holy music could ever reach. He was incapable of feeling much of anything right now.

Maybe that was for the best, he thought. Somewhere among the factoids of his medical education were abstractions about the human mind and how it shifts into modes it requires for self-protection. When suffering becomes too severe, the mind often has a way of obstructing its own circuitry, and when reality becomes too oppressive, the mind can block it out to substitute a more acceptable creation of its own.

How else could Nicole's reappearances be explained?

Then he stopped. Before him a row of black limousines outside the quaint Wee Kirk of the Heather Chapel cast a spell over two thousand somber onlookers. They were her fans and he understood their deferential silence. If anyone noticed him they would assume that he was just another admirer here to pay his respects.

Several people moving among the attendees were handing out copies of a homemade flyer. Zack nodded appreciatively as he accepted one from a young man whose dour countenance revealed the intensity of grief that he was feeling. Upon glancing at the paper Zack recognized a poem that Nicole once posted on Facebook, calling it the consolation that helped her when her parents passed away.

It was Colleen Hitchcock's beautiful "Ascension."

And if I go,
While you're still here...
Know that I live on,
Vibrating to a different measure
—behind a thin veil you cannot see through.
You will not see me,
So you must have faith.
I wait for the time when we can soar together again,
—both aware of each other.
Until then, live your life to its fullest.
And when you need me,
Just whisper my name in your heart,
...I will be there.

Zack read the words again and allowed himself to marinate in them. Nicole cherished Hitchcock's message and knowing that fact was a gift, particularly in view of his precarious psychological and emotional state. Looking at the people around him, he saw that it had been her present to them, too.

The hymn inside the church concluded and for a time there was no sound except for the frolicsome chirping of sparrows and finches in the surrounding trees. Finally, the tower bell intoned its barren proclamation of Nicole's fate. And each forlorn ring seemed to carry Zack further and further from personal involvement in the proceedings. It was ironic being removed from it all, yet so intricately involved.

If people only knew how involved...

Zack thought about the obituaries in *The Los Angeles Times* and *USA Today*, and the endless online postings that had enraged him. Their sneering innuendos about the overdose were disparaging, as if rumor and fact warranted equal handling under the catchall called Freedom of Speech. Nicole did not deserve such treatment, he resolved. It had taken him too long to come to his senses about that, of course, but the simple truth was that the autopsy results had not been published. Until then, everything was bullshit.

At that moment someone beside him spoke, "Remarkable, is

it not?" Zack turned to find a thickset fifty year-old Hispanic man in a black cassock and white clerical collar gazing at the large gathering.

"I'm sorry... what?" Zack asked.

"The impact that one individual can have, it is inspiring," the priest continued as he offered his hand. "Forgive me for intruding on your reflection. I am Father Luis Solano from Saint Teresa's church."

"Zack Raskin," he responded, returning the handshake.

"Miss Branson's passing is an extraordinary event," Solano added as mourners emerged from the sanctuary. "But of course, you know that," he added pointedly, "being more than a fan."

The statement landed hard and Zack reacted more quickly than he intended. "What do you mean?"

"Your face speaks volumes," the priest stated simply. "You and Miss Branson were close, were you not?"

Zack answered as convincingly as he could, but the priest's perception unnerved him. "Actually... I didn't know her that long."

Solano met his look with penetrating scrutiny. "And yet I detect something else. Something much deeper. More than grief."

"No, grief pretty much sums it up," Zack said hoping to end what was starting to feel like a cross-examination. "Well, I've got to run. It was nice meeting you, Father."

But Solano had more to say, which came more forcefully this time. "Zack, I am not a conventional parish priest," he began, impeding Zack's departure. "I see things that others do not." As the potential meaning of the words registered on Zack's face, Solano took the homemade flyer from his hand and wrote on it. "Here is my number if you ever want to talk."

Zack could no longer deal with the priest or the gloomy scene around him. All he could think about was getting out of Glendale and back on the freeway heading home. He would return another day, he promised himself, when he could be alone at Nicole's grave. He mumbled something unintelligible as he shoved the flyer in his pocket and left.

As he hiked up Cathedral Slope to his car, Zack yanked his tie and collar open, wishing that he could move faster without looking like he was running. Even though run was exactly what he wanted to do. Father Solano's words had upset him, to be sure. Unhappily, his getaway from Forest Lawn was hampered as he approached a young woman who seemed to be waiting for him.

How anybody could have missed Sandy Phillips was another story. Ten years older than Zack, she was a tough product of New York City streets with overly processed red hair and a tendency to pack her voluptuous figure into skimpy outfits, not to mention her penchant for long artificial fingernails, which she wore like weapons. At the moment they were shiny black, though Zack would have reason to doubt that their color had anything to do with reverence for the event Sandy was attending.

"Mind if I walk along?" she inquired, hitting her vowels so hard he thought she might be joking.

"I'm not going far," he told her as he hurried on.

Sandy stayed at his elbow even though his pace was taking the wind out of her. "You were at the hospital with Nicole, am I right? The paramedic?"

Zack reacted with surprise. "One of them," he offered without explaining the difference between a certified paramedic like Angie and an EMT.

"Truth is, Mister Raskin, I've been lookin' for you," she offered while extending her hand with a smile. "Sandy Phillips, from *Rolling Stone*."

Still recovering from Father Solano's apparent ability to see into his soul, Zack tried to mask his panic over the idea of a national magazine finding out about Nicole and him and hounding him forever. His mind conjured up tabloid covers with sordid photographs of the couple naked on a rooftop lounge chair at the Greek.

And on his bed three hours ago.

Upon arriving at his beloved Honda Prelude, now rescued from impound and incongruously parked among a fleet of luxury vehicles, he turned to her politely. "Well, this's as far as I go. Nice to see you."

But she remained persistent. Putting a restraining arm on the door, she held her ground. "I'd like to talk about Nicole. Can I spring for lunch?"

"I don't think so. Thanks anyway."

"Okay, then you buy," she added with an indifferent shrug, still holding the door.

He yanked the car open. "I meant that I don't want to talk about this." He climbed inside more roughly than necessary to accentuate his irritation.

"You were there when she died."

"Maybe you didn't hear me," he stated firmly, "I'm not interested." But interested or not he was a captive of this nag because the damn engine would not start. More panic filled him as he envisioned Sandy sabotaging his spark plugs in a diabolical plan to make him tell all.

She leaned closer, her oversized breasts brushing against his arm. "You don't have a clue how important your perspective is, do you."

"No more important than anybody else's," he insisted while coaxing the ignition. *Please... start... start!* No such luck. His mind contemplated other getaway options, like locking her in the trunk and catching a cab outside the cemetery gates.

"Come on, Raskin," she whined, "Ya gotta have thoughts about the overdose."

"Yeah," he declared. "It never happened." With that the engine cooperated and Zack drove off in a cloud of exhaust that engulfed the young woman at the curb.

Powell Library at UCLA was busier than usual that afternoon, as an onslaught of research papers and exams descended on students campus-wide. Tucked away in a corner of the third floor sat a most unlikely occupant: Zack Raskin. He could count on one hand the times that he had visited the venerable building, but it was a lot more private than the medical school facility. He desperately needed whatever seclusion he could find. The crushing finality of the memorial service and disquieting implications made by the priest had brought home the full impact of his two recent encounters with

Nicole. Especially making love to her again. The repercussions of their renewed intimacies were turning him inside out.

It was time to pull himself together.

Zack had come to the library for explanations because the Internet only offered so much reliable specialized information. He steered his search to a category of books with such titles as *Life After Death, The Paranormal Handbook, Ghosts & Spirits Among Us, Secret Dimensions, and Mysteries of the Unexplained.* Books that suggested interpretations of Nicole's return that he would have never previously considered. *"There is much that mankind doesn't understand about the supernatural phenomena around him,"* one passage assured him. *"From UFO's to the great pyramids to reincarnation and ESP, conventional science is at a loss. Unfortunately, some people dismiss what they cannot explain about their universe..."*

He read that last part back, how people reject what they cannot substantiate, and wished that he been accorded that option. *Why couldn't he shelve the events of the past few days and move on? Why and how had Nicole come to him so dramatically? And how the hell could that priest at Forest Lawn know so much about him?!*

His best hope was to uncover insights that might shed light on what was happening, and he was prepared to study every book on campus if necessary. After all, he was accustomed to a medical world of absolutes, where epidemiological study defines a person's health, so explaining an ongoing romantic relationship with a deceased woman was not going to be easy. And yet, he reminded himself, none-other than Albert Einstein once published a theory about twelve dimensions that are observable from the third dimension that humans occupy.

Failing a scientific discovery, Zack would look for a remedy that did not involve Rolling Rock beer or anything stronger. A book called *Guided Imagery* seemed promising, since the once-marginalized visualization technique was becoming a legitimate adjunctive tool for the treatment of medical and emotional issues.

Zack was well into his research when he was interrupted by a familiar grating voice, "Well, I'm impressed..!"

Startled, he glanced up to see none other than the garrulous Sandy Phillips towering over him munching from a vending machine bag of potato chips. He contrived a thin smile and shut his book. "If it isn't Lois Lane. How are things at the *Daily Planet*?"

"*Rolling Stone*," she corrected as she helped herself to a seat. The heavy wooden chair scraped noisily as she hauled it into position.

"Kidney Stone would be more accurate," he glowered.

Sandy picked at the remaining chips in the bag with one of her monstrous fingernails. "You aren't gonna make this easy, am I right?" she asked loudly. Her voice was like that, he determined, always torqued as if she were communicating with the hard-of-hearing.

Nearby students glared at the unwelcome breach of library etiquette. Zack answered in a quieter tone. "That depends. Are you going to badger me again?"

"When did I badger you?" she protested.

"Today. At Forest Lawn."

"I asked you to lunch."

"And when I said no, you didn't take the hint."

Sandy set the bag of chips on the table. "Yeah well, actually I was thinkin' about apologizing for that."

She seemed nicer now without having to pretend, but Zack still wanted to be left alone. "Hey, we all act like insensitive jerks once in a while," he retaliated. "How'd you know I was here?"

"Brilliant investigative technique."

He was not buying it. "Right."

"Okay, your roommate told me," she admitted. "But for some reason he doubted you'd really be here. What's that all about?"

"An allergy I have to book bindings. Tragic malady..." he began, and then faked a cough before gathering up his materials. "I'd better split before the open sores appear."

A second later he was heading across the room, forcing her to scramble after him as he had at the cemetery. "Raskin, wait. One question, okay? Then I leave ya alone."

Zack slowed, eyebrows raised. "Forever and ever?" he asked derisively.

"May I get hit by lightning if I'm lyin'."

He shrugged before exiting into the hallway. "Works for me."

As Sandy scooted through the door behind him her brassy

voice seemed to shriek in the high-ceilinged passageway. "What'd you mean before, when ya said the overdose never happened?"

Zack measured his response. She was analyzing him and he knew it. "A figure of speech," he explained.

"It was more than that, alright? I'd like to know what's up."

"I don't believe Nicole used drugs, that's all."

"And...?"

"I just don't buy it," he concluded at the elevator.

Her skepticism was obvious. "Based on what?"

"Based on nothing."

Sandy's frustration grew as she saw the interview dying on her. "But you can't take a position like that without somethin' to stand on."

The elevator bell sounded with a soft ping. Zack turned to face his interrogator for what he hoped would be the last time. "The lady was a friend, Lois. I cared about her."

As the vacant elevator car opened, he stepped inside. Sandy edged to the door. "All right, let's say a skinny kid with holes in his jeans knows more than the county coroner. How'd she die?"

"Unpleasantly," he replied as the doors closed.

Zack flopped against a wall of the cubicle, closing his eyelids. As he shut out the world, the far-away clanking of pulleys and rhythmic rattle of the elevator floor proved calming.

But his isolation was short-lived. The sound of Nicole's voice ruptured his tranquility. "You really told her off."

Zack turned to find her watching him carefully. "She deserved it," he said, not knowing how he was supposed to acknowledge her presence. "I hate ball busters like her." A barrage of questions flittered through his brain: *were there rules for conversations with a dead woman?* Albert Einstein had failed to cover that eventuality.

"It was nice of you to stand up for me," she offered sweetly.

"I'd do anything for you. You know how I feel."

An eternity passed.

"I'm not sure I do."

"What are you talking about?" he disputed.

"Of course you do."

She took her time choosing her words. "Zack, you know

Nicole Branson through songs, videos, and our one night together. You don't really know *me*."

"I know enough to have fallen in love," he shot back, startling her as much as himself with the pronouncement. He had blurted it out without thinking, but he meant it. And it was something he had never told any other woman. Zack believed with all his heart that he shared something special with her and that they would have continued to see each other if she had lived.

Of course, she *hadn't* lived, and further reminders of that fact were not necessary. Her death had permeated his thoughts and movements for days. Nicole practically died in his arms and yet here she was with him again, every bit as stunning as the moment he first comprehended whom he nearly spilled hot coffee on. Their amazing sexual liaison today, which she conspicuously failed to mention, and her appearance in the elevator mocked the finality of her death that everyone else in the world had accepted.

The fragrance of her perfume clutched his throat and the urge to hold her and never let go was overwhelming. *What the hell was he supposed to do now?!*

"Love..." Nicole repeated skeptically. "Are you sure?"

"How can you ask that, after what happened with us today?" he came back.

"Emotions are complicated, Zack. Learn everything about me," she implored, inching closer. "Then tell me what you feel is love."

"I already know everything I need."

"No, you don't," she insisted. The argument had a dire ring. "Find out who I am and what happened at the concert. It might change your mind."

Just then the elevator doors opened and a gaggle of students crowded in. He glanced back at her, but he need not have bothered. Nicole was gone.

NEWS ITEM:

KCBS-TV News Transcript, April 28

Even as the shock waves of entertainer Nicole Branson's death from a heroin overdose continue to reverberate through Hollywood, a press conference was announced today by Miss Branson's attorney, Dwight McKinney, to discuss the terms of her will. Advance word is that her estate of a reported thirty million dollars is to be divided among various charities and environmental causes. A separate provision is said to establish an educational fund for the children of a distant cousin, Miss Branson's only surviving relatives.

Chapter Six

A FedEx jet screamed overhead as Zack cupped a hand over his ear to facilitate his call from the noisy baggage claim carousel. "Yo, Dougie," he chirped with less than his usual perkiness. "It's me."

Doug was in the apartment, making a sandwich with whatever he could scrounge from the refrigerator that did not look like a failed lab experiment. "Zack, where the hell are you? You missed the Med Ethics seminar."

"I'm in Youngstown, Ohio," Zack told him.

Doug set aside the mustard jar with the overdue expiration date. "Funny, I thought you just said you're in Ohio."

"I did."

Doug paused. "Okay, I'm game... why?"

"Nicole grew up here," Zack explained. "I have to find out what I can about her."

An awkward silence followed. Zack knew there was no chance of Doug understanding his motivations.

"So, how long's that going to take?"

"I dunno," Zack told him.

"A few days, a week."

Once again Doug was caught short. "Zack..." he began, "I don't mean to be unkind, but don't you think you're acting a little strange?"

"You always say I'm strange."

"This time you're pinning the needle," Doug went on. "You see that, right?"

Zack knew what Doug was getting at, of course, since he had been wrestling with that very concept for days. "I can't describe it... I know she wants me to do this."

"Who does...?"

"Nicole."

There was that name again. "You talk like she's still with us," he finally broached.

"Sometimes it seems like she is," Zack explained.

Doug glanced at the stack of medical books waiting for him

on the dining room table. "Don't take too long, okay? Even you have to show up for class occasionally."

Zack's rental car was a silver tin can that the car rental company jokingly passed off as a passenger vehicle instead of what it was, which was something that clowns might pack into at a circus. But it was inexpensive, which pretty much covered his list of requirements. It also had a name he had never heard before, something the Korean marketing people must have thought had a dynamic English-language ring to it, but to Zack sounded like *Cirrhosis* or *Sclerosis*. And that made him smile. Anything that could make him smile these days was a good bet.

As he drove his Korean Sclerosis into the Mahoning Valley, the landscape around him changed dramatically. Zack could see the deserted factories that riddled Youngstown's approaching skyline, persistent victims of the decline of the Midwestern rust belt in the 1980s and bad economic conditions in the time since. He sipped from a cup of bitter mud-like gas station coffee and glanced at men on street corners with nothing to do but smoke cigarettes and wait. While some industrial cities managed to reinvent themselves over the years, Youngstown was still searching for a new identity.

Zack juggled his drink with one hand and steered with his knee so that he could find something on the radio. The tuner was awful. Ultimately, he located a station where an announcer with affected mellifluence and too much reverb was reminding listeners that tonight was *Bra-less Blonde Night* at a place called The Love Machine, where blonde women without brassieres would be admitted free.

The radio signal worsened with a thick cloud of static that came across as he imagined a nuclear holocaust might sound, but when Zack moved to change channels a woman's hand beat him to the control and turned it off. Curiously, he was not surprised to find Nicole in the car—in fact he had been hoping to see her. And now there she was, in faded jeans and an oversized black pullover sweater, looking like anybody else taking a road trip.

"My parents moved to this country because they wanted a better life," she began as if resuming a previous conversation. Her voice was soft as she contemplated the scenery. "They never found it in Youngstown. Not many people did."

Zack did not know how to respond, something told him that now was not the time. She had appeared for a reason.

"Everyone's had it bad," she continued. "Factories closing, people unemployed... you can see the sadness in the air."

"I'm seeing lots of things these days," he muttered. "Not all of them add up."

She turned to read his reaction. "Are you mad at me?"

"No, I'm not mad. Unless you're using the psychological term, then my roommate thinks I'm certifiable."

"What's wrong?" she asked.

"Well, you're still in my life for one thing and that doesn't make a hell of a lot of sense." He shot her a hard look. "That makes me pretty messed up."

"You deserve answers," she said in a near-whisper. "I don't have many, I'm afraid."

Zack could see that she was trying to be candid. "Then let's start with this: why the hell am I in Ohio?" he asked as simply as he could.

"Because you care about me," she offered cautiously. "You're my only hope to clear my name." She rolled the window down to inhale a lifetime of memories that seemed to saturate the landscape.

Zack shunted his attention back to the road. "What about you, Nicole?" he probed further. "Why are you here?"

"What do you mean?"

"You know what I mean." He studied the oncoming yellow lane dividers as they strobed toward him until taking on the effect of a solid line. "Are you a ghost?"

"I don't know."

"Well, if you don't who does?"

"Some things aren't easily explained," she said apologetically."

He was watching her. Screw the oncoming traffic. "Come on," he snapped. "You've gotta do better than that."

"But I can't."

"Try."

"Zack..." she began as tears filled her eyes. "I don't know what's going on any more than you do. One moment I'm feeling sick on stage... then I'm fighting to breathe... I can't explain what I don't understand." She turned to look at him. "But you were there and I could tell you were just as scared. The next thing I knew... I was gone."

"Aren't you forgetting something?" He waited for more but nothing came. "You also came back and made love to me like you meant it. Then you accused me of not really knowing you. Why won't you just level with me?!"

"I am leveling with you," she insisted.

"Then why don't I feel better?" Once again he trained his concentration on the highway and saw that his fingers had turned white from gripping the wheel. Loosening his grasp, he turned to Nicole once more but she was gone.

He drove on in troubled silence for what could have been ten minutes before a peculiar feeling came over him. It was then he saw that Nicole's window was still rolled down. *She really had been there!*

Gulping the cold remains of his coffee, his heart pounded. Her ghost was here because she needed him. But just as important, he understood how much he needed her. He felt complete when she was with him and empty when she was not.

Pushing those thoughts from his mind, he concentrated on keeping the car moving in a straight line. As he pointed it at the recesses of town, a weighty cloud hung prophetically on the horizon.

Zack's days in Youngstown were disorienting. Despite his efforts to visit the places where Nicole grew up, the city and its people were little more than a collective blur that he could never quite bring into focus. As if the momentary detachment that he felt at the funeral had permanently disabled his sensory abilities.

Zack's teachers would have called his visit a subconscious experience. Like a Fellini movie that he could not turn off, the trip was a disjointed and confounding event.

It began on a cracked sidewalk into which had been etched the date, 1947. He was absorbing the tired appearance of a residential street when an elderly man's voice injected, "I don't have any use for Nicole Branson's kind, young man..."

Inexplicably, Zack had been deposited onto a neighborhood porch stoop. Without knowing how he got there, he was sitting beside the man while children dressed in clothes and hairstyles from the 1980s played hopscotch on the sidewalk. Zack gawked at the illusion taking place around him.

The elderly man nudged him with a bony elbow and pointed a finger at one of the children. "People like her, they forget where they came from," he charged. "You think she ever did anything to help this city?"

Zack followed the man's look to the girl he was talking about—*it was young Nicole!* He was astounded by the sight. The man continued to lecture, but his words were just vapors escaping from a rusted pipe. They were nothing to be saved.

Zack climbed from the stoop as the child tossed a pebble into one of the boxes drawn in chalk on the sidewalk. His pace was purposeful; he didn't want to disturb her. The scrawny girl hopped from one uneven square to another and Zack could see that this adolescent Nicole was far from the mature figure she would become in later years.

Moving closer, however, he could make out more clearly the womanly promise that her face exhibited even then. There was a degree of sophistication about her that set her apart from the other kids. Zack also noted that she had a pasty complexion, which he guessed came from poor nutrition.

Little Nicole glanced up at him and frowned. He felt compelled to say something, but when he opened his mouth *young Nicole and her friends had already vanished.*

An instant later Zack was gone from the neighborhood and relocated to an inexpensive motel—where he was in bed with Nicole making love. The bed frame was squeaking loudly and he could not comprehend how he had been transported here without knowing it, let alone be with her like this. When she cried out that she loved him he reacted with no small amount of relief—*at last!*—only to discover later that she was no longer there. He was alone in the bed and drenched in sweat.

His fingers touched the pillow beside him and found it warm. Pulling it towards him, he could smell her lingering perfume. He would have to accept Nicole on her terms, as confusing and unconventional as they might be.

The next thing that Zack knew, his location changed once more and day plunged into night. He was now standing in a graffiti-scarred doorway that shielded him from a driving rain as a frosty woman's voice spoke from a place unseen, "The way she defied her parents' wishes was terrible. It broke her mother's heart."

Zack followed the voice through the door into a neighborhood dress shop where an old woman worked an ancient sewing machine. A Kiwanis calendar on the wall said it was 2017, though the place felt more like the 1950s. And Zack was in a conversation he had not remembered starting. "Was Nicole really so terrible?" he was asking.

The woman grunted her antipathy as the variable speed motor sped up and slowed in response to her foot on the floor control. "To Frances she was," she said condemningly. "Lord rest her soul. Nicole knew how she felt."

Zack followed her stare to the window, where a middle-aged woman was adjusting a display. Her face was drawn and her shoulders heavy. If ever there was medical evidence of a broken heart, Zack thought, this woman was it. He immediately knew her identity, though it was impossible. It fit the pattern of events associated with this odyssey: he was somehow looking back in time. *The woman was Nicole's mother.*

Zack approached her uncertainly, seeing right away her resemblance to her daughter. Although she was only a few years older than Nicole, still in what should have been her prime, she seemed much older. The years of hard work and poverty had taken their toll. And so, apparently, had the maternal heartache that the old woman spoke about and the mental illness that Nicole described in their dressing room discussion.

Frances Branson paused in her work to glance briefly at Zack. He saw the same caring in her that he loved in Nicole. He wanted so much to bombard her with questions but he never had the opportunity.

He was abruptly deposited in an unkempt park on an overcast day, wandering through the weeds beneath decomposing playground equipment as a distant church bell rang. Another disembodied voice spoke to him. "She was a quiet girl, and sickly. Always had the flu or some darned thing..."

Suddenly, Zack was dispatched again, this time to an elementary school classroom located in the bowels of an old red brick building. An elderly woman was talking as a class of children worked on a math problem. "She fell behind in her studies, days here, weeks there," the woman said, motioning towards little Nicole. "The time she got rheumatic fever we had to hold her back an entire grade. It's hard to believe she ever became a sex symbol."

He looked at Nicole, perhaps half the age she was when she played hopscotch in the street. She looked back and smiled. But then, as before, the teacher and her students evaporated from sight. Zack was standing beside his car near an uninhabited steel mill. He watched teenagers throw rocks at broken windows, then got in his rental car and drove away.

He needed a drink. Badly.

"She started out on that stage thirteen years ago..." the bartender was saying. Zack sat at the bar as country music he didn't recognize boomed from a jukebox. He was no longer stuck in the grotesque Youngstown time warp that previously held him prisoner, this time he was having a conversation with a real person. The trace of Jack Daniels in the bartender's personal aroma was proof enough of that.

The bartender, whose *Middy's Roadhouse* bowling shirt identified him as Dave, was in his late-thirties and every inch a local guy who had probably never ventured very far from this tavern, the consecrated spot where he more than likely tied on his first drunk and lost his virginity in the parking lot.

Sipping a cold bottle of Rolling Rock, Zack felt at home in

the well-worn surroundings, where generational rites of passage play out with dependability and oats are regularly sown. Where blue-collar guys drink domestic brew and local women pretend they are something they are not.

He glanced at the stage as Dave told him about the band that Nicole fronted years ago, Mahoningly Yours. It was less a stage, really, than a carpeted platform a few feet higher than the booze-stained pool tables.

"I'll bet it was something," he suggested to Dave, "seeing the start of it all."

The bartender thought about that as he wiped a mug. "It was for a while."

"What do you mean?"

Dave slid the mug onto an overhead shelf. "Well, you know," he said with a tinge of regret, "people change."

Zack wanted to ask more, but the jukebox was fading prematurely while other music faded in—*live music*. He turned and his jaw dropped at the sight of *fifteen year-old Nicole* and her young band plowing through a rousing version of Pat Benatar's 's 1980's smash "Heartbreaker." She was cute and energetic as she belted out the classic lyrics.

But seeing young Nicole perform was not Zack's only confounding discovery: in the room's improbable transformation the old pool tables had been replaced by a capacity crowd. Everyone was attentive to each vocal turn that she dispensed.

Zack was absolutely mesmerized. Nicole's distinctive vibrancy was already shining through the unpolished edges of her teenage exuberance. She was a star in the making.

As the song ended, the bartender's remark was still dangling in the air, "... *people change*." Zack pulled his attention back to the present, "How did she change?"

Dave's continued stare at the stage suggested that he, too, might be seeing her up there. "In the beginning she was just a shy kid," he began. "Nobody paid her much mind. But in a year or so she grew into her looks, if you know what I mean. She was pretty hot stuff." He trailed at the memory and then finished his thought. "And did she ever know it. By then she treated everybody like garbage."

Zack stole another look at the stage. Young Nicole was still there, strutting her stuff for the crowd. *Could this nubile girl be the same woman he had been making love to?* The answer was no, of course, but he could not help watching with a certain dark interest. Did his fascination with the woman this child became now make him some sort of pervert? *Jesus Christ, as if he didn't have enough problems already! Now he was heading into pedophile territory?!*

As he wrestled with that unsettling question, Young Nicole was pouring out in a killer rendition of the iconic rock ballad "Will You Still Love Me Tomorrow?" It was as if she were singing it just for him.

Zack wanted to keep listening, but remembered that he owed Dave a response. "Treating people that way doesn't sound like the Nicole I... heard about," he observed.

"Neither did that drug addict who killed herself in Hollywood, I'll bet." Dave shook his head sadly. "Once she hit around here, she was on the road outta town. Nicole didn't give a damn about the friends she had after three years of gigs."

The room plummeted back into silence and Zack took one more peek at the stage, which was empty. The bartender wiped another mug. "None of us."

Zack's curiosity about the inference was brief. Dave's eyes said it all. Zack understood that he had been in love with her, too. And for all he knew, she had loved him back. Right outside in the backseat of his car. Dave's sentiments were more than those of a casual acquaintance.

Before Zack could follow up on the point, Dave moved off and revealed Nicole sitting on a barstool, scrutinizing him. "Deflates the image a bit, doesn't it," she remarked.

"He sounds pretty jealous."

"I hurt a lot of people, Zack. I thought I was better than them."

"You are better than them."

"Who says?"

"I do," he argued.

She was filled with sorrow. "You heard Dave. I'm not who you think I am."

But before Zack could dispute it, Dave reappeared with a case of bottles that he began transferring into the cooler. Zack slouched in disillusionment. Nicole was no longer anywhere to be seen.

In the darkened United Airlines 737 coasting through the clear midnight sky, high above the mosaic of miniature cities dotting the Midwestern plains, everyone was asleep except for one passenger. Zack sat under an overhead light, mired in the thoughts that haunted him. An iPad screen filled with Nicole's pictures glimmered up from his tray table. There was no escaping his situation and nowhere for him to turn.

"*You know Nicole Branson through songs, videos, and our one night together,*" she had told him in the library elevator. "*You don't really know me.*"

The words curdled in Zack's stomach like food poisoning. Unable to look at images any longer, he closed the iPad and switched off the light. No one had the slightest idea of what he was going through—except for the mysterious priest at the funeral. Father Luis Solano seemed to know things that he could not possibly have known and Zack was committed to avoiding finding out how he did.

In the rear of the plane, a large man stood to stretch his legs. He located Zack's location several rows ahead and determined from his fidgeting that he was having trouble falling asleep. Returning to his seat, the man settled back and closed his eyes. He would have no such problem.

NEWS ITEM:

E! Entertainment Telecast, May 1

The untimely death of Nicole Branson may have, in the minds of the mainstream American media, cast another cloud on the reputation of rock and roll music. But can the tragic legacy of deaths and suicides related to substance abuse among rock artists really be linked to the music? Is it a consequence of fame? Or could it be a commentary on the performers themselves? From Jimi Hendrix, Janis Joplin, Jim Morrison, Sid Vicious, and Elvis Presley in the distant past to Whitney Houston, Michael Jackson, Amy Winehouse, Prince, and Nicole Branson in recent years, it seems that the dark places within them could only be temporarily illuminated by their art. It was then that the darkness seized permanent and final control.

Chapter Seven

A match tip blazed to life lighting the Marlboro cigarette that trembled between Zack's fingertips. Sitting in the empty corridor of the Factor Building at UCLA, he dismissed the fact that he had not smoked since high school. So what if he was negating years of abstinence? His physical well-being seemed irrelevant. All he cared about now was seeing Doc Sandberg. She, he had concluded, was the one person who could help him with the more troubling matters at hand.

A petite young woman with long black hair, ear gauges, and an assortment of eyebrow and lip piercings emerged from an office suite and hesitated at the sight of Zack's haggard appearance. Ultimately, she motioned him inside.

He lumbered down an inner hallway of faculty offices to an open door, but when he paused in the opening the professor addressed him without taking her eyes off her computer screen. "You'll have to make it fast, Zack," she said, making a notation on a legal pad. "I'm not even supposed to be here today." Then she looked up and immediately recognized that there would be no rushing this. Her student was in trouble.

The first thing that Sandberg did was disregard the campus smoking ban. If body language offers clues to human behavior, then Zack's demeanor was clinically noteworthy. She motioned for him to sit. "So... how can I help you today?"

He descended into a chair and grimaced from the muscle soreness caused by sleep deprivation. "I don't know exactly where to start."

Sandberg observed him thoughtfully. "Why not start at the beginning?"

He responded with a desperation-filled stare, the depths of which made her uncomfortable. "I... I'm coming unglued."

Ordinarily, she would have rejected such non-specific jargon, but Zack was obviously in discomfort and being *unglued* was his way of describing it. "What makes you say that?" she asked matter-of-factly.

He hesitated as the words that he rehearsed on the drive over deserted him. Thankfully, they eventually reinstated themselves. "A friend of mine died nine days ago..." he began guardedly. "A really close friend." He paused again, doubting himself. Doc Sandberg could never understand the bind he was in. And now that he was talking, he was convinced that there was no way to explain it.

Sandberg moved her chair closer. "It's okay, Zack. Take your time."

He took a long, tired inhalation. "Anyway, she died..." he resumed, "but now she's back. What I mean is, I can see her."

"I'm sorry for your loss," she said honestly. "How many times has this happened?"

"A bunch."

Sandberg accepted the statement. "It's not as uncommon as you might believe."

"I'd really like to believe that..." Zack replied.

"Sometimes our subconscious minds try to help when we're in distress," she continued." After my father passed away he came to me in dreams, asking me to stop grieving."

Zack finished his cigarette and dropped it in an empty Pepsi can that he retrieved from a wastebasket. "But these aren't dreams," he countered. "Nicole's real. We talk... we argue..." He did not know how to say the rest, so he just went for it. "We've even made love."

Sandberg watched him closely, absently fingering her Navajo necklace. "Go on," she encouraged.

He looked away but knew that her eyes were trained on him. Hopefully she would not misconstrue his averted gaze as an evasion, rather than a neurological reaction to searching for words. He desperately wanted to tell her everything. "At first the idea of seeing a ghost freaked me out, ya know?" he confessed. "But what scares the shit out of me is how much I like being with her." He could have gone on, but there was little point. He sounded like a complete lunatic.

"It's hard to lose someone we're close to, Zack," Sandberg offered. "Your anxiety is understandable, but I doubt that you're coming unglued, as you call it."

"But I'm having sex with her – how twisted is that?!"

"Everyone handles loss differently. Your mind is processing

yours the way it needs to."

Zack envisioned the emotional memories in his amygdala, hippocampus, and medial temporal lobe short-circuiting all at once in a melodramatic eruption of sparks and smoke. "So... I'm delusional?"

Sandberg did not have an easy answer. "Some people believe in ghosts, but in my experience there are things that wishing for can't make happen," she told him. "No matter how hard we might try."

His disappointment was obvious and she waited for her comment to sink in before resuming. "I recommend that you take some time off. Recharge your batteries." But she could see from Zack's depleted condition that he needed more than that. "Do you have anyone to share your feelings with? A minister or rabbi, perhaps?"

The image of Father Solano approaching him at Forest Lawn flickered through his mind. "I met a priest the other day and he offered to talk to me."

"Maybe you should give that a try."

"I don't know," he answered. He could not bring himself to admit why Solano was so troubling for him. "I mean, I don't really know the guy. Besides, that's why I'm here."

"And I'm glad you came. But I think that someone who specializes in grief counseling would be more effective."

Zack could not imagine anyone being drawn to a job filled with death and misery. Patients would always be like him, scraping the depths of their emotions.

"However, there is another avenue that you might want to consider," she suggested before turning to a shelf behind her desk. "I know it isn't what you anticipated from me, but it's the best I can do."

Zack felt a surge of hope as Sandberg found a small book.

"When I was your age a lot of us were seeking answers to life's big questions," she explained. "I spent years in a commune doing exactly that." Pleased by the spark of interest that she saw in him, she went on, "I know the whole commune thing sounds unorthodox, but it was highly instructive. You may not be a religious person, but that particular book is one of my favorites. It describes Buddha's four noble truths."

As she handed Zack a copy of *The Enlightened* he fought the urge to deflate. After all, he did not want to offend Doc Sandberg. *How was she supposed to know he wasn't into this stuff?* "Sounds great... thank you," was the best he could do.

Sandberg knew he was resisting the concept. "What I'm getting at is that your problem may be better solved spiritually than scientifically. That's why Buddhism and other faiths exist, to help us find peace at times like this."

He felt bad about his earlier reaction. She was, after all, offering assistance. "I guess I never thought about that. Maybe I'll give that priest a call, after all."

A few minutes later Zack was walking to the construction area for the Molecular Science addition where he stashed his car. This secret place, located behind a dumpster and piles of bricks, was one of his most imaginative illegal parking discoveries ever. If only he were in the mood to appreciate it, he thought. But his session with Doc Sandberg had not improved things, and now he may have to deal with Father Solano and what he apparently knows about him.

Then things got worse. As he approached the Terasaki Life Science Building on Charles E. Young Drive East, Sandy Phillips fell into step beside him. Her thick flaming red hair had been cut short and colored luminous purple.

"Raskin, how's it hangin'?"

"Lois, what are you doing here?"

"Came to see you," she pronounced. "You don't look so good."

"You've got room to talk."

"You don't like my hair?"

"I hope it wasn't expensive," he answered, picking up his pace.

She forced a smile. "I'm not kiddin', Raskin. Are you feeling okay?"

"Is there a reason you wanted to see me?"

"Do you still think Nicole Branson didn't O-D."

"Didn't you promise to leave me alone?"

"That was bullshit," she allowed. "The evidence is overwhelming, don't ya think?"

"Why do you care what I think?"

She eyeballed him like a poker player holding a winning hand. "The cops found more stash in her house. Coupla grand in white lady, syringes, you name it."

The assertion threw him, but he covered it as much as he could. "So? Her band leader said on TV that she didn't even take prescription drugs."

"What'd you expect him to say, that his friend was slammin' junk in her arm?" She waited for a response and when none came she shifted gears. "Anyway, I was thinkin' we oughta work together on this."

He threw her a look. "I'm not working on anything."

"Is that why you flew to Ohio?"

"How'd you know about that?" he hesitated to ask.

"Brilliant investigative technique."

"I had business to take care of," he said, recovering from her surprise move.

"No shit?" she challenged. "In Youngstown."

"I have a diverse portfolio."

Sandy nodded as if accepting a wager. "Easy enough to check out."

Zack stopped at Manning Drive. "Who the hell are you to be checking me out?!"

"A reporter on a big story."

Without warning he grabbed her purse and began digging through it. Sandy lunged to get it back. "What are you doin'?!"

"Getting answers," he snarled, turning to keep the bag from her grasp. "You see, I wanted to make sure you didn't quote me in some moronic article, so I called *Rolling Stone*." The color drained from her face. "And they never heard of you."

Sandy retrieved her purse, but the resistance in her was gone. "That's because I don't work for them."

"You said you did."

"Sue me, I lied."

"Then how come you're hammering me about Nicole?"

"I want to be a reporter, okay? I'm sick of proof-reading for hacks."

Zack did a double take. "Wait, you're a fucking proof-reader?!"

She shrank. If there had been a hole to crawl into, she would have. "Was... at Starmagazine-dot-com."

Zack pivoted and walked off without responding.

"Gimme a break, Raskin," she called out. "I'm an awesome journalist."

"Star Magazine?!"

"Come on, we're both hotwired into this." She answered scrambling after him.

"You're not wired into anything," he tossed over his shoulder as he arrived at his Prelude. "You believe that crap about an overdose."

"So, convince me otherwise."

Zack's answer came when his car fishtailed from the construction site, leaving Sandy in a cloud of dust for the second time in their relationship.

Zack could not remember ever being this uptight. He had not planned to come to Forest Lawn today, but he had no choice. He needed a breakthrough from the anguish that he felt since the trauma team opened the E.R. curtain to reveal Nicole's sheet-covered body.

Anguish. Maybe that was the word he had been looking for to describe his condition, he recognized. As he steered his Prelude through the lush cemetery grounds, past the endless rows of graves, Zack comprehended how much that word and its derivatives had been ruling his life lately: anguish... torment... punishment.

Yes, *punishment* said it even better, he decided. Punishment was more active than anguish, and it had that special element of torture, which nicely described his current existence. The ghostly and erotic visitations and Nicole's allegation that he did not actually know her. *Punishment is what he'd been living with.* And that is what he was determined to stop.

But only she could free him.

As he drove along Cathedral Drive past the Wee Kirk of the Heather Chapel where the memorial service was held, Zack thought about the book that Doc Sandberg gave him, *The Enlightened*. He stayed up late reading it, though he was not sure how much he understood. While he had never been very good in philosophy classes, finding meaning in Buddha's writings was of considerable importance. Sandberg's opinion mattered and if she thought Buddha had answers for him then he would figure out what they were, one way or another.

He did his best to remember Buddha's four noble truths:

1) Suffering was always present in life and,
2) Desire causes suffering and,
3) Suffering ends when desire is overcome and,
4) Freedom from life is achieved by nirvana—
the release from the cycle of birth, death, and rebirth.

He paused to mull over the second and third noble truths. *Was his desire for Nicole the cause of all this? What had he done that was so terrible, anyway? He was a fan who was there when she needed him. They shared a moment of intimacy. What difference could that possibly make to the universe?*

Surely, he reasoned, the great Buddha had not intended to associate Zack's lovemaking with Nicole's death. The first connection was more logical: that Zack's desire for her had by some means brought her spirit back from the dead. Maybe not letting go was causing him to suffer a bad case of limerence, the psychological term for an uncontrollable emotional hangover.

That may be what Father Solano inferred when they met at the funeral.

Parking outside the mausoleum above Benediction Slope, he examined it respectfully. It was an elegant building, not nearly as macabre as he had anticipated. It was also the site chosen by Nicole to safeguard her remains and those of her parents. He was curious about what went through her mind when she made her selection. Had she glanced at the map and questioned Forest Lawn's decision to assign burial sections such cloying names as Babyland, Slumberland, and Lullabyland? Had Nicole felt, as he did, that they sounded more like attractions at Disneyland than someone's final resting place?

Maybe it was fitting that Walt Disney himself could be found interred just a few yards away, Zack gathered.

Still, Forest Lawn was her wish and it was a most beautiful place. Since the graveyard was transformed into an art-filled memorial park in 1906, it had become caretaker to countless stars. In addition to Disney, Michael Jackson and Elizabeth Taylor were buried there, as were W.C. Fields, Humphrey Bogart, Spencer Tracy, Errol Flynn, Clark Gable, and Carole Lombard, among many others.

Leaving his car, Zack crossed Arlington Road and approached the stately Freedom Mausoleum. The silence around him seemed to grow with each step, making the thick sound of his respiration feel more labored than it was. His footsteps slowed as he passed through the Courtyard of Freedom and arrived at the towering statue of George Washington facing the entrance.

He hesitated at the oversized brass door handle awaiting his grasp. *Could he go through with this?* Even after all he had been through, the truth still frightened him. Nicole was gone. Opening that door threatened to make him feel as if he were giving in to the very thing that he had been resisting: the finality of her death.

He gathered himself and opened the door.

Inside the Grand Hall, the soles of his Reeboks squeaked on the polished marble floor and warm sunlight glowed through stained glass windows that enhanced the carved names with a serene luster.

Zack clutched the assortment of wildflowers that he purchased from a vendor at the entrance and proceeded along the rows of bronze crypt plates searching for her name on the second tier. One inscription was followed by another and then another, as markers that he passed and the lives they represented soon melded into the insignificant detail on a mortuary mural. Like the columns of names in a phone directory, they meant nothing to him.

Then there it was: *Nicole June Branson*. Arrayed on the floor were dozens of floral arrangements, candles, CD cases, and framed photos from fans.

Zack's pace ground to a halt as the strength began to leave his legs. He slumped on a bench and stared at the lettering of her name beside those of her parents, Lawrence and Frances.

He did not know what to do next. Whatever he thought

would be accomplished by coming here was no longer relevant. He could not ask Nicole to stop the tragedy that was consuming his life. It was not her fault that his fate had become entwined with hers. He understood with new clarity that there would be no relief for him until he completed the investigation into her death.

It had been a long time since he attempted the Lord's Prayer, but that is what involuntarily emerged from his lips. "Our Father, who art in heaven, hallowed be Thy name..."

A moment later he stopped. A now-familiar sensation was coming over him, the awareness that he was not alone. That is when he saw the slender outline of a woman standing motionless against the room's magnificent patriotic stained glass interpretation of Colonial women sewing an American flag. There were no facial features to be seen in the radiant light's shadow and no words offered to suggest her identity.

Of course, Zack did not need to be told who it was.

His mouth parched. Gathering the flowers from the bench beside him, he clumsily dropped several. After stooping to pick them up, he stood to face her. But when he looked up she was gone.

Not far from where Zack parked his car in the Haven of Peace section near Benediction Slope, a big man crouched to place flowers at the headstone of *Agnes Terrell, Beloved Wife And Mother.* The man never knew Mrs. Terrell, but her grave was a most efficient place from which to monitor Zack Raskin's movements.

Two hours later, Zack was watching a family of ducks swim in the pond at Kenneth Hahn State Park in Baldwin Hills when Father Luis Solano approached along the shallow embankment. He had to chuckle at the thought of his mother's reaction had she lived to see the day that he was voluntarily seeing a priest. After years of nagging him to attend Mass with her, this occasion would have been absolutely triumphant.

"I was pleased to hear from you, Zack," Solano began with a smile. "Thank you for making the drive. It made slipping away from

Saint Teresa's possible. Our new building campaign has proven to be very demanding."

Solano's voice was more welcoming than Zack remembered from the funeral, with warmer tones and fewer traces of a Mexican accent. For some reason even the flecks of gray in his hair that Zack had not previously noticed made him seemed less intimidating. "No problem, Father. I appreciate you making time for me."

The priest became more serious. "I could hear the urgency in your voice on the phone. Please tell me, how may I be of assistance?"

Zack was not sure how far he wanted to go. After all, it was difficult enough talking to Doc Sandberg. Finally, he remembered what she advised and pushed his concerns aside. "At Forest Lawn you told me that you see things other people don't. Would you mind explaining that?"

Father Solano opened a wrinkled paper sack and tossed a handful of bread crumbs to the ducks. "I believe you already know the answer."

"No, I don't," Zack insisted.

The priest weighed him with dark appraising purpose. "You have been visited by Nicole Branson, have you not?"

Zack's mouth opened but no words came out. While he was aware that the priest perceived something about them, actually hearing the words was downright disturbing.

"How... could you possibly know that?" Zack probed.

"It is my job," Solano responded gently.

"But you don't even know me."

"I know more than you think," he began. "You see, my role as a priest involves more than attending to the souls of my parishioners. I have been blessed with what can only be described as a special connection to the departed."

Zack suppressed the urge to panic. "The departed..."

"I cannot explain it other than to say that the Lord had a most remarkable purpose in mind for me," Solano added. "Ten years ago that resulted in training at the Regina Apostolorum Pontifical Academy in Rome. As an exorcist."

"Exorcist... like in the movies?" Zack blurted, his fear intensifying.

"Something like that."

"I didn't think any of that was real."

"It is, I assure you," countered the priest. Just then a group of giggling school children arrived to see the ducks and the priest emptied the rest of his paper sack on the water. "Let's walk, shall we?"

As the two men moved across the grass to a paved path Solano chose his words carefully. "Church doctrine tells us that spirits move among us, Zack. Most major religions agree... Judaism, Islam, Hinduism, Shinto, Buddhism, and Christianity. I have been blessed with a heightened awareness of such things, and at Forest Lawn when I saw you I had the overwhelming sense that Nicole has returned."

"You could really tell that? That's amazing."

The gravity in Solano's voice became more intimidating. "Clearly, her soul is not at peace. I believe that God brought you to me so that I may learn why."

"She said she wants me to find out how she died," Zack revealed. "The drug overdose story on the news is wrong."

"I see..." the priest replied with concern.

"So that explains it, right?"

"While it is true that souls are sometimes released from Purgatory to complete unfinished business from their mortal lives..." Solano asserted, "We do not know if this particular spirit has malevolent intentions."

Zack bristled. "Malevolent?! No chance. She was a fantastic person."

"In life, perhaps. Remember that what you have seen is not Nicole, but her essence. Unfortunately, some spirits have nefarious purposes." Solano lowered his voice, as if sharing classified information. "You must be extremely careful. If she takes any action beyond the need to clear her name, then it may not be her at all."

"What do you mean? Of course it's her."

"The specter may look and sound like Nicole, but that could be an illusion designed to deceive you," Solano warned. "What you are experiencing could very well be the corrupt handiwork of the Devil."

Zack stopped cold, as he roiled uncontrollably inside. "Okay,

Father... look... I know you mean well, but now you're talking science fiction."

Solano turned to face him. "She appeared to you after her death. Would you have previously thought that possible?"

"Of course not."

"Then this is hardly science fiction," the priest declared. "To what extent have you interacted with her?"

"Oh, not much..." Zack answered evasively.

"Yet she has spoken to you."

"A few times, yeah."

"Then this is critical: has she encroached on your personal life or initiated any sort of physical contact with you?"

Zack glanced away. "That part's a little foggy... I had a few beers in me at the time..."

"You do not have to be Roman Catholic to accept what I am saying." The priest was resolute. "There is a war between good and evil being waged all around us, and I am a combatant in that war. Believe me when I say that Satan exists and he may have designs on your soul. Nicole could be a cruel deception."

"Or maybe she has unfinished business, like you said," Zack came back. "Let's not get carried away."

"The point is, you must be extremely cautious until we know for certain," Solano warned. "It is vital that you never trust anything that she says. Can you do that?"

"I think so," Zack said. But of course that was a monumental lie.

"Then may the Lord have mercy on her soul and yours," Father Solano offered, extending his right hand and making the sign of the cross in the air. "Mary, Mother of Jesus, and Saint Joseph, father of Jesus and Terror of the Devil, I beseech you to protect and defend this man against all that is harmful or evil. In the name of the Father, Son, and Holy Ghost... Amen."

Zack had never been inside the Los Angeles County Medical Examiner's facility in Lincoln Heights, so it took a while to find his way through the maze of hallways. The vestiges of death and its accessory chemicals were everywhere. Distinct from the hospital smells he was used to, he guessed that these noxious odors had become so ingrained in the building that no amount of cleaning could make a dent in them.

Inside the Specimen Section, he paused to take in the dozens of bottles on display in a glass case near the door. Organs and other body parts floated in murky fluid for the viewing pleasure of anyone who cared to look, though not many civilians ever would. This was not a place for the uninitiated. After all, this was where the county's twenty-three staff pathologists determined how people died in the course of conducting over eight thousand five hundred autopsies every year.

Curiously, it was also where visitors could visit the coroner's gift shop, *Skeletons In The Closet*. Zack tried to visualize the marketing genius who devised that particular branding strategy as he helped himself to a stale peanut butter cookie from a plate on a stainless steel lab cart. He did not heed the *Donations Welcome* sign as he picked up a chipped mug with the Medical Examiner's logo on it—the chalk outline of a dead body—before noticing that there was nothing to put in it. Without anything to drink, the homemade treat went down like a clump of sand.

Just then a chubby young man in a lab coat rounded a corner with a tray of test tubes. He was the same age as Zack, though his gnarled mop of red hair and translucent Irish skin made him appear as if he might be comedian Conan O'Brien's long lost little brother. His name was Lee O'Connor.

"Zack? What're you doing here?"

"I came to see you."

"You look like hell, man. You want somebody to put a toe tag on you or something?"

Zack smiled. "Nah. I'd have to wash my feet first."

An awkward moment passed between them. Lee broke the ice. "How are things at school?"

"The same," Zack volunteered. "How about you?"

"What can I say? I wish I was still there, but when I get out of specimens and into autopsies it'll be better."

Zack concurred, even as he wondered how conducting autopsies day after day could ever be regarded as better than a laboratory position. But he had to admire O'Connor's determination to stay in medicine after flunking out of UCLA last year.

"With so many cases stacked up around here training and promoting people is one way to fix our accreditation problems," O'Connor explained. "That's good for guys like me."

A group of doctors entered the area, preoccupied in conversation as they closed in on the cookies. Zack motioned to his friend, "Is there someplace we can talk?"

In a cramped storage room down the hall, the former classmates were surrounded by cardboard file boxes containing information on cases handled by the coroner. The sign above the door advertised, *OUR CUSTOMERS NEVER COMPLAIN.*

O'Connor was stunned by Zack's request. "Are you out of your mind?! If I got busted smuggling a file out of here, they'd cut off my nuts and put 'em on display!"

"Come on, Lee. I really need a favor."

"Christ, the Nicole Branson autopsy...!" But then he caught himself as he read the seriousness on Zack's face. "I take it this isn't for a paper you're writing."

"No."

"Then if you want me to risk getting shit-canned, you'd better come across with more than that. There are people watching every move we make around here."

Zack sagged with resignation against a wobbly IKEA particleboard shelf. "She was a friend," he ventured. "She was onstage a half hour before she got sick. I was the EMT on scene. If it was heroin, I want to know why she didn't overdose sooner than she did."

When the young man did not react right away and Zack gripped his arm. "Please, Lee. I can't tell you how important this is."

NEWS ITEM:

National Institute on Drug Abuse Report, May 2

- *Over 250,000 people die of drug overdoses in the United States each year.*
- *Hospital emergency room visits related to heroin have more than doubled in the past decade.*
- *2.4 million Americans admit to having used heroin at some time in their lives.*
- *54.3 percent of graduating high school students report having used an illicit drug.*
- *Heroin use among 12-17 year olds has increased four-fold since the 1980s.*

Chapter Eight

When Zack got home at seven thirty he was dismayed to find Sandy Phillips preparing a meal in his kitchen, though somehow not shocked to learn that it was his roommate who let her in. Taking advantage of Doug as he packed to visit his parents, she talked her way into their home with a bag of groceries and the pretense of reconciling with Zack. Evidently, Doug neglected to ask how it was possible to reconcile a friendship that never existed.

Fortunately for Sandy, having visited Nicole's grave and his classmate Lee O'Connor, Zack's mood was less hostile. Moreover, his resolve to get to the bottom of Nicole's death had been reinforced by Father Solano's dire warning of Satan's possible designs on his soul.

And while Sandy's personality was irrepressible, he had to admit that he might actually benefit from her aggressiveness. He understood medical things, but nothing whatsoever about investigative procedure. The elaborate feast of taglierini pasta with fish and lemon sauce did not hurt, either. Unlike the hot dogs and junk food that he usually lived on, this dinner was exquisite.

Sandy also proved to be unexpectedly pleasant company. In the process of holding up her half of the conversation, she revealed enough about her background to give Zack a clearer impression of her and why she behaved the way she did. He learned that after dropping out of high school with her boyfriend, she found herself broke and abandoned halfway across the country. Returning home, she earned a GED diploma before completing two years of community college. She had been struggling to launch her writing career in Los Angeles for three years when Nicole died.

Zack wondered why she had been hiding her more appealing traits, until he recognized that her conduct was not much different than his own. As he had confessed to Nicole: he lived behind a smoke screen to keep outsiders at a distance. The only distinction, he decided, was that Sandy's fakery was a whole lot more effective than his own.

"It was great your pal got all this stuff," she exclaimed after the dishes were cleared. "What'd he do, clean the whole file cabinet?"

Zack glanced up from his microscope to see her toss a medical folder onto a stack of similar documents that she had skimmed but not understood. He smiled at the return of her antagonism. "I told you it'd take time, Lois. Relax."

Her eyes flickered impatiently, reminding him of a teacher in high school whom he had not thought about in many years. While Mrs. Braeden was probably a decent person, she had what the kids claimed to be a permanent sneer on her face, which the teen rumor mill decided was a birth defect. The students were wrong about Mrs. Braeden, of course, just as Zack had been wrong about Sandy.

"By the way, you can stop callin' me Lois any time now," she sniffed the way Mrs. Braeden did when she was annoyed. "What's wrong with *Sandy*?"

"Bet lots of people ask that," he volleyed, enjoying the game.

"You're a laugh-riot, ya know it? I can't catch my breath over here." She punctuated the aspersion by switching on a thrift-shop lamp in the darkening room, as if more light had anything to do with breathing.

Zack ignored the oddity that was their partnership and took a sip of tea before turning his attention to the tissue section mounted on a slide. He would have preferred coffee, but Sandy had brought her favorite apple cranberry blend and he appreciated the gesture. "You're the one who wanted to team up," he reminded her. "There's an answer here and I'll find it, with or without you."

She reacted to his challenge by flipping a file open to a page she had seen moments earlier. "Then start with this, hotshot..."

"Start with what?"

"This." The long bright purple nail pointed accusingly. "This toxicology sheet says there was enough smack in Nicole's blood to kill several people."

"Delicately put, thank you."

"Facts are facts."

"Blood samples can be spiked."

"You mean... stuff is added later?"

"It happens."

"You wanna explain why anybody'd do that? She was only a pop star."

Zack's face hardened. "She was a lot more than that."

Sandy reacted to his edgy tone. She had momentarily forgotten that Zack had not only tried to save Nicole's life, but also considered himself her friend. "Raskin, I didn't mean nuthin'... okay?"

"Forget it."

"I had no call talkin' that way."

Zack glanced at her a beat then motioned to the microscope. "Take a look at this."

She crossed to the table. "What is it?"

"Lung tissue."

"Yuk."

"Just look at it. Tell me what you see."

"I dunno, everything's pink," she observed upon peering into the eyepiece.

"That's right, pink and healthy. Heroin addicts usually have scarring from cotton fibers in their injections."

Sandy stood upright. "Meaning?"

"Meaning, if she was using then why's this lung section normal?"

Zack and Sandy were still working hours later. The lights were off so that photos of the concert on Sandy's laptop could be shown on a wall. The snapshots obtained from online fan sites created an eerie effect in the inky darkness. Like gigantic frescos, they transfigured the bland surface into a visual chronology of what had become the defining night of Nicole's life.

And as it turned out, Zack's.

As Zack and Sandy watched the initial batch of photos, the only sound was the tiny fan venting heat from the Epson projector that Zack borrowed from Doug's room. Finally, Sandy inquired, "What're we lookin' for?"

"Beats me," came the frank response.

She threw Zack a look but was unable to see his face in the shadows. He had become a silhouette set against the amber illumination of a streetlight outside. "You gotta be puttin' me on," she charged.

"Hey, I'm new at this detective shit, all right?"

As the images changed from one to the next, the result was that of witnessing Nicole's approaching death frame by frame, angle by angle. Sandy was intrigued and Zack did everything he could to immerse himself in a patient's final moments with a professional medical mindset, not that of a grieving lover.

The photos continued to unfold, taking Zack and Sandy closer to Nicole's collapse. Blinking away his tears he examined every portion of the photos. Nothing evaded his scrutiny. "Look there," he broke in at one point.

"See her perspiring?"

"That don't look like overdose to you?" she probed.

It did, but he was not about to volunteer it. Though he was striving for objectivity, the process was excruciating. The frames advanced further as Zack steadied his hand and forced himself to press the laptop's spacebar:

Click! *A close up of Nicole looking left and grimacing with discomfort as she sang into her microphone...* Zack felt his teeth clench as he empathized her discomfort.

Click! *Another close shot of Nicole looking right, gulping a breath between verses...* Now Zack's own breathing hesitated as he felt her growing distress.

Click! *A profile angle of Nicole glancing at her musicians with concern...* Zack vividly remembered the moment and a feeling of panic surged through him.

Click! *An extremely close shot showing Nicole's face filled with pain...* It was all Zack could do to not turn the computer off; his connection to her eminent death was immediate.

Click! *A new close angle capturing Nicole singing with her eyes closed, clutching the mic intently...* Zack felt himself begin to hyperventilate, as the helplessness that he felt that night returned with a vengeance. He looked away and fought to gather himself before resuming his torture.

Click! One last image appeared and it made Zack freeze where he stood: it captured *the instant that Nicole looked at him for the last time. As her body succumbed, she was so scared and uncomprehending.* It was the very memory that he saw whenever he closed his eyes. A wave of dizziness passed through him and his vision dimmed. Recognizing the symptoms of syncope, he fell into a chair and hoped to avoid a loss of consciousness.

Sandy reacted with concern, only to have his equilibrium return with vengeance and his focus sharpened. "There...!" he exclaimed.

"Where?" she asked.

"Her index finger," he clarified with mounting agitation. He had discovered something in the photograph. "See how it's clubbed at the tip?"

"Kinda. Does that mean something?"

He was on his feet and pacing. "Lee O'Connor said Doctor Takahashi's a veteran pathologist, but you'd never know it from this."

"What're you talkin' about?"

Zack's mind was spinning; there were so many facts to reconcile. *But where to begin?!* "Her teacher in Youngstown told me she had a childhood bout of rheumatic fever," he finally revealed.

"Come on, Raskin, I'm not following. Stick to English."

Grabbing one of the files, he inspected forensic observations made during the autopsy. "Rheumatic fever leaves a heart defect called SBE," he stated from memory. "Subacute bacterial endocarditis. It's a biggie and Takahashi doesn't even mention it. How could somebody who did autopsies for forty years miss that?!"

"Maybe she didn't have a heart defect."

Zack stood beside the projected image of Nicole's hand. "The human body leaves clues, Lois." His hand gently traced the illuminated shot. "Like clubbed fingers, which are a neon billboard for SBE. Takahashi left that out, too."

Sandy moved closer. The information was coming too fast. "Wait a minute... you knew Nicole, right? Did you know her fingers were like that?"

"No," he hated to admit. He could not tell her that his mind was on other things at the time. Like sex.

"Then ya can't trash the pathologist for it," she finished.

A little after two thirty in the morning Zack and Sandy wearily descended the stairs. After having repeatedly viewed the slides his face was now buried in one of the files. Then half way to the foyer he stopped. "Are you fucking kidding me?!"

"You get a hit?" she asked hopefully.

"You better believe it," he continued. "Her blood work-up shows she was pretty damn sick once. There's a low white cell count, probably from bone marrow infection during the rheumatic fever. There's even calcific aortitis."

Sandy shot another look at him as he continued walking, forcing her to rush after him. "What do I hafta do, take a Berlitz course? Calcific what?"

"Scarring of the valves. Nicole had a low-grade heart infection her whole life."

They paused at the entrance to digest his discovery together. "So, maybe the coroner screwed up."

"I doubt it."

"But aren't these the same geniuses who cremated the wrong body a few months ago? It was on the news. Sounds to me like they don't know what they're doing."

"That was a forensic attendant screw up, not a doctor. A first year intern wouldn't make these mistakes."

Sandy let out a low whistle in appreciation, an annoying habit that she acquired in the working class Bay Ridge section of Brooklyn. When she pushed the door open and stepped outside the brisk night air felt good after being trapped in the stuffy confines of the apartment.

Zack, on the other hand, did not notice the temperature. He was still weighing the omissions by the pathologist. *Was there anything that he had misunderstood?* The results were suspicious, yet challenging the Medical Examiner's report would be no minor project. As the investigators in the notorious O.J. Simpson criminal case learned about blood evidence, clinical errors have a way of taking on new meaning.

And that meaning confounded Zack. Nicole's file was so incomplete; he determined that it could not have been the result of mere oversight. It had to be deliberate. *But why would anyone falsify the facts of her death? Why would they destroy her reputation? And more important, how did she really die?*

Those troubling questions only provided a momentary distraction, however, because when Zack and Sandy cleared the front steps he glimpsed something moving inside her Volkswagen convertible across the street. An instant later, his mind synced with his eyesight and he realized that someone was searching the car!

Shouting at the thief, Zack shoved the file folder at Sandy and charged the vehicle. The man extricated himself from the front seat and took off on foot. And even though Zack was not one to seek out confrontations, this was different.

Giving the chase everything he had, he pounded after the large man through the concentrated shadows of the tree-lined street. Zack's left leg, the one that always gave him trouble, started cramping right away. His lousy circulation or pitiful nervous system, whatever was causing his peripheral neuropathy, was not going to improve anytime soon and he knew it. His mind flashed on the dinner that he just ate and hoped it contained enough magnesium and potassium to ward off the worst of the spasms.

Instinct told him the break-in was no coincidence, not after the new forensic revelations. *This was related to Nicole's death!* He ran faster and was amazed to find himself gaining on the culprit. God only knew what he would do if he caught him. He would worry about that if the time came.

Then a block away the mysterious figure vanished around a parked U-Haul truck and Zack immediately knew that the pursuit had failed. There were too many passageways between too many buildings with too much foliage. The intruder was gone.

Zack doubled over as a headache pulsed. He could not tell if it was from tension or being out of shape. Hell, he thought, with his luck it was a brain tumor. He envisioned a malignant and insidious nemesis burrowing cancerous sprouts into his occipital lobe. And that would mean blindness was not far behind. Then dementia and a death devoid of dignity. *Wonderful.*

Eventually, Zack gave up his depressing self-diagnosis. He could not let whatever was wrong with him become a deterrent. His tumor could go fuck itself.

Sandy was looking her car over as Zack hobbled up. "Got... away..." he sputtered, still catching his breath. The headache was worse now and even talking was uncomfortable. "Anything... missing?" he managed to ask.

"Don't look like it."

"Guess... we showed up... just... in time."

Sandy was not so sure. "Maybe." She picked up something from the curb. "But if he was boostin' the radio, what was he doin' with my DMV registration?"

When they returned upstairs Zack swallowed a handful of Ibuprofen and put a cold pack on his neck. He was glad that Doug was unavailable to harangue him about taking more Advil than recommended. Then he dialed Lee O'Connor at home.

In the meantime, Sandy visited the bathroom where she washed the sweat from her palms. The episode scared the hell out of her. To her journalism was about research, interviews, and writing. She was not prepared for feelings of actual fear.

Returning to the living room, Zack looked grim as he finished his phone call. "Thanks, Lee," he was saying. "I'll catch you later."

"What'd he say?" she asked from the window while reassuring herself that her car was still there.

"Doctor Takahashi's on vacation and nobody knows when he'll be back."

"Of course they know."

"Nope. He's retired and they only bring him in when they need an extra hand."

"Then let's call him," she answered.

Zack gingerly shifted the cold pack. "Fishing in the boonies," he grumbled. "No cell service."

A powerful realization came over Sandy as she turned from the window. "... and no questions about autopsies."

"That pretty much sums it up," he confirmed.

On a lower slope of picturesque Kings Canyon National Park in Central California, a frail man in his seventies exited a rustic rental cabin at Lake Bonita. The weathered bungalow, while cramped and poorly maintained, offered Dan Takahashi exactly what he needed: sequestration. Surrounded by acres of thick buckeye, mature sequoia, and blue oak trees, the ancient log structure was nearly indistinguishable from its lush natural setting.

The pathologist gathered his fishing pole and tackle box from the rear deck and carried them to the lake. Adjusting his long-bill cap, a chorus of chirping birds and buzzing cicadas escorted him along the narrow winding path. The beautiful weather and mild lapping of the shoreline were proving to be excellent therapy after the strain of abandoning his professional ethics. Takahashi had never before considered falsifying an autopsy report, but the bribe he was offered was highly persuasive. His divorce had destroyed his financial security, so the money was a welcomed bail-out, indeed.

As for the Branson case, he would simply have to live with his actions. Besides, he reasoned, nothing that he did altered the outcome of her fate. She was deceased either way.

Takahashi stowed his gear beneath the seat of an old rowboat that someone had christened *Lady Luck*, before drawing to a stop. A lizard that had been sunning itself on a rock scurried out of sight. And the cicadas overhead seemed to become more insistent, their buzzing resembling a drum roll.

He sensed that he was not alone.

NEWS ITEM:

KFI TalkRadio Transcript, May 4

In case you haven't heard, Reverend Harold T. Edmund, Founder of the self-described fundamentalist Christian Parents Who Care organization, has announced a demonstration tonight to protest what they claim to be the pervasive influence of drugs in the music business being marketed to our nation's youth. Southland parents are asked to delete from their teenager's computers and phones any music downloads that they deem objectionable, in particular those by the late Nicole Branson, whose lyrics are being vilified by the group for supposedly containing symbolic references to her own drug usage.

Do you believe that Reverend Edmund and his followers have a point? Or does the idea of censorship scare the daylights out of you? Call us... we'd like to hear what you have to say.

CHAPTER NINE

Glen Conway burst to the surface of his swimming pool and was startled by the image of Zack looming over him. Conway had not expected visitors, nor did he desire any. All he wanted was to swim his laps in peace. Between the crush of media inquiries and the overwhelming loss of Nicole, swimming was his only means of escape.

He sized up the young man in a wrinkled EMT uniform with caution. "Can I help you?"

Zack strained to see in the Pacific Palisades sun, but even through the glare he could tell that Nicole's longtime bandleader was a handsome man with an artist's grace. "Mister Conway, I'm Zack Raskin, I attended to Nicole at the Greek."

Conway slowly climbed the blue and white tiled steps to the deck and reached for a thick terry cloth towel. This intrusion was unwelcome, a point that he soon emphasized by pulling a Springfield XD handgun from beneath the towel and aiming it at Zack. "What do you want from me?"

Zack's eyes jerked open and he raised his hands in surrender. "Whoa! I just want to talk about Nicole!"

Conway's face was taut. "For Goddsakes, first reporters and fans. Now an ambulance driver?! When will people understand that I've lost my best friend?"

"I understand that, sir. I really do."

"Then you won't mind leaving my property," Conway cut in as he waved the gun at the yard gate. "Immediately."

Zack inched backwards. "Mister Conway, you told a reporter that she never used drugs..."

Conway stared. "I asked you to leave."

But Zack stopped. There was too much at stake to give up now. "You think she was clean, don't you."

"What business is that of yours?"

"Because her cardiac arrest had nothing to do with an overdose."

"What are you talking about?" Conway demanded.

"I've seen the coroner's report," Zack assured him.

Conway lowered the gun. Whatever upset he experienced over Nicole's death was giving way to the words of this stranger. He was starved for an end to his sorrow. Zack had a captive audience. Conway had been ambushed by the revelation.

"Mister Conway, the pathologist lied and I want to know why."

Conway set the weapon on a table. "I'm sorry about the gun... this has been a really difficult time."

Glen Conway's home was a showplace befitting a millionaire musician. The vista from his adobe mansion on Turquesa Lane was sensational. Santa Monica Bay and what seemed to be the entire Pacific Ocean could be seen through massive panoramic windows. Nicole was once quoted as saying that some of her favorite compositions were found on the glistening blue horizon seen from this property, waiting only to be written down.

Zack ambled along the terra cotta tiled hallway, passing a display of framed platinum and gold records. He knew that Conway had co-written many of Nicole's hits, but the trophies were an impressive sight nonetheless. Then when he entered the book-lined den, something far more intriguing caught his eye: a resplendent mural of Nicole hanging above a glossy white Steinway grand piano.

He approached the work, drawn to it. The details in the towering frame were so realistic they could have been high-resolution photograph pixels rather than brush strokes and pigment. Every gold thread in her metal-mesh gown glowed with individual distinction and her long, thick hair was gathered elegantly on one shoulder, the way she wore it years ago.

The artist's portrayal of her eyes was particularly evocative. They were every bit as enticing as they had been the night Zack met her. So was her mouth. Zack involuntarily bit his lip as he relived the sensation of kissing her.

Sitting on the piano bench he never turned away and he appreciated that if he had never met Nicole he could have fallen in love with her based solely on this portrait. It was that exceptional.

Conway's voice broke in, "I know how you feel."

Zack spun to his feet at finding he was no longer alone. Conway had reappeared, having changed into jeans and a vintage silk Hawaiian shirt, which he wore loose and untucked. "What do you mean?" Zack asked in an attempt to cover his embarrassment.

"Take it from a man who's been there," Conway added thoughtfully. "I fell for her once myself."

Zack managed to choke out a response, still trying to appear detached. He was blushing and knew it. "Did she know?"

"You can't write as many ballads as we did and not pick up the vibes... but she had the decency to never bring it up."

"Maybe she felt the same about you," Zack suggested, hoping that she had not.

"I'm afraid that wasn't in the cards."

"I only met her recently," Zack heard himself say, "but in some ways it seemed like we'd been friends forever."

Conway nodded. "That was Nicole."

They remained preoccupied with their private thoughts a while longer, before Zack steered the conversation to what they were avoiding. "I'd appreciate it if you can remember anything to help me figure this thing out... anything at all."

"A reason for somebody to falsify the autopsy? No way."

Zack read his look and decided he was being truthful. Then he dropped the bomb. "How about a reason for murder?"

The color emptied from Conway's face. "What the hell are you talking about?"

"Nicole had a congenital heart defect," he started. "That means her coronary could've been induced."

"Induced..." The word was even more obscene when repeated. "I can't believe I'm hearing this!" But there was something about Zack, his earnestness, if not his affection for Nicole that indicated otherwise.

"Mr. Conway, I know this is hard but I've got to look at every possibility. You and I know she wasn't shooting up," Zack explained. "Yet somebody went to a whole lot of trouble convincing people otherwise."

Fighting a losing battle with his tattered emotions, Conway excused himself to the bathroom. Zack stole another glance at the wall and gasped as Nicole's image came to life, turning from her partial profile to face him. But her mouth moved in slow motion, as if unable to communicate from the beyond. Zack looked away and a headache once again punched his blood vessels with migraine ferocity. An inundation of Advil, Tylenol, Aleve, and Aspirin had blunted the thing but now it was back.

And so was Nicole.

In light of Father Solano's warnings, Zack was acutely aware of the potential consequences of this. *He had been visited by a dead woman who might be an evil spirit and he had been making love to her!* Rubbing his neck, he wondered how much serotonin, the chemical associated with emotional function, was in his brain stem right now and if his body had produced a bad batch. *Whatever it was, he did not want her showing up here in Glen Conway's house!*

Images of an exorcism in a dingy church basement with Father Solano fighting for his soul jolted through his mind. So did mental pictures of him receiving electroshock therapy at UCLA should Solano fail. As Nicole's unseen bearing became stronger, his mind jumped to the psychotropic drugs that alter human brain chemistry, like the phenothiazines used in treating schizophrenia. If he could not resolve her ghostly visitations, then pharmacology might be his last resort.

Nicole's spirit was overpowering now, and it was not long before she was at the window beside him. "Keep on him, Zack," she opened quietly. "Glen knows more about me than anyone."

Zack tried to respond but could not. The combination of sleep deprivation, stress, headache, and grief was taking its toll. *Or maybe it really was a brain tumor.* He clutched a chair back as a wave of dizziness ran through him. Hanging on until the sensation passed, he hoped that full-blown ataxia, the loss of coordination and control of movement, was not close behind.

Then in the muddle of his thinking he heard Conway's voice once more. "Are you feeling all right?" The musician emerged from the bathroom with a box of tissues.

Zack glanced at the window, only to find Nicole back in the painting where she belonged. "I've got a headache, that's all."

"Having a gun pulled on you probably didn't help."

"Probably not."

"Let me get you some aspirin," Conway offered as he exited.

Zack plopped into the chair he had been clinging to and Nicole's voice returned, "Aren't you glad to see me?"

She was sitting across from him now, motionless and shy, like in the mural. He did his best to draw air into his defiant lungs. "I can't take much more of this, Nicole."

She measured him with concern. "I wouldn't be doing this if I had anywhere else to turn. You know that, don't you?"

"I also know a priest who says you're not who you say you are."

"Zack, please don't listen to that man... I don't trust him."

"Funny, that's what he says about you."

But before she could respond, Conway returned. Zack blinked and was relieved to see Nicole once more reinstated on the canvas. Conway resumed their conversation by inviting him to call him by his first name and the task became easier.

"The night I met Nicole she told me she didn't want to be alone," Zack began. "Do you know what that was all about?"

Conway gathered his thoughts. "She was in a relationship that ended a few months ago," he reminisced. "I know it hurt. Sometimes she'd call me at night just to have someone keep her company until she fell asleep."

Zack's mind flashed to the dressing room when she told him that she had been lonely since she and her boyfriend broke up. "Did you know the guy?" he asked.

"No. She never said who he was..." Conway said before trailing. "But hold on..." He crossed the room and looked through a bookcase. "I found something the other day. She left it here after a writing session."

Setting several items aside he located what he wanted.

"What is this?" Zack asked opening a notebook that he handed him.

"Her think-book," Conway explained. "She wrote everything in there. What came to mind just now is a poem." Conway found the page, dated April 12. "Read the dedication."

"*To S.A. with all my heart.*" Zack swallowed hard as he read.

holding close
to life
and love
isn't life a dream?
whenever
I'm with you
like this
it's the very best
my life
has been
it seems...

The verse hit him hard. These were the words of a woman in love. In love with someone other than him. "Do you think S.A.'s the guy?" he finally asked.

"I do."

Zack looked at the canvas again and thought about his conversation with her at the Greek. *"How can someone like you not be in a serious relationship?"* he had asked.

"I never said I wasn't," she replied.

Then Zack's mind came back to the man before him. "But wait," he said, thinking aloud. "If she kept his identity from you there had to be a reason."

"I always suspected he was married," Conway told him. "I know that doesn't sound like Nicole, but that's what I thought.

Zack's heart nearly stopped cold. The possibility of S.A. taking out his revenge on her after their break-up shot through him like a thunderbolt.

NEWS ITEM:

The Los Angeles Daily News, May 5

In a rare demonstration of unity, the Los Angeles City Council voted unanimously today to supply The Los Angeles Unified School District with $50,000 to be earmarked for a special series of anti-drug seminars. The new program, which follows the drug-related death of singer Nicole Branson last month, is said to be a frank "no-holds-barred" presentation intended to take the glamor out of recreational drug use.

Chapter Ten

Studio B at SongWorks on Melrose Avenue in West Hollywood was filled with guitars, amplifiers, drums, and a retro Seattle grunge band named Groin Pull playing a song entitled "Smells Like Love" with bone-shattering power.

Having installed himself in the control room's comfortable leather power chair, producer Elliot Kefler listened to the rehearsal with a practiced ear that told him neither the composition nor band were destined for the Rock and Roll Hall of Fame. Kefler wore his characteristic white tennis apparel, though he did not actually play tennis, with a lightweight blue cashmere sweater tied around his shoulders. A paunchy sixty year-old, he had an expensive hand-sewn toupee that looked almost natural. He also benefitted from top-notch cosmetic work, the results of which were framed by his coppery tanning bed skin.

He reached for a fader on the expansive mixing console and reduced the musical offenses to a humane level. "The lead guitar and drummer suck," he told the engineer. "But the singer's okay. The label signed these idiots, so let's get clean tracks on everybody and let my session guys baste this turkey later."

Kefler would have said more, but a well-endowed woman in a breezy low-cut summer sundress chose that moment to burst through the door. It was Sandy. "Sorry I'm late, Mister K. I couldn't believe that traffic!"

He stared blankly. "Do I know you?"

Sandy reacted innocently. "Sandy Phillips, from *Rolling Stone*. We met at Nicole Branson's funeral."

"We're in the middle of a session." He turned away to check a cue sheet.

Characteristically, she was undaunted. Crossing in front of the console, she practically demanded his attention. "You told me to come see you today about the piece I'm writing." Kefler did not have the foggiest idea what she was talking about, of course, because it never happened.

"The story on Nicole," she prodded.

"Oh, yes," he mumbled with disinterest. "Unfortunately, you couldn't have caught me at a worse time. I'll have my assistant set something up."

She purposefully inclined forward to give him a generous view of her cleavage, hoping for the same stupefied juvenile reaction that she got from most men. Zack had been unresponsive to the ploy and she admired him for it. Kefler, on the other hand, seemed duly distracted. He knew a great pair of knockers when he saw them.

After waiting for his eyes to relocate to her face, she pleaded, "Mister K, there's a deadline the size of Kilimanjaro breathin' down on me and without a quote from Elliot Kefler I can start mailing resumes. Know what I mean?"

It did not take Kefler long to make a decision. She was young, stacked, and probably available. His mind flashed to what she might do to him with those exotic long fingernails of hers. That alone was worth a few minutes of his time.

On the cozy SongWorks courtyard patio, Sandy was looking at a snapshot of Nicole with a younger Kefler casually draping his arm around her shoulder. "This's trick," she proclaimed.

"Thought it might work for you," Kefler said with an assured smile. "You know, 'Nicole's early days with the man responsible for it all...'"

Sandy blinked at his ego. "Looks like you two were tight."

The muffled repetitive drum beat of a hip-hop group leaked from one of the studios and thumped the redwood decking as Kefler settled back in his wicker chair to light a Monte Cristo-A cigar. His shiny gold watch glistened in the daylight, as if staged for a Rolex magazine ad. "I was with the lady from her first demo," he gloated as hundred-dollar smoke reached his nostrils. "We were even romantically involved for a while, if you want the inside scoop."

Sandy studied the eagerness on his face and saw a repugnant hedonist willing to climb over a corpse if it meant publicity for himself. She pretended to write his remark in her notepad. *Nicole had to sleep with this creep to have a music career?!*

"Obviously, she had good taste," Sandy said with a sly smile.

Kefler accepted the remark as the signal he was waiting for. "There's so much I'd like to share with you. Why don't we talk about it over dinner tonight?"

Sandy deftly sidestepped the offer. "That sounds nice. Unfortunately, I have plans tonight."

"Plans can be changed," he added suggestively. "I'll book the chef's table at The London. Gordon Ramsay owes me a favor."

She adjusted positions to give him another look at her breasts. "Let me see what I can do," she offered while pretending to send a text message. Then she added matter-of-factly, "By the way, do you happen to know somebody with the initials S.A.?"

"Who's that?"

"I think Nicole was dating him but I don't have a name. I'd sure appreciate it if you could help me out."

Kefler thought it over. "S.A..?" he repeated, "No, but I guess there were a few things I didn't know about her at the end. Like the drugs."

"That's a common problem in the business, isn't it?"

"Not like it used to be," he said. "It ain't the eighties anymore."

"So, you had no idea what she was into?"

"I suppose the signs were there," he reflected. "The mood swings, her iffy health... that's drugs for you."

Sandy considered. "What if I told you there's a question about that?"

"About what?"

"There's a guy who found discrepancies with the autopsy."

A more pronounced sparkle flashed in his eyes. "What kind of discrepancies?"

"Cause of death." Kefler broke into a wide grin that surprised her. "Did I miss something?" she asked.

"No, no... sorry. It's a reflex," he explained. "I loved Nicole, I truly did. But this industry goes nuts for controversies. It moves product like we're giving it away."

"No kidding?"

"You better believe it. When George Michael died his sales jumped three thousand percent. Ka-Ching!"

Sandy glanced at her phone, cringing as she pretended to read a text message. "Damn it, my appointment can't be moved. Maybe another time."

Kefler recognized the brush-off, but after one more glance at her chest he decided to give it another shot. "How about a quick tour of the private lounge upstairs? I've got the only key."

Sandy could not flee SongWorks fast enough. She scurried west on Melrose Avenue, wanting to toss Kefler's snapshot into the trash but pocketing it instead. She wished she had thought to bring hand sanitizer and assertively wiped the fingers that Kefler touched on her dress.

It was noontime rush hour in Hollywood, which condensed the pedestrians, bikes, cars, and trucks on Melrose into a clogged mass. As she maneuvered her way through the knots of people on the sidewalk, a large man casually stepped from a storefront and proceeded to follow her.

Following Sandy was not difficult. Eventually easing her pace to look at various window displays, it was evident that she was unaware of being watched. What with that, and purple hair that could probably be seen from space, the man stayed further behind than normal. Moreover, he already had what he came for; he had serviceable audio of her conversation with Kefler on the patio.

Two and a half blocks from the studio, Sandy took a seat outside one of the area's popular coffee houses. Her observer paused a moderate distance away and made a call on his cell phone.

As Sandy read a menu, Zack appeared and repeated something that he had apparently said seconds earlier, but which had gone unheard. "I said, 'Hi, Lois'..."

Startled, she jerked around to face him and there was anxiety in her voice that he had not heard before. "Raskin, don't look up, there's a guy followin' me."

"Are you sure? Where...?"

"On the corner. I've seen him before, but can't remember where."

Zack put a plan together. "I'll head for the john and double back to check him out," he decided as he stood. "If anything happens, make sure you get a good look at him."

She reacted with concern. "Why can't you look at him?"

"I plan to," he said impatiently. "Unfortunately, we don't know if he has a gun."

"Don't talk like that, all right?"

"The police are gonna need a description," he continued. "You down with that?"

"I guess."

"And get a picture with your phone if you can."

Zack entered the coffee house. Once inside, he bolted through the kitchen to the alley, pausing to pick up a three-foot length of metal pipe from the ground. It would make a good weapon if necessary.

The man was still on the phone when Zack inched up behind him. He clutched the pipe nervously and it seemed heavier than before. Blood oscillated in his temples. Only then did it occur to him that he lacked the fortitude to actually use the pipe on anyone. *Who did he think he was, Liam Neeson?!*

He stole a breath and summoned his best simulation of a tough guy. "Excuse me..."

As the man turned, Zack's memory chattered in and he recalled the terse words they exchanged at the backstage reception. But it was a fleeting moment. Ted Gimble wasted no time in driving his fist into Zack's abdomen and running off. The pipe clattered to the ground as he doubled over.

Sandy rushed over. "Raskin, are you all right?"

Zack winced in pain. "... security... guy... from the... concert..."

She clenched his arm. "There he is!"

Gimble was still visible among the sidewalk pedestrians. Trying to catch his breath, Zack took Sandy's hand and plowed into the passing shoppers and tourists. The two picked up their pace, with only sporadic glimpses of the man to keep them going.

Then, just when it looked as if they might be gaining, Gimble disappeared. Zack hauled himself onto the bed of a parked pickup truck for a final look around.

"Do you see him?" Sandy asked.

"No."

"Shit!"

"Please tell me you got something from Kefler." Zack asked as he drove west on Sunset Boulevard. His stomach still hurt from being punched and his headache had returned.

Sandy reacted blankly, unable to hear over the cacophony of troubling new engine noises the old Prelude was making. "What?"

"What-did-you-find-out-from-Kefler?" he repeated at the top of his lungs, daring his head to split open like a ripe melon.

"He's-a-sleazoid," she shouted. "You-shoulda-seen-him-check-me-out. I-don't- know-what-she-ever-saw-in-him!"

"Who?"

She retrieved the photo from her pocket and thrust it at him. "Nicole! She-actually-dated-that-butt-hole. He-hit-on-me, too... like-I'd-ever-touch-his-saggy-flesh!"

He pulled over beside an ornate sign welcoming travelers to Beverly Hills, shut off the engine, and studied the picture in edgy silence. "What else did you find out?"

"Concert security was usually hired by somebody in Nicole's crowd. A guy named Dennie Seifert."

Zack could not place the name. "Do we know him?"

"He's the roadie I scammed my press pass from."

"Great! If he can tell us who the security gorillas were..." he reasoned, "what do you bet we find S.A.?" But Sandy's doubt was apparent. "It adds up, Lois," he argued. "Either Nicole breaks up with S.A. and he flips out because he can't deal with it, or he breaks up with her and she becomes a liability because Glen Conway was right about him being married."

"So, he hires thugs to fake the autopsy?" she interrupted. "Gimme a break."

"Maybe he was being an asshole about everything and her heart gave out from stress." This time there was no interruption. The concept was beginning to sink in. "Medically, that's possible. Her heart was weak and she was already under a lot of pressure. She got dumped on the eve of a major concert tour."

"That still don't explain why S.A. went to all the trouble of creating the overdose story," she said. "I mean, what would he do that for? She was already gone."

"I don't know. Maybe we're back to her dumping him and he's a vindictive prick."

Silence followed as they reflected on that. Sandy spoke first. "Ya wanna hear what else Kefler said when he wasn't staring at my tits? Her albums will sell better when this gets out."

"Whatever," he answered, re-starting the engine. The grating mechanical noise was more deafening than ever. "He won't have to worry about that for a while."

"What do you mean?"

"He can't exploit this until the controversy gets out, right? Other than Glen Conway, you and I are the only people who know about this and we're not going public anytime soon."

She hurled a look at him. "That depends on when soon is, don't ya think?"

"I dunno, eventually."

Sandy reached over and turned off the engine before he could pull into traffic. She was not about to let the discussion end. "Don't screw with me, Raskin. How long is *eventually*?!"

"How am I supposed to know? When we have something."

"The questions about the autopsy are worth a byline in the *New York Times*," she fired back.

"A few hours ago you were still swallowing the party line about an overdose. No way are you blowing this investigation for me."

Sandy glared. "Since when are we doing this for you?!"

"All I'm asking for is time, Lois," he pleaded.

NEWS ITEM:

The Sacramento Bee, May 6

The Jackson County Sheriff reports finding the body of an unidentified adult male floating in Lake Bonita yesterday. An apparent drowning victim, the deceased is believed to be in his late sixties or early seventies. Local officials estimate that the man had been dead for several days when two fishermen discovered his body tangled in the debris above Bonita Canyon Dam.

Chapter Eleven

Open parking spaces seldom appeared in front of the apartment building, yet tonight there were two. Doug McKay did a double take as he walked past and considered inviting people over solely to take advantage of the rarity. But the notion faded. Having spent several days with his parents for their wedding anniversary, he had fallen behind in his studies. There would be no guests for now.

Stopping to check the mailbox, he found little of interest and headed up the stairs. Flipping through envelopes with one hand while carrying his suitcase in the other, he found a glossy museum catalogue addressed to a long-departed tenant that he thought might be worth looking at when he had time.

It was not until he arrived at the door that he discovered it was slightly ajar. Curious, he shouldered it to reveal the darkened space. Light from the ornate wall sconce in the hall punched a hole in the shadows, just enough for Doug to see that the place had been ransacked. He never saw the gun that hit him across his head.

An instant later, his attacker stepped into the light to close the door. But when Ted Gimble turned his victim over, he cursed. This was not Zack Raskin.

"Hey, kid," Angie was inquiring, "who do you like in the west this year, L.A. or Arizona?"

"I dunno," Zack replied, his mind far away from star players and bench depth.

They were in the employee lounge at the Willis Ambulance Company in West Hollywood. Zack sat at a kitchen table making notations about Nicole's case history from a medical textbook while his partner read *Sports Illustrated* in an easy chair and listened to the radio scanner chattering intermittently in the background.

Angie perused a column of statistics. "The American League I pretty much got figured," he went on, referring to this year's baseball prospects, "but those two got me stumped."

"I can't talk about that now, Angie. I need to stay on this."

"No, what you gotta do is take a break. All that work won't mean much if you get sick."

"You're probably right..." Zack conceded as he settled back in his chair and sipped freshly brewed coffee from the expensive beans that Mrs. Willis provided to her employees. "It's hard to downshift sometimes, you know?"

"You know I do," he answered. Then, setting his magazine aside, Angie ambled over. "But let me ask you something," he began. In fact, there was a lot that he wanted to ask but had held back until the right time. "Are you sure Nicole didn't O-D?" He noted Zack's defensive reaction but pressed on. "Now hear me out... I know you were a big fan and all that, but the truth is you hardly knew her."

"I knew her better than you think," Zack replied as offhandedly as he could.

Angie took a seat across from him and looked him in the eye the way he did when instructing him in a medical procedure. "Why, because you nailed her once?"

Zack did a double take. He had never said anything about that. *First Father Solano saw through him and now Angie?!* Angie rested his big hands on the open medical book. "Zack, listen to me. I'm sure it was terrific, but it was a one-night thing, okay? One night."

There was so much that Zack wanted to say, but could not. "I know," was his absurdly insufficient response.

"Then ya gotta let this go."

"That's a lot easier said than done."

Angie studied him for a moment and comprehended that there was more to this than he knew. "Okay, but you at least gotta be objective," he added. "You know as well as I do that even if the M.E. got stuff wrong, her heart could've been weakened from recreational use. Users don't all end up psychotics."

Zack measured the theory. It felt better than he feared to be talking about the case. "Then you tell me... what are the odds of a high red cell count in a heroin user?"

"Same as findin' a virgin at the Playboy mansion."

"She was six point-o." Zack handed him a lab report to prove it.

Angie looked at the documentation. “No increase in erythrocyte volume or hemoglobin/hematocrit? No way was she shootin’ up,” he verified with suspicion. “Not with this CBC.”

“The problem is I’ve got roadblocks everywhere,” Zack added. “She was cremated and nobody can find the pathologist who did the work-up. He was freelance.”

Angie regarded his young friend with renewed admiration. “Don’t you let that stop you, understand? You’re cookin’ here, kid. Angie’s proud of you.”

The discussion was interrupted by a dispatch croaking over the radio across the room: “Unit seven. Delta Response, Code Three. Priority Seventeen D-2 Long Fall Emergency. 2534 Silver Creek Drive, Westwood. Male subject condition unknown.”

Zack’s stomach tightened. “Angie... that’s my address.”

Spectators were gathered outside Zack’s building as the ambulance raced up. A uniformed policeman who knew Angie from his years on the job briefed him the instant he and Zack climbed out. “Looks like the victim took a pretty good beating before somebody tossed him off a balcony.”

Zack stared at the men as his worst fears were realized. “... Doug.”

Running to his roommate lying on the concrete, he kneeled beside him. He was incapable of functioning on a professional level. He was an incoherent jumble of confused sensations without any of the resolve that he usually possessed as an EMT.

Angie was soon at his side, his voice commanding. “We’ll take care of him, Zack,” he said. “I promise.”

Then, turning to his patient, Angie whispered reassuringly while performing a delicate survey of Doug’s neck, spine, and vital signs. “Okay Doug, the cavalry’s here. I’m gonna check you out a little bit and then we’re taking you into the shop. You got nothing to worry about.”

But as Angie listened to Doug’s heart and lungs with his stethoscope, he knew how hollow his words were. Doug had a broken neck, and spinal cord traumas are among the most difficult injuries to treat. Whenever the meninges membranes covering the spine are damaged, the chances for quadriplegia or tetraplegia paralysis are enormous. Injuries to the medulla oblongata itself, that essential part of the anatomy where the brain joins the spinal column, are even worse.

Angie was grateful for the arrival of a fire truck and turned to Zack, who was still in a stupor. "Zack..." he began gently, "fire department's here." He waited for Zack to register that somebody was speaking. "We got this. Why don't you check things out inside?"

Zack made the long walk upstairs with a young Latina policewoman, though he had no specific awareness of her. His perceptions were still a mess, a hodgepodge of frazzled and directionless thoughts. All he knew for certain was that there were more stairs to climb than he remembered. One after another the steps appeared before him in endless succession. His feet and legs weighed a ton as he lifted them.

"Your roommate may have walked in on a burglary," the policewoman stated as they entered the unit. Zack did not respond. The place was completely trashed. "Let me know if anything's missing, okay?"

Zack nodded absently, though considering Doug's condition he did not particularly care if anything was missing or not. His only valuable possessions were Nicole's think-book and the autopsy files, which were stored in his locker at work. "Mind if I have some time alone?" he asked.

"I'm sorry, sir, it's department policy to stay with the resident," she told him.

Zack flopped into a chair. His depletion was so complete he was sure that someone would have to assist him back to his feet. This lady cop might have to do it, he decided.

As he scanned the scattered belongings around the room, none of the anger that he would have predicted surfaced. None of the feelings of indignation and violation that crime victims usually experience. There was only emptiness. There were not even any of the sounds that he was accustomed to: no traffic noise on the street outside, no stereo pulsating through the wall from the unit next door, not even the rasping hum of the refrigerator that drove Doug nuts.

It was a silent world. Artificially, horribly silent, as a series of disjointed memories gushed forward in his mind:

His conflicted reaction to the sight of Nicole coming to life through the oil of the painting at Glen Conway's house...

The tension that he felt when the shadowy figure was searching Sandy's car...

The ecstasy and bewilderment colliding inside him when Nicole made love to him the day of her funeral...

The panic that seized him when Father Solano said that he perceived something more than grief in Zack, and that he sees things that others do not...

The urge to throw up at seeing Doug's body splayed in an unnatural position on the sidewalk...

The stinging pain that he felt when Nicole gave him that final unforgettable frightened look moments before she collapsed at the concert...

Zack rubbed his neck to quell the images and, much to his surprise, the technique worked. At long last he found some peace. He sat there with his eyes closed, savoring it.

But it did not last long. When the policewoman took the opportunity to quietly survey the rest of the apartment, someone spoke. "This wasn't a burglary."

Zack opened his eyes to find Nicole sitting on the coffee table, facing him. "Really?" he answered peevishly. "Well, maybe you'll finally fill me in on what is going on."

Her answer was timid and low. "I can't tell you what I don't understand."

"Don't fucking tell me that..." he said, rising up.

"Zack, she'll hear you!" she warned, glancing in the direction of the officer down the hall.

"I don't give a shit." He was in her face now. "It was rough enough dealing with you coming back, but when Doug went off that balcony the rules changed." There was so much more that he wanted to say but he became strangled with emotion.

She touched his arm softly. "They changed the rules on me, too. Remember?"

"I don't know anymore, Nicole. I don't know what's real and what's not."

"I'm real," she answered, squeezing his hand for emphasis.

He pointedly pulled from her grasp. "And what if Father Solano's right about you? What if this's all some kind of evil satanic shit?"

"Don't say that!" Her face was flushed.

"Then help me."

"I told you, I can't."

Zack blinked away tears. "So, now what? If Doug survives, his life'll never be the same. Is my soul worth that?"

"Zack, please... if I mean anything to you stop talking that way!"

"Why? You know who brought all this on," he argued. "Your boyfriend, S.A."

"You don't know that."

"Fine. Then it's the Devil, like Father Solano says."

Nicole clutched for his hands again. "No..."

"Then prove him wrong. Who's S.A.?"

Just then the policewoman returned. Zack looked from her to Nicole, who was no longer anywhere to be seen. "Did you say something, sir?" the officer asked.

"No... sorry," he mumbled. "I was talking to myself."

THINK-BOOK ENTRY:

A Poem By Nicole Branson, April 16

here I am
standing
all alone
changing with time
as it changes
me
where am I now?
thoughts
are clouding
here within me
sadness comes
and goes
nostalgia
melancholy freedom
happy, pensive
me
where am I now?

Chapter Twelve

Zack sat in his living room dealing with the distinct possibility that Father Solano had been right about everything. The priest vehemently warned him about a war between good and evil, and while he had no clue why the Devil might want his soul, what happened to Doug raised the stakes. Nicole's evil spirit may have been maneuvering him toward the abyss all along.

He had not noticed the retreat of Angie or the fire and police units. Nor did he know how he obtained the business card of an LAPD detective named Bradley Maulden that was on the coffee table. If he was interviewed by the police he had no recollection of it.

Clearly, he was in shock.

Relocating to the balcony, he leaned against the rail and stared at the spot where Doug landed. An hour elapsed before he regained the presence of mind to call Angie to check on Doug. He found his phone in his pocket and slumped in a patio chair. It was too soon for a diagnosis, of course, but he was compelled to inquire. That is what friends and family do, he decided, they become obsessed with knowing every shred of information. No matter how upsetting it may be to hear.

After leaving a message for Angie, his mind pivoted to Doug's parents. Angie would have notified them by now and they would be arriving on the first available flight. He was incapable of imagining what might come after that.

For now, all Zack was qualified for was contemplating a hot shower. He double-checked the front door lock, shoving a table against it for good measure, and trudged off to the bathroom.

Inside the pink-tiled enclosure that he thought was too effeminate, he welcomed the stream pounding his knotted body. The warm vapors rising around him were equally curative. Like a moist security blanket, nothing could bother him here. Even his confrontation with Nicole a while ago began to wane. *He just didn't give a fuck about anything.*

Regrettably, his numbness was not total. In the back of his mind he still heard her plea for him to ignore the priest, and he could see the anxious look on her face when he invoked Solano's name. His memory lurched to her refusal to tell him about S.A. and it landed on his chest like an anvil. *Damn it, he had feelings again!*

He was exasperated that his disconnected mental state had not lasted longer and hoped he could somehow lapse into a deep REM sleep. Zack adjusted the faucet to maximum heat and, amazingly, the world began to melt away along with the tension in his torso. *If he was crazy, fine. Then he would concentrate on mending his body.* The tough tissues of his musculature were so constricted he felt as if all six hundred muscles were strained. He finessed his neck into the spray and waited for his trapezius to let go, inch by inch, all the way down to the deltoids in his shoulders. Before long, similar benefits were spreading through the latissimus dorsi that jacketed his back.

Zack did not know how long stood there but it was a while. He could practically hear his brain waves downshifting through their frequency bands, from the super-beta level of mental activity to beta and then to the alpha level associated with relaxation. He was adrift, floating through theta cycles towards an EEG brainwave of less than delta, which was near brain-dead, when something snapped him out of it: *he was not alone!*

He stared through the fogged glass door to see the blurred image of someone in the room. *Hadn't he put a table against the front door?!* His mind raced for options, but he was trapped. The sight of Doug lying bloodied and bruised seethed with graphic clarity. Zack was unable to move.

Watching the intruder's outline advance, he became aware of the drain at his feet noisily gulping water and wondered if it might be the last sound he would ever hear. Pressing against the wall, he clenched his fists and braced for the worst.

But the trespasser did not attack.

Peeling himself from the tiles, Zack gingerly wiped the glass to see someone disrobing. *Nicole.* A moment later the door swung open to reveal her standing before him, naked and vulnerable. Her eyes glistened as she gazed into his, and they exchanged no words as she stepped into his embrace. Her skin was smooth and cool to his touch, her breasts soft against his stomach. Wet billows of steam engulfed them as he held her tightly and they cried.

If Satan had come to take his soul then he would offer no resistance.

Zack had been in the Ronald Reagan UCLA Medical Center dozens of times, both as an EMT and a student doing clinical service. He was friendly with the night staff and often participated in their after-hours social events. One night he even joined doctors, nurses, and orderlies in a spirited game of floor hockey in the hall, with a roll of white surgical tape filling in as the puck, an assortment of crutches, brooms, and mops serving as hockey sticks, and bed pans as the goals.

But as he paced this hallway, such revelry seemed like events from someone else's life. He settled onto a couch where he sat alone. Medical personnel, patients, and visitors moved past without breaching his solitude. The epic human struggle between life and death, comfort and pain, joy and sorrow was playing out around him and he was excluded from it all.

At last, he saw an elderly couple walking to the nurse's station, the woman being careful not to rush her feeble companion. They were, Zack knew, Walter and Connie McKay, Doug's parents. "Mister and Mrs. McKay," he said approaching them. "I'm so sorry."

Connie McKay brightened at the sight of him. She was an agile woman with a contemporary look most women her age do not possess. "Zack, dear. What happened?"

"Who would do a thing like this to our Doug?" Walter added. The tremble in his husky voice bared his anguish, just as his comportment did his deteriorating health.

"We don't know yet," Zack told them. There was no point in burdening them with theories about Nicole's death and how his investigation—or the Devil's scheme for his soul—might be connected to the assault. "The police don't have much to go on," he explained simply. "Have you seen him?"

Connie drew her husband's arm closer. "He doesn't even look like himself, with all those terrible bruises..."

"Doug's strong, Mrs. McKay. He'll get through this." The grief-stricken couple traded a look, ardently wishing that it might be so. "The staff here is really good," Zack continued. "Especially Doctor Kelada. There's nobody better with spinal injuries."

The McKays nodded, though they were not absorbing medical veracities at the moment. They were still grappling with primal emotions. "Why don't we have a seat?" Zack offered, motioning to the nearby visitor's lounge.

Zack guided them slowly and Walter continued, "I can't believe this is happening. We just had him home with us..."

"He was glad he could be there for your anniversary," Zack assured them as they took their seats.

Connie was watching Zack with compassion. She had always liked her son's roommate. "And how are you doing, dear?"

"Okay," he answered unconvincingly. "As good as can be expected."

"Doug told us he's been worried about you," she volunteered.

The directness of the statement caught Zack off guard. "He did?"

"You don't look well, son," Walter added, wrinkling his brow. "Not well at all."

Zack did not have it in him to pretend. He might have anticipated that Doug would tell his parents about Nicole. They had an enviably open and honest family relationship. After having a baby so late in life, the couple was determined to avoid mistakes that many younger parents make. "My problems seem insignificant compared to Doug's," was the most he could say.

"You're his best friend, Zack," Connie continued with motherly kindness. "He hopes you find the answers you're looking for."

"And so do we," stressed her husband.

Zack thanked them for their support, but the sight of Angie's approach engulfed the moment. Zack tried to read the prognosis on his face but his partner's years of experience masked whatever he was thinking or feeling.

"Mister and Mrs. McKay," Zack began, "this is Angelo Giambalvo. He attended to Doug at the accident."

The McKays held hands in anticipation. "Do you have an update for us, Mister Giambalvo?" Walter asked.

As Angie sat on the couch, there was a softening of his bearing. "You should talk to the doctor about that," he replied. "I just want to see if I can get you anything to make you more comfortable. Something to eat or drink?"

"We would appreciate anything that you can tell us, Mister Giambalvo," Connie pressed. "We know the news isn't good."

Angie saw Walter squeeze his wife's shoulder and knew that he could not deny them information about their son. "Doug is going to live," he started. "But what kind of life it will be is anybody's guess. He has a broken neck. Doctor Kelada is running tests to see how extensive the nerve damage is."

Zack was overwhelmed by Angie's kindness. He knew how complex the relationship was between the spinal cord and its control of other organ systems. His mind flickered to images and statistics of hemodynamic instability and respiratory insufficiency in patients like Doug, and the complications of bladder and bowel control, skin sensation, muscle atrophy, and overall health that can occur. Angie's reassuring bedside manner was exactly what these lovely people needed.

The McKays nodded their appreciation, but said nothing as their emotions hindered their ability to speak.

"Are you sure I can't get you anything?" Angie asked.

"No, thank you," Connie responded, sliding into a daze. "We don't want to be any trouble."

"Then I'll leave you with Zack," he told them, patting his young partner on the shoulder before returning to the treatment room. Zack's stomach tightened as he comprehended Doug's plight. He knew that while advances in nerve regeneration had been made with laboratory animals, human progress was marginal.

Taking the McKays' hands in his, he held them firmly and said a silent prayer. Maybe his mother was right about going to Mass after all. *Screw the Devil. He would have to wait for his soul.*

When Zack stepped off the lobby elevator a short time later he saw a familiar figure crossing the expansive space with a Bible and rosary in hand. He considered turning away to avoid detection, but Father Solano saw him first.

"Zack... what a nice surprise. What are you doing here?"

"I was with some friends upstairs."

"If you don't mind my saying so, you look terrible," the priest said with concern.

"Yeah, well my friends aren't doing so hot."

"Would you like me to look in on them?"

Zack flinched. He did not want Solano learning more about what was going on and he certainly was not ready to admit that the priest was probably right about everything. "Thanks, Father, but I think what they need most is space."

Solano was watching him. "And what about you? Why do I sense that things are more serious than you disclosed to me?"

Zack's apprehension flared. *He could not afford for Solano to be right! As much as it scared him, he had to be with Nicole again.* "Father, I appreciate what you're trying to do, but maybe calling you before wasn't such a good idea."

"Your doubts are understandable, but I urge you to reconsider. There is a threatening specter around you. If you are in trouble I can help."

The words fell flat, as Zack was determined to resist his involvement. "I guess your radar is out of whack this time, Father. There's no trouble here."

"Demon spirits are seductive, Zack. If you are a willing vessel then you are defenseless against them."

"Like I said, I'm fine."

"So you claim."

Startled by the priest's inference, Zack pushed past him. "Goodbye, Father."

Solano held up his Italian-made rosary with its black and silver cross and called out, his voice reverberating in the big room, "God of power and mercy, through the intercession of Saint Michael, the archangel, be his protection in the battle against all evil..."

But Zack was out the door before the priest's prayer ended.

A few hours later Sandy was driving Zack in her Volkswagen past the green ivy embankments of the Santa Monica Freeway on the way to Venice Beach. Still feeling severe discomfort over his encounter with Father Solano, Zack did not notice either the unusually light traffic or the natural beauty along the upwardly sloping banks of the freeway. Nor could he get Doug's parents out of his mind. He had always admired his roommate for having such a supportive home. What was happening now was so unbelievably cruel and unjust.

An open-sided Jeep with a colorful surfboard lashed to the roof sped by. "So, how ya doin?" Sandy asked. "Are you sure you're up to this trip?"

He was only half-listening. "Sure." Another surfboard came into view, this time on a sports apparel ad on the side of a bus. The muscular guy in the picture was hugging the board and beaming inanely through overly-whitened teeth. Zack wanted to punch his lights out.

"I can drop you someplace. The Santa Monica Pier, maybe." she continued, angling to the off-ramp that would take them to Venice. "This guy Dennie's just a roadie."

"Road manager," Zack corrected.

"Whatever. Elliot Kefler might be wrong. There's no guarantee he knows squat about Nicole's security set-up."

"I'm not giving up," he came back. "That's what S.A. wants me to do."

"Okay," she reassured him while turning south on Main Street, "just thought I'd put it out there."

Zack paused in the recognition of how caring she was being. "I appreciate it, Sandy. Thanks."

She shot him a startled gape. "Wait a minute... did you actually call me by my real name?!"

"When?"

"Just now."

"Must be your imagination."

The VW made the turn onto Venice Boulevard and as Sandy's

conversation with Zack continued, a dirty white Dodge van behind them accelerated to maintain proper tailing distance.

Straightening the wheel, Ted Gimble looked at Gunter Strauss who habitually chomped a piece of gum while adjusting the radio receiver in the glove compartment. After a burst of static, Sandy and Zack's voices resumed the transmission:

"Raskin, there's somethin' else we hafta talk about. You weren't up to any more bad news earlier."

"I'm not sure I'm up to it now."

"They found the pathologist. Face down in Lake Bonita."

"Shit..."

"The news service called it an accidental drowning."

"Sure it was, just like Doug thought he could fly."

Gimble glanced again at Strauss, who was attaching a silencer to his Glock 9mm automatic pistol. It was time to end this shit. They would just have to wait for the right time and place.

The morning salt air was thick with odors that nobody ever seems to talk about when they mention Santa Monica Bay, the sewage-like aroma of mildew and rotting seaweed. But then, being as close to the polluted beach as they were, the presence of actual sewage was a distinct possibility. Zack marveled at the stupidity of Los Angeles County routinely depositing human waste and chemical runoff into the coastline's delicate ecosystem. Thanks to enterococci bacteria in the ocean, over a million cases of gastrointestinal illness—stomach cramps, diarrhea, and vomiting—from swimming here are common. And that does not count God-knows-how-many eye, ear, and nose infections.

This was hardly the postcard ocean view that Glen Conway enjoyed from afar at his Pacific Palisades retreat. The water here had an uninviting blue-gray tinge born of decades of abuse. Whenever he saw people fishing along the infamous *Red Zone* of the Pacific stretching from Santa Monica to Seal Beach, Zack had to wonder who they were planning to feed their tainted Pacific Barracuda, Barred

Sand Bass, Topsmelt, and aptly named White Croaker. The image of vendors in crisp lab coats strolling the surf hawking Loperamide, antibiotics, and chemotherapy doses like peanuts at Dodger Stadium flashed through his mind.

Zack and Sandy approached the dilapidated Venice bungalow that faced what had once been an alley but now served as a street. Sandy silently admired the black Harley-Davidson parked in the tiny joke of a yard. How appropriate that the model the roadie chose would be a *Rocker*, she thought as they knocked at the door.

Several minutes lapsed before a burly man appeared behind the chain lock. Seifert's name had not rung any bells for Zack, but the unfiltered Camel dangling from his lips triggered his memory: *this was Ox Man, the guy he observed checking cables before the concert.* While Seifert appeared unhealthy that night, in action he seemed to be a confident professional. But as the morning sunlight glared on his pale complexion, he was a very different person; this Dennie Seifert looked much older. A man at the wrong end of a binge.

"What do you want?" he spit out.

"Hey, Dennie," Sandy started. "Remember me? Sandy Phillips from *Rolling Stone*."

Seifert clutched the door solidly. "Yeah, sure. Listen, I was just heading out."

"This'll only take a minute," she added. "We wanna talk about Nicole Branson."

He narrowed the opening. "I gotta get going... sorry."

Zack jammed a straight-arm against the door. "She died in case you didn't hear about it. The least you can do is answer a few questions."

"Do you know who hired security staff for the tour?" Sandy jumped in.

Seifert reacted with panic. The paranoia of a drug abuser, Zack deduced. Or something more.

"Look, I told you... I don't have time to talk."

He pushed the door again and Zack was unable to hold it.

Sandy pressed her body against it, as well. "Why does somebody want us to stop looking into her death?" she demanded.

The big man's face reddened. "I wouldn't know." Then he forced the door shut.

At the end of the street the dirty white Dodge van sat unobtrusively in the shade of a lime green stucco building. As Zack and Sandy headed for the Volkswagen, it leisurely pulled away.

By the time Zack walked onto the stage of the Greek Theatre, the sun was directly overhead. Painted risers and colorful flats prepared for a musical tribute to Broadway gleamed in the light. They created a vastly different effect than the elements of Nicole's rock show.

Pausing at the sight of the rows of empty red seats, Zack could almost hear Nicole's audience leaping to its feet, cheering as the band cued her entrance. He recalled the musicians exchanging buoyant glances with each other. And he felt the energy. *God, that energy! It had been everywhere.*

He was transported back to that night three and a half weeks earlier. The band was riding an up-tempo groove behind Nicole and when she caught him watching her she smiled. As she approached the wings during her performance she never took her eyes off him. She was a vision of all things desirable in a woman.

And she was interested only in him.

But wait, that's not how it was. Or was it? He no longer knew. Zack was unable to move, as his relationship with Nicole became a grotesque hallucination: *she was a few feet away from him when illness overcame her, she faltered, the band stopped playing and the audience went silent, and Zack watched in horror as she reached out for him, filled with fear. Her outstretched arms were inches away... but could not touch him.*

Unnerved by the punishing distorted images, he turned to leave, but Nicole was everywhere he looked. Like the photographs projected on his apartment wall, she was before him now, pleading for his help, reaching out to him, dying one frame at a time.

"No....!!!" he bellowed.

Sandy rushed to his side. "Raskin, what's wrong?"

He did what he could to pull himself together. "You don't want to know."

"The hell I don't," she countered. "When was the last time you slept, anyway?"

He turned away, avoiding her. "Beats me."

"Raskin..." she admonished before cutting herself off. It was then that she finally understood why he had been driving himself so hard. "She was more than a friend... wasn't she," Sandy concluded.

He met her look, relieved that his secret had found its way into the open. "She still is," he confessed.

NEWS ITEM:

The National Enquirer, May 8

In a stunning revelation, a medical student at UCLA has challenged the Los Angeles County Coroner's findings surrounding the recent death of pop star Nicole Branson.

Chapter Thirteen

The glaring tabloid headline said it all: *POP STAR'S DEATH QUESTIONED!* Positioned directly beneath the pronouncement were publicity photos of Nicole singing and a lurid shot of her on a gurney in the morgue.

Zack stared in disbelief at *The National Enquirer* issue being extended for him to see by an exasperated Doc Sandberg. "I don't believe this..." he sputtered.

"You aren't the only one," she added as she read from the article, "UCLA David Geffen School of Medicine student Zack Raskin challenges the Los Angeles County Coroner." She sighed with weary resignation. "I'm sure Mister Geffen will be thrilled to have his good name associated with this."

"I don't understand how they found out," Zack mumbled.

She reacted, not quite comprehending. "Do you mean to tell me this's accurate?"

"I'm not challenging anybody," he told her. "They made that up."

Sandberg studied him guardedly. "Does this have anything to do with what you told me the other day?"

"Nicole's who I was talking about, yeah."

"Well, you've certainly come a long way from ghostly visitations and sexual fantasies," she remarked. "Why didn't you tell me about her pathology issues?"

"I didn't know much then," he said, shrinking in his chair. "I still don't..." He vacillated mid-thought. There would be no defending this catastrophe to Doc Sandberg.

She continued to assess him before reading from the tabloid once more. *"Raskin accuses officials of a cover-up in Miss Branson's death, though some sources are speculating that she did not die at all and may be hiding in seclusion."*

"That part's ridiculous."

"It's all ridiculous," she declared, handing him the newspaper. "Who are you to be conducting post mortem investigations, anyway?"

"Nobody," he admitted, incapable of absorbing the printed

words before him. "I sort of fell into it."

"Do you remember what you said when you came to see me? You were seeing a dead person, you were having conversations with her. You were even making love to her." Sandberg held his look firmly. "Does that sound like reality to you?"

"No."

"Good answer," she replied, leaning forward. With the change in posture came an adjustment in tone. "Forget the fact that people are furious that our school has been linked to this. They'll get over it," she continued softly. "What I want you to consider is how much you're putting at risk. Hospitals, medical groups, and universities who hire doctors don't like scandals. Do you understand?"

"Yes."

"To prove the point, someone in Washington even called the Dean questioning how we're spending federal grant money they send us."

"Grant money?"

"We are a public institution that depends on government support. So does your scholarship."

Zack did not respond as confusion and defeat reverberated inside him. The headline seemed to get bigger every time he looked at it.

"You're the most promising student I've seen in a long time, Zack. You could be an absolutely wonderful physician." Sandberg paused to reinforce her meaning. "So I'm not suggesting this, I'm telling you. Pull your life together."

"I don't know if I can," he told her. "It's more complicated than you think."

"Evidently," she noted with more sarcasm than she intended. "I did you a disservice when you first came to see me. I should have helped you get into counseling."

"I don't know if that would've changed much."

"It's worth finding out."

"It's a little late for that, isn't it?"

"There are no deadlines when it comes to mental health." She handed him a business card. "Duane Ellerbe has a psychiatric practice in the Valley. He's the best there is and he'll be waiting for your call."

As Zack examined the inscription, Sandberg handed him another card. "Take mine, too. I've written my mobile number on the back. I'm worried about you."

Zack emerged from the building and his mind was on overload. Not only was *The Enquirer* feeding on Nicole's death, but he knew that every newspaper, magazine, radio, and television station in the country would now be unleashed.

Sandy was waiting on a concrete campus bench, where a brass plaque indicated that it was dedicated to the memory of Herbert W. Sertok, Ph.D., an esteemed professor. Zack's grim attitude was apparent. "Well, you don't look very good."

He shoved the tabloid at her and her jaw dropped as the headline registered. "How the hell did they get this?!"

"Like you don't know," he shot back before storming off into the noon hour multitudes on the walkway.

Sandy raced after him. "It wasn't me. I'd never sell out to a rag like this!"

"They nailed us on everything!"

"Okay, they scooped us," she snapped. "I can't believe you suspect me!"

"You sure were panting about filing a story," he continued. "Man, you really sucked me in."

Defiantly grabbing his arm, she spun him around to face her. "Read my lips, Raskin: I didn't do it!"

"Then, who did?"

"How would I know?!"

"Who else had anything to gain by leaking this?"

That is when an epiphany struck her. "Elliot Kefler... remember? Controversies sell records."

Zack considered. Sandy's idea was reasonable and either she was a world-class actress or the hurt that she projected was authentic. "I'm sorry," he relented. "I shouldn't have jumped on you."

Sandy shrugged, taking pleasure in mimicking his earlier

assertion, "Hey, we all act like crude, insensitive jerks once in a while."

"Sounds familiar."

"Oughta... asshole."

"You've got a way with language," he said putting an arm around her. "I can't imagine why your writing career hasn't taken off."

Sandy sneered as they crossed Charles E. Young Drive. Suddenly, Ted Gimble's dirty white Dodge van materialized from a service area and veered directly at them!

Pedestrians screamed and dove for safety, but whether it was the element of surprise or his exhaustion Zack did not budge. He was a deer in headlights. Then, with the vehicle nearly on them, Sandy yanked him out of the way at the last moment. The van jumped the sidewalk in pursuit, but she and Zack landed safely in the flowers of an above-ground planter.

The van glanced loudly off the brick enclosure and disappeared around a corner. Its tires could be heard squealing as an echo might in a canyon. As people emerged from their hiding places they vented about the maniac who lost control, but Zack and Sandy knew better. They got a good look at Gimble behind the wheel and were keenly aware that this was no accident.

And why.

Zack plopped onto the planter, rubbing his left leg, which he strained in the fall. "You saved my life." he told her.

"Yeah," she quipped. "What was I thinkin'?"

The near-death experience left Zack with an urgent desire to see Doug. Some people might have gone directly to the police after a blatant attempt on his life, but all he could think about was his roommate suffering in intensive care.

As he and Sandy approached the lobby of the medical tower, he phoned the nursing station to make sure he would not be intruding on Doug's parents. He was relieved to learn that the McKays had gone to the cafeteria. That meant he could have some private time with his friend. Sandy would wait for him downstairs.

Zack had not seen Doug since he was admitted to the hospital, so he was not fully prepared for what was awaiting him. As he peered into the room's observation window he was overwhelmed by sight of the battered motionless form hooked up to the grouping of IV bags, respirator, and vital sign monitors.

Could this human wreckage be the same person who so fiercely wanted to become a doctor? Who spoke passionately about one day volunteering his services to a global organization like the International Red Cross or Doctors Without Borders?

Could this damaged young man be the guy who had been such a caring friend?

Removing a surgical mask and gown from the neatly folded stack on a hallway cart, Zack stepped into the room. Unlike his previous visits to the ICU as a student and emergency medical technician, he did not look at the monitors or medical chart. He was simply here to reciprocate Doug's friendship.

Then something in the corner of his eye grabbed his attention: the sight of Father Solano in a surgical mask, sitting in a chair, immersed in prayer. "Father, what are you doing here?" Zack asked in an accusatory tone.

"The hospital chaplain is an old friend. He told me what happened."

"Oh," was Zack's tight response. His displeasure at encountering the priest was evident.

"I'm extremely troubled by this turn of events, as you might imagine," Solano said as he rose to his feet. "Why didn't you tell me?"

"Truthfully?" Zack answered. "I wasn't up to another lecture about your cosmic war between good and evil."

"What is happening is unholy, Zack. Every instinct that I have tells me so," the priest declared. "I am worried that you could be the next victim... if indeed you are not already."

"Look, I'm grateful for your concern but I'm doing okay."

"And Doug? How is he?"

Father Solano gestured to the bed. Doug's complexion was chalky. The only color on his swollen face and arms was from his many bruises, which had turned dark purple and blue as the red blood cells in his skin broke down. This was wrong. So incredibly wrong...

"I think it's time for you to go," Zack said dismissively as he opened the door.

"The evidence could not be more clear. What happened to Doug is the work of a demon spirit."

"No," Zack argued. "Somebody doesn't want me looking into Nicole's death." He held the door open wide. "Thanks for stopping by, Father."

The priest shook his head sorrowfully and gathered his rosary and Bible from the bed. "Doug may be in good medical hands, Zack, but all the antiseptic in the world cannot eliminate the contaminants of evil." He crossed to the door and paused. "The taint of evil is in this room... and it envelops you," Solano concluded before making the sign of the cross. "I'll be in the chapel if you want to talk."

When the priest finally left, Zack tried to shake off his unworldly assertions and moved to the chair. Doug's eyelids struggled open as he became aware of someone in the room. When he finally identified his friend, they both did their best to hold back their emotions.

"Hey," was all Zack could get out. "It's me."

Doug blinked once slowly.

"I wanted to see how you are," Zack added.

Doug blinked again and pursed his dry lips. A tear trickled down his cheek.

"I know, McKay," answered Zack, unable to hold back tears of his own. He gently took Doug's hand, squeezing it gently as he sat beside him. "I know."

Walking back to Zack's place from a city parking lot on Broxton Avenue where they stashed the VW, Zack and Sandy stopped short at the sight of a bright blue *Eyewitness News* truck from ABC-7 sitting out front.

He ducked behind a row of hedges. "Terrific," he snarled. "Who's next, *TMZ*?"

"The article went viral," Sandy moaned. Another vehicle cruised past, a silver Ford Transit Connect with the logo KNX 1070 NewsRadio on the side. "Now what are we supposed to do?"

"Find a back way in and lock the damn door."

"Holy shit!" were the first words from Sandy's lips as they entered the living room. The place was still a shambles from Doug's supposed encounter with burglars.

"You should've seen it before I straightened up," Zack remarked as he crossed to his blinking answering machine. Doug never understood why Zack insisted on keeping a landline phone or this ancient machine, but to Zack they represented symbolic independence from technology. He owned a smart phone, of course, but as a matter of principle nobody knew how to reach him. A trivial victory over progress, Zack supposed, but a victory nonetheless. Like his insistence on playing sonically superior CD's on his stereo rather than the inferior compressed MP3 files the rest of society inexplicably found acceptable. Apple, Samsung, and HTC would have to work a whole lot harder to turn him into one of their lemmings.

A woman's voice played on the machine, "Mister Raskin, Jeannine Alexander at KKRB-FM. I'd love to get you on the air with this Nicole Branson story. Twitter has really blown up over this, so if you've got things to say we want to help you get them out there. Call me at 323-555-8100."

The machine beeped to signal the end of one message and the beginning of another. There were seven more reporters, ten radio hosts from around the country, and two muckrakers from England, all expressing support for what they called Zack's *cause.* It was enough to make him sick. The media sharks were circling, waiting to pick the flesh off his carcass. Hopefully, it would not be long before there would be other human entrees to pursue for their voyeuristic dining.

Sandy, meanwhile, turned on the television where a local channel was carrying a news conference featuring a spokesperson for the medical examiner. "...We assure the public that there is no merit to these unsubstantiated allegations being made by Mister Raskin. Ms. Branson's case has been treated with the utmost care and professionalism..." Sandy picked up the remote to increase the volume as the official continued. "Regrettably, this story is yet another example of fake news being disseminated by Mister Raskin and a willing media on an unsuspecting public."

As Sandy turned off the TV hoping that Zack had not heard it, one last message appeared with a beep on the answering machine. "Uh, this's Dennie Seifert..." he began. "We hafta talk." He paused before continuing in hushed tones. "I know what's goin' on. Meet me at the observatory at eleven tonight. A park ranger I know'll leave the gate unlocked. Whatever you do, don't let anybody follow you."

The line disconnected with a loud *click!* Sandy turned to Zack with fascination. "I wonder what that's all about..."

Zack shoveled a spoonful of instant coffee into a mug and filled it with tap water. "You're welcome to find out."

She reacted defensively. "What's that supposed to mean?"

He shoved the cup in the microwave and punched the keypad before answering. "I'm hanging it up, Lois. Just like Doc Sandberg told me to."

NEWS ITEM:

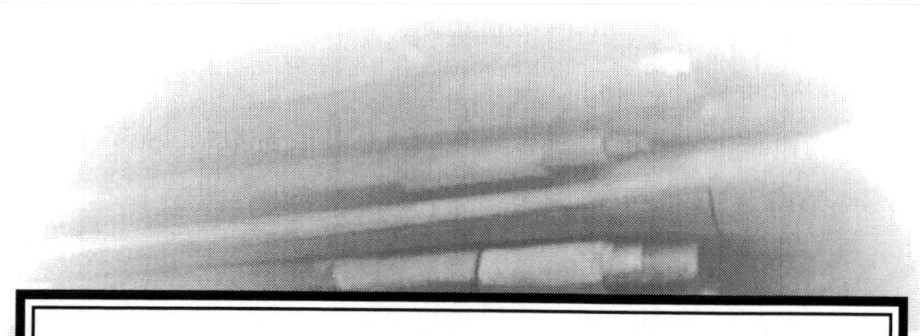

The San Francisco Chronicle, May 9

The Medical Examiner of rural Jackson County has identified a deceased male found last week at Lake Bonita as Daniel Takahashi, MD, a retired forensic pathologist. Takahashi, 72, who was born in Whittier, California and resided in Sierra Madre, and who received his medical education at The University of California, Berkeley, was determined to have fallen from his boat and drowned while vacationing at the popular lake.

Dr. Takahashi most recently assisted the Los Angeles Coroner's Office in the autopsy of entertainer Nicole Branson.

Chapter Fourteen

Walking past numerous cluttered workstations in the busy squad room of the West Los Angeles Community Police Station, Sandy shook her head. "I can't believe we're doin' this." The dozens of men and women wearing side arms and crisp blue uniforms were as removed from her life as astronauts on the moon.

Zack shot her a look. "You wanted my help; this's all I've got."

"But the cops won't do anything," she protested. "You know how they are."

Zack cornered her outside an empty cubicle. "We ripped a pretty big hole in this, Lois. The police can run with it now."

Sandy was unconvinced. "What about Dennie Seifert?"

"The cops can deal with him." Zack was adamant. "He's their problem now."

"But Raskin —"

"Let it go, will ya? Your story's blown, in case you missed it. The tabloids beat you to it."

She did not respond. It was hard letting go of her dream and so much of it had been linked to a medical student who refused to take no for an answer. But now here he was, shutting her down. "You serious?" she finally asked.

"Do I look like I'm kidding?"

"Unfortunately, no."

"Then let's tell this guy what we know," Zack decreed as he held up the business card of LAPD Detective Bradley Maulden. He did not recall receiving it the night Doug was attacked, but obviously the man gave it to him for a reason.

A short time later thirty-year law enforcement veteran Brad Maulden motioned for them to be seated in an interview room. "I'm glad you decided to come in, Zack. How's your roommate?"

"Okay, I guess. It looks like he might've dodged a high-cervical injury," Zack answered tentatively. "I'm sorry, Lieutenant... I don't actually remember meeting you."

"I'm not surprised. You were pretty out of it," Maulden explained. "That's why I left my card."

"Have you found out who attacked Doug?" Sandy interjected.

Maulden seemed to notice Sandy for the first time. "And you are...?"

"Sandy Phillips. I'm a journalist."

"And friend," Zack pointedly added.

Sandy smiled at the reference, but it was short-lived. Detective Maulden removed a copy of *The National Enquirer* from a folder and slid it across the table to her. "Then I take it this is yours?"

"No way," Zack answered. "Neither of us had anything to do with that."

"They messed it all up," she added.

"Funny, that's what the M.E.'s been saying on the news," Maulden countered.

"Only according to him it was you who messed it up."

"The medical examiner's wrong," Sandy shot back. But when the defense she hoped for from Zack never came, she backed off. "We just wanna turn over what we've got."

"Okay. But first explain to me what the Nicole Branson case has to do with the attack on Doug McKay," Maulden requested.

This time Sandy did not bother waiting for Zack. "Somebody wants to stop us from investigating her death."

Maulden considered the headline again. "I can give you five minutes."

"It's all here," Zack assured him about the files that he pulled from his book bag.

Looking at the information, Maulden revealed no reaction. "Okay. According to you, Branson had a disease. How do you say this...?"

"Subacute bacterial endocarditis," explained Zack.

Sandy added, "SBE... it's a heart defect."

"What's that got to do with drug abuse?" the detective asked as he shifted stiffly in the chair that was supposed to be ergonomically correct but was not.

Zack was resolute. "She didn't abuse drugs. Nicole didn't use them at all."

"The coroner said she did," the detective came back.

"The coroner's wrong," Zack declared.

"So *The Enquirer* got that right, after all?" Maulden remarked dryly. In three decades he had seen his share of conspiracy fanatics. No matter how thoroughly a case might be handled, there was always somebody who knew more than the experts.

Zack saw what he was thinking. "They run thousands of cases through the M.E.'s office every year," he added. "She had a heart attack that was never reported."

"How do you know?"

"We've seen the autopsy report," said Zack, pointing to a section of the folder. "The omission was deliberate."

"How'd you two get your hands on this?"

"We can't tell you that."

Maulden checked his watch. His impatience was growing. "And the coroner would falsify the report... why?"

"That's what we were hopin' you'd find out," Sandy told him. "Somebody lied through his teeth and his name's right there: Daniel Takahashi."

"He's a retired pathologist they brought in for the autopsy," Zack explained.

Maulden flipped to another page, wondering how much more time he should spend on this. "Have you told Takahashi about your concerns?"

"They found him floating in a lake up north yesterday."

"Face down," Sandy added.

The assertion got Maulden's attention. He looked his visitors over one more time.

"You seem to know a lot about this."

"Nicole was a friend of mine," Zack responded.

"We think Takahashi got whacked to keep him from talking," Sandy continued.

Maulden settled back in his chair. "So, now it's a cover-up, two murders, and the attack on Doug McKay?"

"There've also been attempts on us," Zack added.

Sandy nodded. "Two security guys from her concert were

behind that. They tried to run us over."

"We think they work for someone Nicole was dating," Zack added. "His initials are S.A., that's all we know."

Maulden had heard some far-fetched tales but this one was pretty wild. No surprise that the tabloid ran with it, he thought. Closing the file, he placed the newspaper on top. "The initials are all you know."

"That's right," Zack confirmed. "She wrote about him in her think-book."

"Her what?"

"It's like a diary."

The detective smiled. "So, she wrote down the killer's initials so the police could catch him? That was thoughtful."

Fuming, Sandy glared at Maulden. "Let's get outta here, Raskin."

Once assured by Detective Maulden that he would look into their allegations, Zack and Sandy paced the sidewalk outside.

"Well, that's the worst idea I ever had," Zack scowled.

"Shoulda listened to me," she reminded him. "He didn't believe a word we said."

"Doc Sandberg was right," he sighed. "*The Enquirer* blew our credibility. Now we're just two head-cases with a convoluted theory."

"Maybe you are," she cracked, hoping to distract him from his plummeting spirits.

"And you...?"

"Me? I'm a stubborn bitch who won't give up on a great story." She waited for a response and when none came she smacked him on the arm. "This's where you tell me you still want in."

"Sorry, Lois," he answered wearily. "This's where I haul my ass home. Maybe you should do the same."

When Zack returned home he grabbed the last beer from the refrigerator and made a note to buy more. He would need it, he reasoned as he checked the answering machine. There were more media inquiries, of course. No amount of insecticide would ever make a dent in that cockroach population, he decided. Skipping dozens of messages, he stopped at the sound of one particular voice. "Zack, this is Luis Solano. I regret parting company at the hospital the way we did. I know that you must be frightened and confused. It is most critical that I see you as soon as possible."

A shadow appeared on the floor beside him and Zack looked up to see Nicole standing by the balcony window. She was agitated and tense. "Zack, don't call him back. Please. He wants to keep us apart."

"Don't worry," he assured her. "Solano's not getting anywhere near us."

"But he knows about me! He won't stop."

"Trust me."

Just then, there was a firm knock at the door.

"Zack, it's Father Solano. Did you receive my message?"

Nicole looked at Zack filled with terror. "It's *him*!"

Gesturing for her to be quiet, he hoped the priest would become discouraged and leave. But instead, the knocking became more insistent. "I know that you're home. Your neighbor saw you arrive. Let me in."

She hugged Zack in fierce desperation. "Please don't open the door!"

But Father Solano was not giving up. "I know you're confused. The evil spirit is trying to seduce you, but we can defeat her. Together with God's help we are stronger than she is!"

Zack squeezed her tightly and called out. "Go away, Father. I'm not interested."

"She is with you now, isn't she," the priest countered. "We are running out of time. You must reject her!"

Nicole was sobbing now. Holding Zack's face in her trembling hands, she implored him to resist. "I love you so much... I beg you... don't let that terrible man destroy what we have!"

Zack was not sure what to do, but when he looked at her again he regained his strength. "Go away or I'll call the police," he called out.

Without warning Solano kicked the door open. Nicole

screamed and Zack charged the priest as he pressed his way in. "What are you doing?! Get the hell out of my house!"

But like a soldier on a mission, Solano would not listen. His face was flushed as he moved around the living room in his surplice and purple stole, panning his unblinking stare into every corner. "I can feel her! The essence of evil is everywhere..."

Zack panicked at the proclamation, then quickly grasped that Nicole had gone into hiding. "I said I don't want your help!"

"I am pledged to save you. Nicole must be freed from her bonds before you are both destroyed."

"Nobody's destroying anybody," Zack countered, pulling on Solano's sleeve.

"That is what Satan wants you to believe." He spun to yank his robe free. "Look around you! He is making his move... Nicole's death, the assault on your roommate, the attempt on your life today..."

The reference stunned Zack. "How'd you know about that?"

"Our Lord and Savior told me," the priest answered quickly as he sprinkled holy water with an antique aspergil.

"For Goddsakes... stop!"

Solano spurned him and commandingly began his prayer. "Holy Father, whose nature is ever merciful and forgiving, accept our prayer that this servant of yours..."

"Father, please..."

"... Bound by the fetters of sin, may be pardoned by your living kindness," The priest continued.

"But I love her!"

"Protect this home from the devil's contamination and free this man from demons possessing Nicole Branson's soul."

Unable to take it any longer, Zack finally shoved him towards the door with all his might. "Goddamn it, I said stop!"

Solano staggered from the impact. "I will not abandon you, Zack," he declared. "Oh, merciful God, exorcise from this place the most unclean spirit!"

"I don't want her to leave!"

Solano made the sign of the cross. "I command you to depart, impious one," he continued before his surging emotions caused him to involuntarily lapse into Spanish. "¡Te ordeno que te vayas, impío!

Salir, maldito. Be humiliated and cast down. ¡Salgan con todos vuestros engaños!"

Zack's mind was spinning now and he felt as if his head would explode any moment. Utterly horrified and disoriented, he bolted from the room. Even the horde of reporters waiting outside would be better than this.

A few minutes later, Sandy approached Zack's building in her car to find him speed walking two blocks away from the apartment as an energetic media swarm pursued him. "Raskin, are you okay?" she yelled over the cacophony of reporters' questions.

"I've been better," he groused as he headed her way by squeezing between two narrowly parked cars.

"What happened?" she asked, pulling to a stop.

"You wouldn't believe me if I told you," Zack replied as the pack began to catch up with him.

"Get in," she directed. Her windows were soon filled with cameras and disagreeable faces. Sandy hit the gas and forced a group of indignant journalists to dive for safety. "So, what's up?"

"There's a priest in my apartment doing an exorcism," he returned sourly. His hopelessness was manifest and it worried her.

"You gotta be kidding!" she fired back. "What's that all about?!"

"You don't want to know," he answered as he wiped away a tear. The likelihood of never seeing Nicole again had taken its toll. He was spent.

Sandy pretended to concentrate on driving as they sped down the street, all the while furtively studying her troubled friend. After a hasty turn at the corner, she finally offered him a deadpan look. "So, did the exorcism make you any less of a jerk?"

Zack knew she was trying to cheer him up and he appreciated it to the degree possible in his distressed frame of mind. "Probably not," he answered as she veered dangerously across two lanes of traffic onto Wilshire Boulevard to evade the news vehicles that appeared in her mirror. "Where are we going, anyway?"

"I wanna hear what that strung out roadie has on his mind."

NEWS ITEM:

Reuters, May 10

In a wide ranging interview today, the mayor of Los Angeles adamantly denied having any knowledge of a law enforcement cover-up in the death of singer Nicole Branson. He assured the public that the investigation into allegations being made by a UCLA medical student is getting the full attention of authorities.

Chapter Fifteen

The Griffith Park Observatory straddles a hilltop perch overlooking the largest municipal park with natural wilderness areas in the United States. The majority of the park's 4,210 acres of terrain is a rough landscape of chaparral and canyons with elevations rising to 1,625 feet, providing stunning views of the sprawling Los Angeles basin to the south and west when the city's obstinate smog layer allows.

A favorite Southern California tourist attraction, the depression-era facility offers telescopic views of the planets as well as astronomy exhibits, presentations, and a spectacular indoor light show. The distinctive triple-domed art deco structure is perhaps best known, however, as a location featured in movies, including the climactic fights in James Dean's classic *Rebel Without A Cause*, Steve Martin's Hollywood spoof *Bowfinger*, and the magical sky dancing sequence in *La La Land* with Ryan Gosling and Emma Stone.

One section of the parking lot also provides one of the city's best views of the famed Hollywood sign above Beachwood Canyon on Mt. Lee.

The observatory is also the site of a pine tree planted in honor of the late George Harrison. Unfortunately, the famous Beatle's original tree was killed by an infestation of beetles, an irony not lost on Zack as he and Sandy cruised past the Greek Theatre amid hundreds of cars and a fleet of limousines departing the evening's concert of Broadway show tunes. Doug would have loved that show, Zack thought before forcing his mind away from such upsetting territory.

They passed through an open yellow security swing arm gate in the darkness of Vermont Canyon Road, and when Zack climbed from the car to close it, he realized that it had been three years since he paid the observatory a visit, though he did not know why it had been that long. After all, the observatory and park were popular destinations for locals and tourists alike. Few urban centers encompassed such a colossal parcel of wilderness, including rugged peaks and miles of equestrian trails, let alone an operational observatory.

The Prelude soon entered the shadowy confines of the park and struggled up the steep ascent of the snaking two-lane road. As its rusting frame flinched upon hitting one of the many crudely patched potholes, the park seemed more rundown than Zack had remembered. And the incline was considerably more severe. The clattering of his pistons was reminder enough of that, as the grating metallic noise ricocheted loudly off stands of passing trees and rock walls on their right.

When they approached the arched concrete Mt. Hollywood Drive tunnel, he slowed to consider the narrow three hundred twenty eight foot passageway ahead with dismay. That was soon superseded when he looked to his left and noted that the only thing separating them from a fatal plunge into Vermont Canyon was an unpersuasive six-inch concrete curb.

When he and Sandy pulled into the observatory parking lot at long last, Zack bought the car to a stop. The overhead security lights surrounding the area were not on, but although his headlights barely made a dent in the blackness as he circled around, it was apparent that no other cars were present. Only a smattering of small light fixtures around the observatory building perforated the murky night.

He was uneasy about the setup, to say the least. "Well, when Seifert picks an out-of-the-way spot, he doesn't mess around," he remarked, hoping to be reassured at any moment by the sight of Seifert's park ranger friend—or a whole group of them. But there were none.

"See him anywhere?" Sandy asked, ignoring his derision.

"Of course not. That'd be logical and easy. Since when is anything logical or easy lately?"

Jabbing him in the arm, she told him to pull over. She then stepped from the car without hesitation, which made him feel guilty. What sort of man lets a woman roam the darkness alone? For that matter, what sort of man would bring a woman here in the first place?

As he joined her on the sidewalk the air felt uncommonly heavy with coastal moisture. Though he never understood the reason behind it, this was the kind of night when first responders expect an increased load of emergencies. As if gloomy atmospherics have anything to do with accidents or crimes.

Walking with Sandy past the towering forty-foot concrete obelisk honoring history's most influential astronomers, Zack could not help noticing that the scowling images of Hipparchus, Copernicus, Galileo, Kepler, Newton, and Herschel on the spire reminded him of mummies in a horror film. In fact, many such films were shot at this very place, most featuring fatuous victims who inevitably make the fatal decision to walk into a sadistic killer's trap. He wondered if that is what he and Sandy were doing, and if the services of an exorcist that he knew might be useful.

A flash of lightning erupted overhead, underscoring his concerns while briefly illuminating the mountain with a discharge of haunting white light. A muscular detonation of thunder followed seconds later, shaking the ground as everything around them plunged back into darkness. It was forbidding but they proceeded anyway. Zack made private estimates of how long it would take to haul ass for the car if necessary.

It was not long before Sandy pointed at a motorcycle stashed in the service drive along the eastern side of the building, beside a gate to a rooftop stairway. "Raskin, look."

"Think that's his?" he asked. An isolated raindrop struck his arm, causing him to glance into the clouds.

"It's the same bike I saw at his house," she answered. "A Harley Rocker 1573."

He reacted with surprise. "I never saw a bike."

"You were too busy whining."

"Okay," he answered. "Let's see where Easy Rider wandered off to." He pointed to the descending slope of the eastern driveway. "So, we take a fast tour and split. Deal?"

"Deal."

The service drive was not long, but in the dark it seemed less than inviting. Using the flashlight application on his phone, he could barely make out the tourist lookout at the end of the pavement. The decline down the hill to the forested terrain below was a craggy, bottomless void. A great place to dump two bodies, he surmised.

But there was no sign of Dennie Seifert, only more drops of rain falling on them.

Arriving at the promenade walkway wrapping around the rear of the observatory, they moved along a row of coin-operated telescopes aimed at what can be a breathtaking expanse of city lights. On a clear day, Santa Catalina Island can be seen twenty-six miles from the coast. But tonight's view was obstructed by the overcast sky.

Sandy called out Seifert's name, but the only response was the howl of coyotes roaming the park. Some of them too close for comfort. Another blast of lightning lit the area, making the trees below appear almost alive. To Zack their branches agitating in the gusting wind looked like giant tentacles waving simultaneous warnings: *get out of here!*

But he did not need assistance in the bad-omen department. His apprehensions were escalating rapidly. There were too many ominous aspects to Nicole's case as it was, not to mention Seifert's mysterious phone message. And Zack knew this was hardly the most benign place to be at night.

"Where the hell is he?" he whispered impatiently.

Sandy glanced at him, her own nervousness beginning to show. "You heard the message. The guy's scared."

"Why should he be any different?"

Sandy nodded her concurrence. Their fears now in sync, they returned wordlessly through the increasing rain to the front of the building along its western edge. Their unspoken intention was to head for the car but they had not gotten far when Sandy touched his arm and motioned to a stairway to the roof. The iron door at the base was open, screeching faintly as it swung in the drizzle.

As much as he hated to admit it, Zack knew it had to be checked out. One fleeting look and they would be secure and dry in his Prelude, he promised himself.

Considering how many visitors make the pilgrimage to the observatory telescopes every day, the public stairs taking them there are surprisingly narrow. Zack made a mental note of that as he reckoned how he and Sandy would leave in a hurry if necessary. For all he knew, they were about to intrude on a crack dealer's convention.

They climbed the passageway cautiously. Zack counted forty-eight steps draped around the exterior of the building in a long precarious curve, making it impossible to see anyone who might be a few steps behind or ahead.

As they finally plodded into the open space of the rooftop, cool air blustered and the night sprinkle gathered strength. The area was deserted, at least what he could see. The huge planetarium dome at the building's center and twin telescope rotundas on each end offered a highly restricted view.

Sandy called Seifert's name again, but her voice fell flat in the moist air. Zack's migraine began to make a comeback, which he interpreted as prophetic permission to vacate the premises as soon as possible.

And leaving sure sounded good. "Let's get out of here," he pleaded as the cloudburst arrived at last.

Sandy turned to argue, but thought better of it. It was possible that the motorcycle downstairs was not Seifert's. This whole detour to the observatory could have been a put-on by a cynical roadie. Besides, it was apparent how much stress Zack was under. And while she was not any more confident about the meeting than him, she wanted so desperately to see it through. To believe Seifert might have answers.

"My nerves are shot, Lois," Zack continued as another lightning strike shook the building. It occurred to him that an open rooftop was a dumb place to be in an electrical storm.

Sandy touched his cheek. "You'll feel better when you get some z's."

"I need more than that," he admitted. Then he paused. As minor as it was, the admission felt good. The problem was how to put the rest into words, because everything else involved the implausible details of his romantic entanglement with Nicole before her death and since.

"I let myself get hung up on Nicole," he finally said. "I even thought I was falling in love." Zack hesitated again before saying more. “Do you understand?”

She took his hand. “What, do I come across that heartless to you?” Then she forced a grin. “Anyway, so what if Seifert’s a wash?” she offered. “We’ll find S.A. some other way.”

Zack soon found himself succumbing to a whole new feeling, at least as far as Sandy was concerned, something that he would not have anticipated: the warm feeling of friendship. “You know, Sandy,” he told her at last, “I’m glad we teamed up.”

She was taken aback. “No kidding?”

“No kidding.”

Her delight was clear. “Just for that, I’ll buy you a beer,” she promised. “And by the way, it’s okay to call me Lois if ya want. I kinda like it.”

“You got a deal, Lois.”

But as they moved off, Zack stopped. Something at their feet caught his eye: a collection of cigarette butts. *The unfiltered Camels that Seifert smokes.*

Sandy picked up on the discovery. “He was here.”

“From the look of it, for a while,” he calculated.

They scanned the area from where they stood. Zack’s jaw hardened as he fixated on something in the distance and Sandy read his concern. “What?”

“I thought I saw something,” he whispered. “Over there, by the trash.” She followed his dim flashlight beam to a wall by the planetarium dome. There was a wire mesh trash container like those she had seen elsewhere on the premises, but nothing else.

Zack peered carefully into the shadows. “Be ready to run like hell,” he directed. His pulse quickened as the worst-case scenario he had not wanted to consider began to write itself.

“You’re the boss,” she answered, meaning it.

He advanced guardedly through the gathering puddles. What he had not told Sandy was what captured his attention: the trashcan itself. The others they passed were empty, but the one in the corner was full. Every instinct in him was screaming, but somebody had to check this out and he was the committee of one.

There was nothing unusual about a container filled with soggy newspapers. Though it was possible that the custodial crew had simply missed one can, something urged Zack forward; the magnetic pull of his quest for answers.

As he approached the can he glanced at his shoes and realized that the wetness at his feet was not water. It was dark red. *Like blood.*

He mouthed an expletive and handed his phone to Sandy so that he could lift the top layer of trash. She steadied the light as he gingerly pushed aside some newspapers and uneaten hot dogs—until he took a closer look. *These were not hot dogs, they were fingers!*

Recoiling at the discovery, Zack moved more litter to see an entire hand protruding. Then, swallowing hard, he reached in one more time, lifting enough papers to reveal Dennie Seifert's stark features. A bullet entry wound discolored the center of his forehead.

Zack knew that the gunshot was TNT, paramedic parlance for through-and-through. Ox Man had been executed at close range. Zack's mind splintered into a hundred sensations, but he still had the presence of mind to touch Seifert's thick neck to discover that *his skin was still warm!*

Seconds later Zack and Sandy were retreating fast to the exit. Descending the stairs two at a time they would be at the car in moments. But halfway down, the shadow of someone waiting below was projected onto a support pillar by a dimly illuminated light behind him.

Sandy saw the shadow first and pulled Zack back, nearly yanking him off his feet on the slippery steps. "Somebody's down there..!" she gasped.

"Back up... don't let him hear us."

Now that his victims were trapped, Gunter Strauss proceeded up the steps. Adjusting his waterproof microfleece parka liner against the increasing rain, he chewed a fresh stick of gum contentedly. It would be good to finally clean up the risk that Raskin and his friend represented. The roadie and park ranger had already been eliminated.

Two down tonight, two to go.

Zack and Sandy rushed to the service drive stairs on the building's eastern side only to find the gate locked. Zack noticed rainwater flowing into a gutter at the base of a gabled lower roof. Pointing, he whispered instructions for Sandy to climb over the rail and slide down the forbidding slope.

Every second counted and she knew it. She also knew she might fall to her death, but there was no time for discussion. She did as she was told.

Zack waited as long as he could, in case he had to create a diversion to buy Sandy more time. But when he saw the shrouded outline of Strauss arriving at the western rotunda like the Grim Reaper himself, he hastily followed her over the railing and slid uncontrollably downward.

Strauss panned the area with his powerful tactical military flashlight, narrowly missing Zack's fleeting figure in the thickening downpour. Moving to the trashcan, a succession of lightning hits delineated Seifert's exposed corpse. Zack and Sandy had discovered it, as he assumed they would.

The only question was where they were hiding.

Extended rolling thunder rumbled through the canyon before the roof again became silent. Listening attentively, he filtered out the sound of the downpour until his ears perked at a faint CLANKING sound coming from the other side of the center dome. Clanking, as in the sound of banging metal, he reasoned. And it was thin, like a drainpipe.

Strauss headed for the stairs. He would finish this in the parking lot.

When Zack finished his clumsy descent to the eastern driveway he hustled Sandy past the motorcycle into the open area near the obelisk. Slipping on the saturated grass, he twisted the injury to his calf and cursed as he fell.

She promptly helped him to his feet.

Just then, lights from opposite directions found them in the thick sheets of rain: the tactical flashlight from the western stairway and headlights near the shuttered refreshment stand seventy-five yards away. Zack immediately recognized that the vehicle lamps belonged to something larger than a car—*a van like the one that almost ran them over at UCLA!*

Though both lights were far enough away that they did little more than suggest Zack and Sandy's presence, to Zack it seemed as if powerful lasers had been trained on them. He squeezed Sandy's hand and accelerated their sprint to the Prelude. He could almost feel the deadly glare of the van's occupants as the large vehicle advanced slowly. Like a predatory animal closing in for the kill.

And glancing over his shoulder, he saw a hulking figure raise a gun and fire multiple rounds. The bullets whizzed by his ear so close that he could feel the air movement that they generated. He moved faster than he ever thought he could. But the stakes were higher now than he ever thought they could be, too. Getting to the car was a matter of endurance. *Whoever these people were, they were killers and they were after them.*

The van was practically flying now.

Sixty yards...!

Fifty...!

Zack and Sandy dove into the Prelude and he fumbled with the key in the ignition. Glancing into his mirror, he trembled at seeing Gunter Strauss moving across the lawn, pause and fire again.

"Get down!" he yelled while shoving Sandy down. A deluge of safety glass and rain filled the car as the windshield blew out. "Fuck!"

Sandy screamed as he frantically turned the key but the engine refused to respond. Then, looking back at the van he saw that it was twenty five yards away and closing fast. "Come on...!" he cursed, trying it again.

A gun muzzle emerged from the van's window and the noise of slugs from automatic weapon fire punching the car and bursting windows was deafening, like sticks of dynamite exploding in a steel drum.

Finally the engine turned over and Zack dropped it into gear and fishtailed out of the parking lot. The van stopped long enough to pick up Gunter Strauss and roared off in pursuit.

The Prelude and van careened around the grove of pine trees in the Berlin Forest picnic area, through the tunnel, and nine darkened switchbacks at desperation speeds. Zack managed the first few hairpin turns, but lost control when he crashed through the security gate, sending the car skidding across a shoulder into a grassy rest area. He and Sandy hung on as the car bounced off a concrete bench and several trees before bottoming out hard in a muddy drainage ditch.

Knowing they were easy targets, Zack floored the accelerator in an effort to maneuver back onto the road. A gooey mixture of sludge, rocks, and leaves sprayed out behind them as the tires somehow found traction.

Just then, the van reappeared and the gunman again sprayed the car with his submachine gun. This time Zack noted the gun was equipped with a silencer, making the deafening metallic explosions engulfing the cabin all the more terrifying.

What was left of the windows disintegrated into a hail of glass and Zack ground his gears to pick up speed. But the big Dodge V-8 engine had infinitely more horsepower than his old Prelude. Pulling close, the gunman let loose with the gun one more time, shredding the dashboard and steering wheel inches from Zack's face.

Zack responded with the only counter-action available, abruptly slamming his brakes that sent the car into a dizzying 360-degree slide before it jolted to a stop in a stockpile of construction materials near the bird sanctuary above the Greek Theatre parking lot.

Mercifully, the van was nowhere to be seen. There was only the cascade of dense rain and blinking signal barriers that Zack might have seen had he been paying attention to such things. But his mind was elsewhere. He knew the killers would soon return to finish them off.

They were sitting ducks.

The engine in his Prelude had conked out on impact and there would be no restarting it. Yet while he should have been worried about that, he was, for the time being, swept up by the hermetic emotional aftermath that follows trauma. It was a stillness that echoed. A surrealistic suspension of time.

Neither Zack nor Sandy moved. Eventually, he got some words out, something like, "Christ, that was close..."

Sandy did not reply. And who could blame her, he thought. His own throat was so tight he felt as if he were being strangled. He did not know how long he indulged in his recovery before he noticed that Sandy was turned away from him, listed against the door.

The seat around her was stained with blood.

His mind sputtered. "No... Lois. Please ..." he begged. He reached to check her jugular, but he already understood it was futile. Sandy was gone. The death-stare in her eyes when her head pitched toward him said it all.

He started to cry. He had no idea what to do. Zack was scared, angry, grief-stricken, and confused. Beset by a merciless and suffocating nightmare, he could only breathe the tart scent of Sandy's bloody wounds and wait for it to make him sick. Acrid bile was already rising in his esophagus.

Suddenly, the headlights appeared behind him again, glowering through the prisms of raindrops. Zack cursed loudly in an attempt to clear his mind, but he was a jumble of nerves. As the van gained speed his hand touched Sandy's cheek in a brief farewell.

Then he was scrambling from the car. The gunman fired and bullets chewed the mud around him until he disappeared into the camouflage of shadows in the empty amphitheater parking lot.

Terrified, Zack plowed through an unyielding obstacle course of shrubbery and trees, but he never stopped. The killers would be upon him soon and they would finish him off. Like they had Seifert and Sandy.

God, poor Sandy... Oh, God!

His only chance was to stay mobile. At the far end of the parking lot he fumbled over a chain-link fence and soon found himself in the middle of Boy Scout Road heading across a picnic area to a small restroom facility. From there it was only a few dozen yards to the residential neighborhood that stretches south for the remainder of Vermont Canyon. Across the street was the Roosevelt Municipal Golf Course, which he quickly rejected as an escape option because of its exposed nature. He would be way too vulnerable there.

He pressed on. Plunging headlong over the first fence that he encountered, he hobbled through a progression of backyards of multi-million dollar homes and their luxurious swimming pools, spas, gazebos, and brick patios, all unoccupied thanks to the rain that soaked him from head to toe. The yards were also buttressed against a steep tree-covered hillside, which reduced his escape options. There was no going left or right, only forward.

Unfortunately, most of the properties were illuminated by decorative lighting, which meant the increased likelihood of being seen. He abandoned the notion of avoiding them, however, and opted for speed. *Speed equaled distance, which equaled safety.*

Speed also meant the dire need to focus. He purged from his mind the horrifying imaginings of professional killers in the corner of every yard, simultaneously training their weapons on him as he burst from one pool of light to another like a target in a carnival shooting gallery.

He kept moving, and in the process his head and arms were lacerated by a gauntlet of thorny rose bushes and hedges. But he felt none of the pain that accompanies such injuries. For the moment he was a machine programmed to live. Even the devastation of Sandy's savage murder was beyond his comprehension. He remembered it, of course, but with the remembering came so much doubt...

Was it really possible?

Could he have imagined it?

The idea of Sandy being gunned down was preposterous. *She was just a proof-reader, for God's sake. A nobody. Who would want to kill her?* Logically, no one. That meant Zack had to consider the possibility of something else taking place here: *Maybe Father Solano was right about everything!*

Zack's mind wrestled with that as he glanced over a wall and scaled it.

Maybe Nicole really was the emissary of the Devil. Maybe his soul was already lost. Maybe this was hell. The question was what to do about it. Here he was, running for his life in a torrential storm, praying that he could shake the killers from his trail, now being forced to consider the idea that his doomed fate was inevitable.

Just then he stumbled in darkness and fell, striking his head hard. Dazed by the impact, it took some time to figure out what happened. At first he thought that he DFO'd, the paramedic acronym for *done fell out*, which is slang for having lost consciousness.

Eventually, Zack realized that he had tumbled into a watery trench, which had been prepared for a backyard construction project. His head hit a wooden concrete form and his cognizance was spinning. Even simple movement was unachievable. Instead, he stared blankly up at the rain descending on him in what could well have been, he decided with macabre fascination, a shallow grave prepared exclusively for his arrival.

He became aware of sirens speeding into Griffith Park. They were responding to the gunfire and chase, no doubt. But running into the street to flag down a squad car was impossible. *Maybe he should just wait for the killers to catch up. He could save them a lot of trouble. They could simply execute him right here and bury him.*

No muss, no fuss. Or given his luck, he projected, one of the abrasions on his body from his malicious yard tour would be contaminated with necrotizing fasciitis, commonly known as flesh-eating bacteria. Zack's mind flickered to the popular college professor who lost several limbs to the infection and then her life within days of receiving a minor scratch while gardening.

Great, let's make it the most agonizing death possible.

And then a most bizarre thought flickered through his mind: *what if he was already dead?* What if this entire nightmare was nothing more than his life flashing before his eyes?

Some life, he thought. Instead of the reassuring memories that people were said to have in their final moments, his were a dystopian flurry of horrors. *Or maybe he was suffering from Cotard's Syndrome, where a person believes he has died and is now a zombie walking among the living.* Whatever might be happening, Zack decided that the specifics of his grip on reality, or lack of it, no longer mattered. The intensity of his misery was real enough.

An undetermined period of time lapsed until thunder growled and a dog barking in the family room window of a nearby house got his attention. His reflex was to get up and run, and inexplicably he found that his legs worked again. Soon he was back lurching through the residential labyrinth, and his head began to pound worse than before. He tried to massage his temples, but that only threw off his sense of balance.

He was not sure why he was resisting the eternal damnation that had been designed for him, only that he was not going out without a fight. He momentarily considered doubling back to seek police protection, but the notion was short-lived. The killers would be waiting for that. They had not set up the trap at the observatory only to fail. *He had to keep moving. He had to get away.*

A cacophony of vehicle horns abruptly jolted Zack to a startling discovery: he was somehow standing in the middle of busy Los Feliz Boulevard and vehicles swerved to avoid hitting him. He had unaccountably travelled a mile without being aware of it, only to falter into four lanes of traffic. He immediately recognized symptoms of post-traumatic stress disorder and cursed himself for succumbing. *PTSD?! Get it together, asshole!*

After making it across the street, Zack discovered that one of his hands was covered with blood. He relived the smell of death in the car before noticing that even as rain diluted the red on his hand, it was too rich in color to be anything but from a fresh wound. *It was his.*

Rattled by his finding, he ran into the densely populated residential district at the same time Gimble and Strauss pulled into the Chevron station at the corner.

Strauss saw Zack's fleeting image and gnawed his ever-present wad of gum with increased vigor. He tucked his Heckler & Koch MP5 submachine gun under his jacket and was glad that he brought this particular weapon tonight rather than his Chinese Norinco Type 64. The MP5, with its built-in silencer, was just right for this particular prey.

He wordlessly climbed from the van to follow Zack on foot and Gimble wheeled south down the continuation of Vermont Avenue. They would catch their victim in an old-fashioned baseball rundown on one of these streets and they would dispatch him.

BACKGROUND ITEM:

Nicole Branson Facebook Fan Page Transcript, May 10

JOJO: What do you guys think about all this stuff about Nicole Branson? Too weird for words or WHAT?!

CHATMAN: I think the Russians are playin' mind games on us.

DABOMBER: DON'T BE A JERK, OKAY? SHE'S TRYIN' TO BE SERIOUS HERE!!!!

ALLTHAT: It really bothers me that people won't just let Nicole rest in peace... she was a great artist... why can't that be enough?

SWEET-1: Cuz she wuz a druggie and we all know how much everybody hates THEM.

CHATMAN: But that guy at UCLA says she wasn't, did you read about that?

SWEET-1: Yeah, right. And if it wuz in The Enquirer then it MUST be TRUE! :)

JOJO: According to them he's a medical student, isn't he? Maybe he knows something...

DABOMBER: ALL I KNOW IS, I'M DEPRESSED. I WANT NICOLE BACK.

Chapter Sixteen

Zack tried to run but no longer could. His legs stubbornly refused to lift his feet. Weaving from the sidewalk onto the sodden lawn of a two-story residential building on Greenwood Place, he tried the handle of the glass security door but it was locked.

Then, after pressing the intercom buttons for various apartments, he finally received a response. "Who is it?" the sleepy woman's voice crackled.

"Help me... please..." Zack cried out. "Somebody's trying to hurt me!"

"Get lost," the judgment returned as the intercom went dead.

"No—WAIT!" he pleaded before the futility of it registered. This was a waste of time. Nobody would let a stranger in their building at this time of night. Grabbing his phone he tried to make a call, only to find the battery depleted. He knew his only chance was to get away from the area and locate a pay phone, if such a thing still existed.

He headed for a gravel path between two buildings and climbed a low brick wall into a row of carports. Peeking into cars in the hope of finding keys in an ignition, he cursed his lack of skills that would enable him to steal a vehicle. *Where the hell was he when guys he knew growing up were tinkering with engines?!*

Engines. The word lingered incongruously in his mind until his consciousness honed in on the throaty rumble of an engine advancing in the alley. He plunged into a crouch in the greasy wetness behind a dumpster an instant before the white Dodge van crept past. He was just a few feet away from the van's muddy finish, and he dared not move. Zack's heart pounded when the vehicle stopped a few feet from his hiding place.

Had the killers seen him?

Was a river of his blood flowing from behind the dumpster, giving him away?

A glut of such thoughts fluttered through his mind, which

was now almost functioning again. Even as he waited for what was certain to be his murderer's approach, Zack was again aware of his emotions and physical discomfort: his head was splitting, he was wet and demoralized, his leg stung like hell... and his gut was still knotted at the stark memory of Sandy's lifeless face.

His hands began to tremble at the truth of how harrowing the chase through Griffith Park had been and how stark his comprehension of eternal damnation was proving to be. Staring at his twitching extremities, he wondered if he would be able to sit still long enough for the killers to put a bullet in him. It flashed through his mind that while Feliz may be the Spanish word for *Happy*, the notion of him finding happiness in Los Feliz was beyond absurd.

The delay was interminable as Zack waited. For no apparent reason he thought about the one hundred twenty million red blood cells that die in humans each second and he found himself wishing them well as the seconds ticked by. The problems of their seventeen-week lives would soon be over, there would be no more invasions of renegade bacteria and viruses to worry about, and no more depending on those big and strong white blood cells to come to the rescue. *Screw those white-celled leucocyte bastards with their funny-shaped nuclei! Where were they now that their red brothers were dying in wholesale numbers?*

Zack snapped back to reality. *What was he doing thinking about blood cells?!* His difficulty in maintaining clarity scared him. *He had to get his shit together.*

And that is when he noticed something amazing: the killers were pulling away! They had not found him and Zack wanted to say a prayer of thanks, but his most important priority now was to keep moving. He would thank God later.

When the van disappeared around a corner, he rose from his position and shuddered from the tear in his gastrocnemius muscle. It was unbearable to walk but he had no choice.

After limping to Dracena Drive and ducking into a recessed doorway, he angled his body to allow a partial view of an alley but found no sign of anyone. Only the rain and a glum orchestral movie soundtrack playing through the slightly open window of a nearby apartment could be heard. Zack glanced at the awning above and speculated what the movie watchers would say if they knew about the genuine drama unfolding outside their home.

Leaning out further, he still saw nothing. He took a long steady inhalation and warned himself to remain focused. Then he heard what sounded like footsteps sloshing through water. *Or maybe his imagination was getting the best of him...* he could not tell. Zack flattened himself in the shadows and snuck another look, catching a glimpse of a beefy, dark-haired man moving from car to car looking for something.

Or someone.

Goose bumps prickled Zack's skin and he was overwhelmed with a cramp of his bowels. He resisted with all his might. This was no time for a panic attack. A moment later he thought he recognized the figure as one of the security men, Gunter Strauss. The prick who let Nicole die. The killers had obviously split up to search separately.

Then he saw that the weapon Strauss was holding looked a lot like a submachine gun and a gush of ice water ran up Zack's spine. He locked in on the barrel, *the same long bulky barrel that spewed its fusillade of death at Sandy.*

As Strauss moved closer, Zack found that his feet would not react to commands. He was dumbfounded by the phenomenon. As intimidated as he was, there was now a part of him that wanted to stay and fight! To get revenge. But this was neither the time nor place. He would not stand a chance. Finally, his feet responded to reason and he slipped away in the rain.

Strauss arrived at the alcove where Zack stood moments earlier and examined the area. Stooping to the blacktop, he found beads of blood. Protected by the awning from the rain, the blood did not contain dust or other contaminants. He spit out his gum and slid a fresh piece into his mouth, savoring it.

He was closing in on a wounded target.

Emboldened by his detection, Strauss added renewed vigor to his mission and it took on an unrelenting pace. As soon as Zack emerged from a passageway between buildings, he would look over his shoulder only to see the hulking figure enter it.

Things continued that way for nearly an hour. Through

courtyards. Down darkened streets. Across flooded parking lots. Evading the occasional passing car, slipping on wet leaves, whenever Zack became hopeful of shaking his pursuer his hopes were soon crushed by the silhouette in the distance.

The pursuit continued to take its toll. Zack's body ached and his legs became increasingly inflexible. Whatever was wrong with him was worsening by the minute, along with the gale that was battering him. He had hated rain events like this ever since he was obliged as a boy to go camping with his father. Upon finding themselves assaulted by the leading edge of a category two hurricane on one occasion, Zack received trifling reassurance from the man intent on using the experience as a character-building lesson.

This time, however, bad weather was Zack's salvation—as most local residents were confined to their homes and he was able to run unseen. Fallen trees and branches prevented the assassins' van from having unhindered access to the neighborhoods, and with a little luck he might enable him to elude the killers after all.

Unfortunately, Zack had become disoriented. For all he knew he had been running in circles. *Why the hell didn't he listen to Doc Sandberg's warning to drop this case when he had the chance?! Was this still Los Feliz or was he now in Hollywood?*

At the intersection of Franklin and Vermont he was careful to avoid the lights and activity surrounding the 24-hour House of Pies Coffee Shop before continuing south. He finally sandwiched himself between two parked cars to catch his breath and wondered what Angie would recommend if he were with him now. But even as the question was raised the answer came back: Angie would wax nostalgic about yet another Steve McQueen movie and how all Zack needed was to, "*think McQueen.*"

Fat chance, he refuted before reminding himself to stay focused. No more wandering thoughts allowed. He had to be alert. This was the time when he would most likely get killed, when his defenses had grown sloppy.

Zack peered over the hood of the glistening Mazda at his back, surveying the sidewalks and yards for any sign of his executioner until his abdomen clenched. *The killer could be seen under a streetlamp!*

With Strauss nearly upon him, Zack spent the remaining energy he had on his diminishing chances for a getaway. He reversed direction and stumbled, block after block, through the declining district near Hollywood Boulevard where there was an increase in iron bars covering ground-floor windows and gang graffiti on aging buildings. But he never stopped. He was desperate and becoming more paranoid by the second.

Slogging on, he improbably remembered that Janis Joplin died of a drug overdose in a motel not far from here. How ironic that he was going to die while trying to disprove the drug death of her music successor.

After more dark alleys than he could count, he had no strength left. His exhaustion was total. With his injured leg inflamed and his head ready to burst, he had to find a place to rest.

And that is when he made a disastrous mistake.

In his confusion Zack slipped into an alley—only to discover too late that *there was no exit.* A wall topped with concertina wire eliminated any possibility of getting away. It was a dead end. Frantically, he looked for a place to hide. Finding nothing, he used a rock to break an overhead security light and picked up the only weapon he could find: a dented aluminum trash can lid.

Moments later Gunter Strauss appeared in the narrow mouth of the impasse. Sneering haughtily, he knew that seeking refuge here was the blunder of a rank amateur. His MP5 at the ready, he proceeded expertly into the grimy space. Sliding a fresh piece of chewing gum into his mouth, he chopped on it. Strauss enjoyed the feeling that always accompanied a kill. And this one had put up a pretty good fight; he had to give him that. The chase through Griffith Park and excursion to this kill zone was an effort to be admired.

Zack was hunkered down on a second floor fire escape, pressed tightly into the indentation of a window casing. Unlike before, when he was numb to all feeling, he was now alive inside. Thanks to the engagement of his brain's stress system, the hypothalamus, cingulate gyrus, pituitary gland, and amygdala, Zack's mind was exceptionally clear. His senses were now heightened to the point of being acutely aware of the odors around him, which were uncommonly potent in their dampness. He could distinguish the smell of animal feces from oil stains on the concrete and the rotten food in the dumpster was as identifiable as the mildew arising from the ground beneath a slow-leaking water pipe.

Zack was exhilarated by the return of his competency. *So what if the pain in his leg was excruciating?*

As he watched the killer stalking him below, a feeling of anticipation coursed through him. He was scared, sure, more than he had ever been. But this other sensation was something new: a primal instinct of empowerment. An excitement. Excitement over being in control again, or at least of not being victimized.

Waiting in his hiding place, Zack was no longer the hunted.

Unfortunately, he did not have the faintest idea what to do with his newfound power. Clutching his trash can lid, he wished it were more substantial. Without a more impressive weapon his odds of walking out of here were not good. He would probably be wheeled out on a coroner's gurney. A perverse scene flickered in his mind, in which his friend Lee O'Connor would arrive at work tomorrow to find Zack's smiling face floating in a jar of formaldehyde.

But then he was back in the moment. Zack knew he had one strategic edge—*no matter how slight or temporary, he had a goddamned edge! He had the element of surprise. Lee would have to bottle somebody else's body parts. Zack Raskin was fighting back.*

Strauss was directly beneath him now, searching behind empty shipping crates stacked by a door. Zack's body palpitated at the recognition that he had nearly hidden behind those same boxes, only to notice the retractable ladder at the last moment.

Thank God this was one of the old buildings that still had an upper floor exit. Many new structures did without them.

But it was still a rancid alley and that, he decided, was a hell of a place to die.

Staring at the man below, he noticed that his adversary's thinning hair had not been remedied by a bad dye-job. Even in this poor light it was evident that his reddish hairdo did not match his eyebrows, beard stubble, or complexion. How odd, Zack thought, that an aging hit man would make such a pathetic grab for youth. *Did the murders he committed fail to provide the required ego gratification?*

Was he so vain that he was willing to embarrass himself with tacky grooming?

Then it was time to act.

With no sign of his prey it would be a matter of seconds before the predator thought to look up. Zack squared his shoulders and sucked in a lungful of air before inching out from the alcove, gripping the aluminum trash can lid, and dropping from concealment.

He landed on Strauss with both feet thrusting down as hard as he could kick them. Searing heat discharged up his left leg and spread throughout his body on impact. But the sneak attack worked. Strauss staggered off-guard long enough for Zack to remember the lid in his hand and maintain the offensive. Clutching the handle for dear life he smashed the killer full in the face and followed with a knee to his testicles.

Strauss wheezed through the bloody agony of his freshly broken nose, disoriented, dropping his gun before recovering his faculties and coming back at Zack with everything he had in his fists.

But Zack's adrenaline was pumping furiously and it was producing an opponent Strauss never thought he would encounter. Possessed by unchecked rage, Zack repeated his vicious kick to the killer's groin while bringing the trash can lid down hard on his head, over and over and over again.

Zack heard himself yell, "You son of a bitch! You goddamned son of a bitch!" But it must have been someone else's voice, he thought, as he experienced a baffling detachment from the violence. It was almost as if he were watching someone else doing the bludgeoning.

All in slow-motion, as if he were having a dream or watching a movie. But, of course, it was neither. This was reality.

Strauss fell to his knees, dazed and choking on the gum that had lodged in his throat. He was unable to fend off the blows raining down on him. And Zack kept them coming without hesitation. He was flying on pure instinct and it was unbelievable.

Knowing that it takes two one-hundredths of a second for a nerve impulse to travel from toe to head, Zack wondered how much faster these head-to-head sensations were registering. Then he remembered that lacerating the middle meningeal artery above the ear would cause acute subdural hematoma and a speedy death.

As far as he was concerned this prick was a prime candidate for the most prolonged end possible, but it was the final result that he had to hope for. *Death.* Any suffering beyond that would have to be meted out by a higher authority than Zack Raskin.

He kept up the onslaught and with each punishing strike of the metal lid Zack could feel the killer's temporal bone softening—until he realized that bones do not soften. Certainly not the human skull, one of nature's most amazing engineering feats. The bone was crushed and what he was hitting was tissue and ooze.

The man was not moving. *Zack's heart pounded and his limbs shook. Bewildered*, he wiped the sweat and splattered blood from his brow. *He had taken a human life!* Convulsions seized his body and he doubled over to vomit. He leaned against a graffiti-covered wall for support, gulping for air, struggling to clear his mind.

The death scene triggered memories of what happened to Nicole, Sandy, and Doug, as the haunting images of their undeserved fates were reprised over and over. Glancing at his hand against the wall, he noticed that it, too, had been sprayed with blood as if a bomb had killed Strauss rather than a trash can lid. He had to remind himself that the bastard got what he deserved.

Then a chilling prospect struck him: *What if he's not dead? What if he's lying in wait, preparing one final attack?* Zack stared at his victim, who was lying face down. The possibility, as horrible as it was, had to be investigated.

Approaching the motionless figure he convinced himself to roll him over in the gathering pool of blood. Strauss's face was constricted into an evil rictus and his vacant stare was like a knife through Zack's heart. In death the man was every bit as loathsome as he had been life, but he was a human being, too. *And Zack killed him!*

His filth-covered hands quivering as he reached down to close the hateful eyes, Zack was unable to complete the task. No way could he bring himself to touch the person whose existence he had just ended. He removed his blood and rain-soaked jacket to cover Strauss's head.

All ability to function drained from his limbs. Collapsing to the ground, he sat against the wall and looked at the corpse. He again thought about hell and wondered if this was what it might be like. The truth was, as he sat in the grimy alley looking at the man he had slaughtered, Zack could no longer remember how it was to live a normal life. To be carefree. Before killers and killing, and loving an evil spirit who had doomed him forever.

Christ, he'd really done it! He destroyed a man!

Soon Detective Maulden would find out and track him down. Maulden would not care about the facts. Zack's blood, fingerprints, skin, hair fibers, and footprints were a road map to his complicity.

"Was it necessary to kill him?" Maulden would ask.

"What kind of doctor beats another human being to a bloody, inanimate pulp?"

"Zack Raskin, that's who. Doctor Death. The newest member of an elite club of notorious physician murderers including Nazi torturer Joseph Mengele, French mass murderer Marcel Petiot, and of course Conrad Murray, the asshole who killed Michael Jackson with acute propofol and benzodiazepine intoxication."

The shrill intrusion of a siren passing on a nearby street brought him back to reality. He had lost everything that he once valued. The prospect of waiting here for the police and the idea of bringing all this to an end seemed darkly appealing.

Then a sharp tingling in his shoulders brought the unsettling feeling that *he was being watched*. Zack jerked his head to find Nicole standing alone in the rain twenty feet away.

"Haven't you done enough? Leave me alone..."

Her voice was deliberate. "You know I can't. I'm counting on you."

"Then you'll have to be disappointed," he told her.

"You could never disappoint me."

He did not respond. His tank was empty. Conversation was out of the question.

"There's one thing you haven't tried," she offered.

He looked at her. *How could she be so calm after all the death and destruction that she caused?*

She continued, whispering two words that would change everything. "My poem."

"What are you talking about...?"

"In my think-book, remember?"

"I'm afraid not."

"The last page."

He blinked as the memory of his visit to Glen Conway's house clumsily returned, and the entry that provided the clue to S.A. But he had studied so many other things in the book, too. Lyrics, poems, and short passages. In his present condition he could not recall the specifics to any of them.

Inching closer, her voice was soothing as she recited her poem to him:

holding close
to life
and love
isn't life a dream?
whenever
I'm with you
like this
it's the very best
my life
has been
it seems...

A glimmer of recognition began to register as she continued:

sunlight falling
on the bed
your heartbeat
matching
mine
and as my head
floats
on the pillow
the seed of love
grows
for all time

Zack reacted blankly.

Nicole kneeled and wiped away the mascara that was streaming down her face as she repeated one particular line, "The seed of love."

His mind stopped as her ballad on TV the day of her funeral came back to him:

Baby, you've just got to believe
it was hard to conceive of life without you
But loving you just isn't enough
to find the words to say quite how I feel
And now you're gone—all I have of you are my dreams
of your kiss, your smile, your eyes on me
loving you

He gaped as the lyrics churned inside him. The revelation finally spilled out. "Jesus... you're pregnant?!"

"I was," she answered sadly.

Zack hobbled along more residential streets in a daze. He was still not sure where he was until he arrived at Sunset Boulevard. Turning right, he knew that he was heading west. And that meant Westwood was just twenty miles away. Concentration was nearly impossible, however. His vision and focus were distorted, as his visual acuity succumbed to the tunnel vision that many trauma victims experience. But Zack did not care about his peripheral visual fields. He was stricken by a wave of renewed heartache for Nicole and the loss of her unborn child.

The pointless and tragic loss.

He would have to remain alert to have any hope of getting them justice. Remembering the Metro station on Hollywood Boulevard he headed north and began to fantasize about a dry subway ride to the Expo train that would take him to Culver City, which was not far from Westwood. He picked up his pace.

When he saw the Hollywood/Western Metro station sign in the distance, however, he stopped. One of the killers was taken care of, but there was still at least one more out there. There was no telling how many there might be. Someone could be waiting for him on the train platform.

He reversed direction and again headed south to the area around Sunset Boulevard. As wary as he was of storefront doorways and alleys they would have to suffice. At Fernwood Avenue near De Longpre he passed a fetid homeless encampment littered with tents, tarps, boxes, and trash. Incredibly, its downtrodden occupants did not find the sight of a scruffy-looking drenched man carrying a submachine gun especially interesting.

Zack had been to this neighborhood on ambulance calls several times and did not remember it as being this impoverished. But given his current frame of mind and the intense storm it seemed pretty damn hostile and bleak now.

The agony throughout his body had intensified to the point where he imagined his muscles resembling shredded pieces of string cheese. His body hurt from head to toe, his lower back nearly as much as his leg. He did not know what that was all about, stress, injury, or both. He might be *circling the drain*, as hospital trauma teams often said of patients in dire condition, but right now he had more to worry about than his physical maladies—or the putrid stench of urban decay that corroded his sinuses. He had no choice but to gamble on his body not giving out entirely.

At a battered pay phone that miraculously appeared beside the rusting security gate of a closed liquor store on North Saint Andrews Place, Zack stuffed the MP5 under his shirt and struggled to drop a quarter in the slot and punch in a number. Staring at his quivering hand, he recognized his deteriorating motor skills as the inevitable result of his fight with Strauss. Repeatedly trying to direct his finger to the correct keys, he succeeded on the fourth attempt. He fell against a wall at hearing Angie's voice announce, "Willis Ambulance Service."

"Angie, thank God I found you..."

Angie was relieved to hear Zack's voice, too. But he was also worried. "Kid? What the hell's going on?"

"You can't imagine what I've been through!" Zack screaked.

"Just slow down and tell me about it. The LAPD found your car all shot up."

"You won't believe what happened! We thought we had a lead and all hell broke loose... Angie, the bastards killed Sandy!"

Angie broke in, unclear about what he was hearing. "Slow down. I can hardly understand you."

"Okay, I'm sorry... sorry."

"What was that about Sandy?"

"They fucking murdered her!"

Angie's heart dropped. "Where is she now?"

Zack had to stop and think. The question confused him. "In my car. I thought you said they found it."

"They did," Angie reported, "but they didn't find anyone. Just a lot of blood."

Zack's stomach grabbed hard. The thought of Sandy's body being taken by the killers was too much for him. His voice cracked. "Those fucking assholes...! Goddamn them!"

"I know, kid. I know."

"But I got one," Zack went on. "One of those shitheads came after me, too, but I got him first."

Angie was stunned by what Zack was telling him. "You what...?"

Once again Zack faltered. His anger was surpassed by the awful reality of the act itself. He began to sob. "I... beat him to death. Oh God, I killed a man. What am I gonna do?!"

A long silence followed as Angie let him cry, correctly figuring that the outlet was the best thing for the moment. Then he offered some basic advice. "Okay, kid, the first thing you gotta do is breathe."

Zack tried without success. He was beyond the basics. "Angie... there's something else. Nicole was pregnant."

"Are you sure?"

"Yeah."

"I'm so sorry, Zack. That's rough."

As Zack began to pull himself together, a piece of the puzzle unexpectedly dawned on him. "Somebody didn't want anybody knowing about his kid."

"We gotta get you to the police," Angie came back.

But before Zack could answer something moved in the thick sheets of rain, fleetingly. More motion than substance, yet it was enough to throw his survival switch. Instinctively, he leapt from the phone an instant before it detonated in an onslaught of bullets!

Zack vaulted with a diving roll over a cinder block retaining wall into an empty lot filled with puddles of water and the rubble of a demolished building. As another spray of bullets stitched the area, he scooted on all fours as far as they could take him through a weed-choked maze of mud, wood, and pockmarked chunks of concrete adorned with massive deformed rebar strands that loomed over him like giant insect antennae.

Ted Gimble was combat-ready, his 9mm Glock with a 100 round beta c-mag poised for the kill. Huddled behind a mound of debris, Zack tried to shoot back but the gun from the alley jammed. As he struggled with it, a sopping wet brown rat darted from its hiding place among the concrete chunks inches from his face, pausing to briefly look at him as if mocking his ability to survive.

Gimble inched closer and as Zack awaited death, his thoughts flickered to his father, the cold military man about whom he usually avoided thinking. Zack had affirmed to Nicole that their relationship was strained. What he did not say was that he also suspected the reason for his father's brittle manner was something other than disappointment in his son. That reason was the unparalleled stress of combat. Colonel Raskin lived with more war-caused suffering than he ever let on. *If only Zack could see his father again, to let him know that he finally understood.*

He contemplated what course of action the old man would recommend now. The Colonel had opinions on everything and Zack desperately wished that he had one to cling to at this moment. Fighting was out of the question. There was no possibility of surprise. Besides, Zack had spent whatever physical reserve that he had back in the alley.

Once again survival was the thing. He had to get away. *But how?* He saw that his only chance was a tiny opening in the wall at the rear of the lot. If the storm obstructed the killer's vision enough he might make it.

Then, despite being unconvinced that his shivering body would hold up, he bit his lip hard enough to make it bleed and hugged the sodden ground as he crawled through rocks, mud, scrubby weeds, and shards of broken glass.

Gimble was standing by the largest pile of wreckage, seconds away from terminating his victim. He climbed the uneven mound for a better look, examining shapes in the darkness, waiting for one to reveal itself.

Just as Zack made it to the wall Gimble spotted him. The bricks and mortar around the opening were violently devoured by a torrent of bullets a second after Zack jammed his body through the narrow cavity. Gimble cursed the driving rain and his footing on the slippery concrete that altered his aim.

Then he saw the discarded MP5 on the ground. It was Strauss's and Gimble knew the only way anybody would have disarmed his partner would have been to kill him. This was a major development. He would have to report in and he was not looking forward to how the news would be received.

NEWS ITEM:

Billboard Magazine, May 10

Amazon.com reports an explosion of interest in everything by Nicole Branson. While industry insiders predicted strong sales after her death, nothing could have anticipated the surge of fan activity when the element of controversy was added to the late artist's legacy. Downloads and product orders have gone up an astonishing nine hundred per cent since the tabloid press first claimed a cover-up in the circumstances surrounding Ms. Branson's autopsy.

Chapter Seventeen

The drive to Culver City was less than ten miles from Westwood, but to Zack it seemed farther. A few hours of sleep, shower, dry clothes, and food had been somewhat restorative—but Zack knew the principal explanation was the magic pill that Angie gave him after picking him up at the Fountain and Vermont onramp to the Hollywood Freeway. Zack guessed it was Hysingla ER, the extended-release opioid analgesic that was twenty times more powerful than Vicodin. Whatever it was, it dulled his shaky emotions and most severe memories for the time being.

The drug also muted the pain that had spread from his injured leg to the rest of his body, but he did not care about physical discomfort. What Zack needed now was absolution from Father Solano. *If only the traffic on Overland Avenue would get him there efficiently!* Unfortunately, everyone in the city seemed to be on Overland this afternoon, which subjected him to the monotonous succession of bland mid-century stucco apartment buildings with concrete yards and open carports that they passed.

It was a good thing that Angie was driving.

Zack coaxed his mind through the numbness of his medicated state to the prospect of seeing Solano. *What could he possibly say to the man who had tried so determinedly to rescue him, only to be rejected?* The priest was polite when Zack called him earlier, but there was a chilly barrier between them that had not existed before.

He knew that he alone was to blame. After all, he rudely resisted the priest's repeated offers of assistance and even assaulted him to impede his efforts at the apartment. Zack strenuously fought to keep Nicole in his life and his current plight was the result—a lethal cloud of evil had descended on him; Doug was in critical condition and Sandy was dead. And he had taken a human life. The haunting tang of Sandy's blood and the explicit images of beating a man to death permeated his consciousness.

Satan had won. There was no doubt about that. Zack's existence had crumpled beneath him and he was in free-fall. Worse, he knew that he had not yet hit bottom. Satan was not done with him, he was now quite certain. *Why didn't he listen to Father Solano in the first place? Why the hell didn't he LISTEN?!* He did not know if the priest could save him or would even want to try, but he had to find out before what was left of his soul hemorrhaged out of him.

Angie cast a practiced eye at his young protégé, watching carefully for additional signs of distress. "Kid, are you sure you want to see this guy?" he inquired.

"Sandy died, Angie. That should've been me, not her," he mumbled. "And, Jesus Christ... I killed a man!"

"I get that. But from what you told me, he came on pretty strong before," Angie offered. "I mean, *fucking exorcism?!* If he starts that voodoo crap around me we're outta there."

"I don't care anymore. I need whatever help Solano can give me."

Turning left on Venice Boulevard, they did not speak again until Angie crossed Canfield Street and steered his black Buick LaCrosse to the curb by a small white building with tall church-like windows. But Angie saw right away that it was not a church. "Zack, we got a problem," Angie said as he rechecked the address.

"What do you mean?" Zack asked.

Angie motioned to the building at the edge of Media Park. " Venice. The Actor's Gang Theatre."

"So, where's Saint Teresa's?" Zack wanted to know.

"Maybe you got the address wrong." Angie punched something into his phone as Zack watched. Then Angie's face darkened. "Where'd you get this address?"

"From Father Solano."

Angie held his phone up to see. "There's no Saint Teresa's in Culver City."

"What're you talking about—that doesn't make any sense."

"Maybe not, but Google never heard of it. And that theatre is 9070 Venice."

"Bullshit," Zack pronounced as he climbed from the car. However, before he walked fifty feet his certainty dissipated. There were only generic mini-malls and small businesses to be seen in every direction, and a tiny oasis of a city park. Peering through the cluster of trees he could see a parking structure and more shops, but nothing resembling the grand historic church that Solano described in detail.

Angie approached him on the sidewalk. "Zack, listen to me. I don't know how to say this, so I'll just give it to you straight. I looked up Father Solano, too. There's no listing for him, either."

"That's ridiculous! His number's right here..." Zack insisted as he took the folded hand-out from Nicole's funeral out of his pocket and handed it to him.

Angie looked it over. "Where...?"

"Right there." Zack pointed to where Solano scribbled it down.

Angie examined the paper again and held it up for Zack to see. "There's no number on this."

"Of course there is..." Zack insisted as he yanked the paper from Angie's hands and frantically examined both sides before a wave of panic engulfed him. *The paper was blank.* "I'm telling you... the number was here! I've been calling it for days."

Angie remained calm. He had treated enough unstable patients to avoid saying or doing things that might worsen the situation. "Good, then it's still in your phone," he reminded him. "Let's redial him right now."

"Absolutely," Zack came back, relieved. He hurriedly scrolled through his call list but before long his hopefulness abandoned him. "Give me a minute... it's here..."

Angie watched closely as Zack's assurances withered and his shoulders sunk. His body language said it all: he was never going to locate the number because it did not exist. And the brutal truth of that was crashing down on both of them.

"I don't understand..." Zack finally whispered. *How could Solano not be here?! What about their conversations and meetings? What about that awful confrontation in his apartment?!*

Zack tried to say more but his ears were buzzing with tinnitus and his head was throbbing. Everywhere he looked the unforgiving images of his nightmare in Griffith Park and Los Feliz materialized... *Seifert's body in the trash bin... the chase... bullets strafing his car... the stark look of death in Sandy's eyes... his terror and confusion as he ran from the scene... and the fight for his life in the alley.*

"We'll figure this out, kid. Don't you worry," Angie assured him. "What do you say we get out of here?"

Zack gawked uncomprehendingly at the call list as Angie guided him back to the car. Even through his shock and confusion he knew that only insane people see things that are not there. He could hear blood roaring through his head and he wondered if that might be the precursor to a stroke that would put him out of his misery once and for all. At least, that is what he was hoping for.

Then he thought of Nicole. If Solano was a figment of his imagination then that meant she was, too. *God... not Nicole!*

Her return to him had been so miraculous. Yes, it had been unnerving and at times even taunted him, but the feel of her in his arms was beyond enthralling. *And the lovemaking! The way she knew everything he was thinking...*

But now he knew the truth: his beautiful, phenomenal Nicole had not appeared to him. *This was all one perverse delusion. He had totally lost his mind.* Zack strained for equilibrium. His thoughts were a swirling mass of incoherent illusions. *How does anyone survive something like this? Why would anyone want to?*

The last thing he remembered was the strength draining from his legs and the impact of collapsing on the sidewalk.

At some point he became aware of someone speaking and his attention gradually shifted back to the world around him. To Angie, who was driving west on Venice Boulevard. "You feelin' okay?" he was asking.

Zack tried to answer but could not. He was unable to think or breathe, let alone communicate. "I am so fucked..." was all he could get out. But that summed things up pretty well. Despite his faltering perspective Zack understood that much. *Nicole and Solano existed only in his mind. His unreliable, deteriorated mind.*

But how could he have gotten everything wrong?!

He diagnosed the answer as parts of his brain began to come online again. He remembered attending seminars about post-traumatic stress syndrome and dementia praecox, the latter being an alarming disorder consisting of disorganized thoughts, hallucinations, and delusions. He was right to have worried at the funeral about why Nicole reappeared and he was now grasping that his mind was obstructing its own circuitry to relieve the shock and pain that he felt over her death.

He stared out the window and analyzed himself with a peculiar sensation of bemusement. *Fully delusional... wow.*

"Cut yourself some slack," he heard Angie say. "You've been through a shit storm these past few weeks. Personally, I don't know how you're still standing."

Zack turned to him. He wanted to tell him everything about Nicole, but just could not go there. "I've lost it, haven't I," was all he could say.

Angie thought about his response, opting instead to ask him a direct question. "What would you think if you were me and there was no priest or church?"

Zack returned his gaze to the passing scenery. "I'd fit me for a strait jacket."

"Thirty-six long, right?"

Zack met his look and found a comforting smile waiting for him. "Look, a lot of stuff is jumbled right now. I get that. So, how about we put Solano on hold and just concentrate on solving this thing with Nicole, instead?"

"That sounds good. Thanks."

"Then we got a plan. We'll get the straight jacket later. I'll loan you one of mine."

Three hours later Zack and Angie were cruising Cliffside Drive in Malibu and even through his sedation the opulence of the exclusive area surprised him. He had travelled high-end neighborhoods on medical calls, but the structures here were not merely nice homes, they were walled estates. Where millions of dollars buy a locale with so much privacy that he doubted that people ever see their neighbors.

Driving past Nicole's secluded property, the *For Sale* sign on the lawn seemed out of place. As if somebody driving by would happen to have fifteen or twenty million dollars and say, "Gosh, I think I'll buy a mansion today."

Zack had not seen much of the house during the candlelight vigil on the beach. But as he took it in now he was captivated. Once featured in *Architectural Digest*, the home was a spectacular Annalise Bousquet design that encompassed simplicity of natural materials and colors in a light and airy flow.

"Okay, kid... now that we're here are you feeling any different?" Angie asked as he pulled to a stop. "We can still go to the cops."

But Zack was determined. "I tried that, remember? I can't go back until I find out about S.A."

"Fine," Angie replied. "Then let's get something to eat and come back later."

"Another one of your magic pills is all I need."

Parking in the long driveway of a home under construction at the end of the cul-de-sac that night, the black Buick was invisible in the shadows. Zack and Angie had studied the area on an internet satellite map and saw where they could cut through an empty lot on the bluff next to Nicole's and slip over her redwood fence.

While Angie cased everything out Zack found himself alone on the sprawling multi-level deck surrounded by stylish teak bench seating and angled designer fire tables. He contemplated the surf below and tried to imagine what a welcomed retreat this spot must have been for Nicole after weathering the demands of her career.

Or a romantic night the Greek Theatre with someone she did not know.

He lifted his gaze to the sky and wondered if she had thought about that night the way he was thinking about it now. *Had she stood here, felt the coastal breeze, and remembered the cool air cascading onto their bodies? When ocean moisture collected on her lips did it remind her of their mouths meeting in that fantastic first kiss?*

He wished he knew. Unfortunately, he did not dependably know much of anything beyond his inability to let go of their night together.

Soon Angie was crouched on a low overhang of the roof, whispering down. "Last chance to come to your senses."

"Does that mean we can get inside?"

Angie ran his fingers along the aluminum flashing that framed one of the home's skylights. "Only one way to find out."

Before long, Zack was beside Angie helping remove screws from the skylight. They tugged on the translucent dome and it lifted easily. "No alarm so far," Angie remarked with a reassuring wink as he felt the opening for the magnetic contacts of a home security system. "I'm better at this than I thought."

After lowering themselves through the skylight, they peered through the darkness with flashlights. Angie spoke first. "The first thing we gotta do is find out what kind of alarm this is."

He headed for a hall closet and located a control panel with a diagram of the house. "Looks like only perimeter doors and windows are wired," Angie mused. "There's nothing here about interior pressure pads or cameras."

He turned with a confident smile and found that Zack was nowhere to be seen.

Zack moved slowly through the spacious, shadowy rooms alone. *So, this was where she lived.* The watery pastels, beach-appropriate fabrics, and comfortable low-profile furniture were all of Nicole's choosing. As were the beautiful architectural salvage pieces, like the huge illuminated panel built into one entire wall by a local artist. *They had given her pleasure.*

Zack felt the enduring stillness around him and tried to visualize how it must have been when she lived here. Looking out at the deck, he remembered a charity event that made news a few years ago, when two helicopters filled with paparazzi nearly collided as they jockeyed for shots of Nicole and her celebrity guests. There were many fundraisers here. Zack was reminded of her generous nature and how readily people seemed to forget that upon her death. She had worked tirelessly to help the less fortunate and yet there was no equity in her selflessness. No dividend invested in her reputation for the day that a web of lies would engulf her demise.

Nicole's legacy had become a drug-tainted death certificate.

Disgusted, he turned from the patio doors to discover another injustice: a stream of ants winding along a wall to the kitchen. Her contributions to the world were of no interest to the opportunists of nature, he decided. Be they insects, journalists, or record producers. To them Nicole's heritage was something to feed on and nothing more.

The revelation struck a chord in Zack. As he watched the column of ants split into pillaging offshoots that extended across granite surfaces into sleek white cabinets and drawers, he could feel his dedication to Nicole being renewed. There was little purpose in fighting the insect infestation, but something had to be done about the human offensive.

Sandy had died trying to learn the truth and he had even killed for it. He would get the answers one way or another and shove them squarely up the ass of the inept media and police officials who accepted the cover-up at face value.

Moving from the kitchen, he advanced along a hallway to her bedroom. When he arrived he could not bring himself to enter. The warm caramel upholstery and wood accents were soothing and romantic, an ideal sanctuary. But when his imagination conjured the image of Nicole and someone he assumed to be S.A. making love on the luxurious bed, he turned away.

Suddenly, Zack jumped at finding someone watching him in the darkness—only to realize that he was looking at his own stark reflection in a hallway mirror. And it was no wonder that he scared himself: this stranger impersonating him was unshaven with scraggly hair and puffy eyes. His face was imprinted with fatigue. He looked like someone else and, after considering his image, felt like it, too.

Doc Sandberg had explained that people process grief in their own way, but who would have ever imagined that his process would be like this?

Leaning in for a closer look, Zack stared at the distinctive matrix of capillaries in his sclera, the fibrous white area around his pupils. He paused, as if hypnotized by seeing a familiar landscape on a map. Eventually, he realized that the tiny blood vessels looked a lot like a river he once knew and its tributaries: Grizzly Bay, Suisun Slough, Peytonia Slough, and a dozen others that etch the countryside south of Fairfield, California where his father grew up.

But why would he think of that now?

Then a realization hit him like a brick. *He had an explanation for what happened to Father Solano!*

When Zack hurried back to the living room, Angie was waiting beside piles of possessions that someone had prepared for packing. Zack flopped onto a box of books as fresh waves of depression spread through him.

Angie read his demeanor with trepidation. "Zack, are you gonna make it? Maybe we should go."

"You are not going to believe this. Solano County is where my father grew up. In Fairfield, California," Zack mumbled. "Solano..."

Angie sat. He had seen amnesia patients precipitously recall fragments of their lives and it was an important development to be nurtured. "Good, Solano. What else do you remember?"

Zack looked at him helplessly. "Solano's church was Saint Teresa's. I can't believe I remember this, but Teresa is the Catholic patron saint of headache victims. My mom prayed to her every night because of her migraines and mine."

"Holy crap!" Angie replied in what he instantly knew was the understatement of the year. "This's great! What about the location in Culver City? Any ideas about that?"

"Yeah... and it's totally nuts. The Actors' Gang Theatre is one that Doug likes. He's always asking me to go with him, but I have no idea how I knew the address." Zack shook his head, baffled. "Where did all this shit come from, Angie?"

"I think you just had a breakthrough."

Zack reacted to the term, suspecting that his friend might be trying to make the best of a bad situation. "You mean *breakdown*, right?"

"Could be," Angie replied. "How do you feel about that?"

"Exhausted, pissed off... sad. I don't know." He felt guilty about not telling him everything about Nicole, but once again could not bring himself to say the words.

"You're entitled," Angie assured him. "There's no right or wrong emotion to feel."

"Thanks," Zack answered as he continued to process the disconcerting associations that had unfolded between the past and his current circumstance. "But I'll tell you one thing," he continued as he gently ran his hand across a container of knickknacks. "I feel better about being screwed up than I do seeing all this... Nicole's whole life's been reduced to a stack of damn boxes."

"Happens to all of us sooner or later, kid."

"Not like this. Not like they did to her."

Angie thought about that as he picked up a tiny glass rabbit from a gathered pile. Zack recalled the assortment of glass animals in Nicole's dressing room.

"Strange, isn't it?" Angie remarked. "This rabbit isn't special as far as figurines go. Couldn't have cost more than a few bucks. But something made it worth keeping. It was a connection that made her feel good." Angie paused again to make sure that Zack was following his observation. "That's why she kept it around," he added, "because it's those connections that make things easier when you need them. When our time comes it all comes down to the connections we made. Like the one she had with you."

Zack glanced from the rabbit to Angie and felt better for his friend's thoughtful words. He welcomed the idea of a special connection to Nicole because it provided a bit of acquiescence for the disturbing phantom presence of Father Solano.

Angie gave him a moment then cuffed him on the shoulder, "Might as well get back to it."

For the next two hours, Zack and Angie searched the mountains of possessions. The house remained dark to keep anyone from wondering what might be taking place, but the lack of light did more than highlight the drama of their effort; it fueled Zack's frustration.

"What's the use?!" he finally blurted as the futility became too much for him. "We're never going to find anything."

"Maybe not," Angie answered.

"You don't have to agree with me."

"I'm not gonna lie." He met Zack's troubled look. "For example, I've been thinkin' S.A. might not be the father."

Zack scowled. "Yes, he was."

"You don't know that."

"Look, the night she spent with me was..." he began before trailing. He couldn't elaborate, it was too difficult. "She was rebounding and I happened to be there, okay? It meant more to me than it did her. I know that now. But believe me, she wasn't the type to sleep around. She was a one man lady... and S.A. was that man."

"Whatever you say," Angie submitted. He had his doubts about Zack's assessment but chose not to debate the point.

Zack resumed digging through boxes while Angie wandered into the entry hall where unopened mail overflowed from a basket beneath the mail slot. He flipped through the letters, stopping at one with a smile. "Now we're cookin'!"

"What's up...?" Zack asked.

"An insurance statement for lab work they covered for Nicole: Beta HCG," he proclaimed, referring to the medical test used to determine pregnancy.

Zack was slow to catch on. "But I already told you she was pregnant."

"Only now we got specifics to work with," Angie explained. "Where's all that desk stuff we saw before?" He dug through the contents of an open box.

"What are you looking for?"

"This..." Angie replied as he held up an appointment calendar. Flipping through the pages, he talked through the logic. "She had the HCG last month, right? That means she shoulda had her period a couple weeks before." He continued his search then paused. "Here, she circled the third."

The details of Nicole's pregnancy were difficult for Zack to hear. Despite his earlier declaration of understanding that his night with her was a one-time event, he was still uncomfortable with the thought of her making love to somebody else.

"How's that get us any closer to finding S.A.?" he asked Angie in an effort to contribute.

"Let's backtrack fifteen or twenty days and find out," Angie suggested. And he was right. Of all the mysteries within the human body, the fertility cycle of a young woman is extremely dependable.

When Angie found what he was looking for he glanced at Zack and wished that he could cushion the discovery that he was about to share. "Take a look."

Zack shined his flashlight on the calendar. The sight of entries in Nicole's handwriting sent a pang of regret through him. The events of her daily routine were there, the meetings, rehearsals, and errands. All the things she would never do again.

He tensed at the item Angie was pointing to: a weekend dedicated to *New Orleans with S.A.* "There's who she was with at the peak of her cycle, kid. S.A. The police are gonna want this."

The impact of the evidence hit Zack like a punch to the heart. The more they found out, the less he wanted to know. Yet he had to keep pressing. Nicole and Sandy were counting on him. "We still don't have a name."

"No, but you can almost feel the son of a bitch startin' to sweat," Angie answered as he entered a number printed on the HCG invoice into his phone.

"Who are you calling?" Zack asked.

"Sometimes women tell doctors things they won't say to anybody else," he began as the call began to ring. "Maybe this guy, Doctor Glasner, knows the father's name."

"But it's the middle of the night."

"It's also an emergency... let me handle this."

Zack stared at the invoice in awe of Angie's expertise. Even the sound of Angie's commanding voice on the phone with the answering service was reassuring. Zack knew that if he were working alone he would have fumbled around forever.

Then Zack observed how silent Angie had become and the grim expression on his face as he thanked the operator. Zack could almost guess what was coming.

"Jerome Glasner died last week," Angie explained. "Electrical fire took out a whole floor of his Calabasas office. He was working late."

"And all his patient records were destroyed, I'll bet."

"You got it."

Zack stared at the invoice. "We've got to stop S.A., Angie. Before he kills anybody else."

The search continued for another hour as they powered through other rooms, digging through boxes with renewed purpose. But by the time they reached Nicole's studio the effort had not yielded any new results.

Zack closed the last box angrily. "How can this be?!" he complained. "How can some guy father a child and there's no mention of him anywhere?!"

"Maybe he got here first."

Zack fired him another look. He did not want to hear more bad news.

"He took care of the doctor, didn't he?" Angie reminded him.

"You're right," Zack acknowledged. "I just don't want to admit it."

"Hey, I understand. But the man plays hardball. That overdose deal he pulled on Nicole was just a warm-up. You oughta know that better than anybody."

Zack shook his head, unable to refute the harrowing memories of Griffith Park and Los Feliz. "Yeah," he agreed. "Besides, nobody thinks twice about rockers on drugs."

"Except you."

"A lot of good it's done." Zack moved to leave, but stopped as Angie paused beside a stack of artwork leaning against a wall. "I already checked those," he said. "They're movie posters. It was one of her hobbies."

"Nice ones, too," admired Angie. "Originals from when Hollywood still knew how to make good flicks." He flipped through the framed posters. "This's some classic collection, kid. Every one autographed by the star. Paul Newman... Sinatra... William Holden... man-oh-man, I'll bet these are worth a bundle." Then a smile spread on his face, "Hey, my man McQueen..!"

Angie lifted the poster from *Bullitt*, starring Steve McQueen, which was prominently signed for its original owner, *Best wishes to my close friend, Ernie.*

"Wow, look at that!" Angie admired. "I wonder where she picked this one up."

Zack limped over to the poster. "It's a poster, so what?"

"So, whoever this Ernie was," Angie admired, "he was one privileged guy!"

Zack watched his friend without comprehending the scope of his wonder. "Sorry Angie, but it'll take more than Steve McQueen's signature to impress me right now." Angie nodded and was returning the poster when he paused again, his mind goaded by something that did not fit. "Wait a sec..."

Zack took the cue seriously. He had seen Angie like this a hundred times as a paramedic. "What's wrong?" he finally asked.

Angie lifted another poster from the stack. "This one's not for a movie."

Glancing at the graphic, Zack wasn't intrigued:

Elect Ron Chandler
United States Senate

"She was politically active, so what?"

Angie set the poster aside and studied it. "In twenty-five or thirty posters, it's the only one. The rest are movies."

"I don't see the connection," answered Zack.

Angie gestured to the smiling photo of Senator Chandler, a handsome man in his forties. "A guy like this'd have plenty to lose if word got out he was having a baby with somebody other than his wife."

Zack sank at the speculation of the identity of Nicole's lover. But he felt obliged to refute the idea. "That's ridiculous."

"Why?"

"Because she'd never sleep with him."

"A senator with bigtime ambitions would have a lot to lose if the truth about Nicole got out. And he'd have the muscle at his disposal to run a big time number on you."

The comments registered, as much as Zack hated to admit it. He remembered his meeting with Doc Sandberg about *The National Enquirer*, when she told him that someone from Washington was questioning how UCLA spends federal grants. *Questioning it after one of their students threatened to blow the lid off this!*

Then he was taken back to the video on MTV, when Nicole sang her ballad "Silent Partners" at a fundraiser. His mind lurched through his memory, past the haunting lyrics about a love that could never be, past the young woman singing them, settling on the banner behind her: *Ron Chandler for President.*

It WAS Chandler. *Ron Chandler had to be S.A.!*

Zack was slammed back to the present and kneeled to examine the poster more closely. The possibility of discovering who was responsible for so much violence was consuming. "A politician... why didn't I see that before?"

Angie crouched beside him. "Because he didn't want you to. Now we still got one big question: how do we *get S.A.* outta *Ron Chandler*? That part don't line up."

Zack tried to work out the connection and failed. The initials obviously did not correspond with his name. His flashlight played across the face of the poster one more time as he studied every detail.

Then he saw it.

"Angie, check it out," he said excitedly, "This's the only poster that's not signed." He flipped the frame around and focused the light on the backing. The revelation was not long in coming. "Shit!" his voice cracked.

Angie adjusted the light to read the inscription that Zack found. The rounded beam flared off the glossy white poster board. *"To Nicole, with all my love,"* he began. *"Your straight arrow, Ron."*

Zack met his look, astonished. "Straight Arrow... S.A."

"Well, I'll be damned," Angie growled with pride. "You just nailed the bastard."

NEWS ITEM:

KCBS-TV News Transcript, May 11

Police made three grim discoveries in Los Feliz last night... first, in the block of Fountain Avenue, the badly beaten body of a man identified as Gunter Strauss, a former agent with Interpol, the international police organization. Then, less than an hour later, the bodies of Park Ranger Darvell Sims and an unidentified Caucasian male at the Griffith Park Observatory. Both had been shot in the head, execution-style.

Thus far, no witnesses to the crimes have come forward and no suspects have been named. A number of calls to 911 last night, however, reported hearing weapon fire in the area. Police did locate a bullet-riddled car near the Greek Theatre, but investigators have declined to say whether or not it's related to the murders.

Chapter Eighteen

At the corner of Constellation and Avenue of The Stars in Century City, the massive entertainment, shopping, and office complex near Beverly Hills, sits the Hyatt Regency Century Plaza Hotel. The acclaimed nineteen-story facility occupies land that was once home to the Twentieth Century-Fox Studio backlot sets for Tom Mix westerns and Shirley Temple tearjerkers. Created by architect Minoru Yamasaki, who also designed the World Trade Center Twin Towers in New York, the hotel forms a grand sweeping crescent that faces magnificent fountains on the Avenue of the Stars. Many notable events have taken place there, from presidential visits to celebrity-filled galas.

On this night a special marquee erected by the Creative Artists talent agency outside their headquarters across the street heralded yet another, *Welcome Senator Ron Chandler!* Special outdoor lighting at the hotel and a phalanx of media personnel highlighted the sort of glamorous activity that luxury resorts crave.

Inside the 13,230-square-foot Los Angeles Ballroom downstairs, film star Calvin Farnell was addressing a sizable audience. "I don't know about the rest of you," he proclaimed, "but I'm feeling magic in the air!" A thousand supporters screamed as Ron Chandler's California presidential campaign conference ignited. The large room overflowed with boundless energy and goodwill.

Farnell, a well-known social activist, grinned at the eager faces and television cameras. "We've received word about the new *Times* poll confirming what we have known all along, that we have the man with a vision for America. And here he is, my friends, the great Senator from Ohio and the next President of the United States... Ronnie Chandler!"

The crowd went wild as Chandler strolled onstage and a college pep band played the unofficial Chandler campaign song, "That's The Way (Uh-Huh, Uh-Huh) I Like It" by K.C. and the Sunshine Band. The catchy disco anthem amped the vitality of the proceedings to intoxicated heights. Farnell grabbed the candidate in a hearty bear hug.

Chandler shook the actor's hand and turned to his supporters as the music played. Ron Chandler was forty-five years old and ideal presidential material. Even his policy critics in Washington had to admit that they liked him personally. His intellectual grasp of legislative issues was second to none and his ability to work long hours without rest was legendary. With two terms in the United States Senate behind him, the former Cleveland criminal prosecutor was another Kennedy, his party strategists were saying.

As he watched from the wings a man wearing a *Chandler Security* badge hoped that was true. Ted Gimble wondered what it would be like to work inside the White House. There would be perquisites of every kind: money, power, and secret information. Unlimited ways to accomplish the political dirty work he was paid so well to administer.

But to get to the White House, Gimble reminded himself, Ron Chandler would have to first win the nomination. And that meant stopping Zack Raskin.

The utility area behind the hotel was congested with buses, cars, and news vans. Angie edged his Buick LaCrosse through the clutter until he found a spot just a few dozen yards from the receiving dock. Turning to Zack in the seat beside him, his frustration was boiling over at not having talked him out of what he knew was a harebrained idea. And he had spent the entire drive over trying. "This's still a dumb fucking idea, Zack."

"I know."

"Then what the hell makes you think hotel security's gonna listen to you when the cops wouldn't?" he challenged. Even though Zack looked different now that he had showered, shaved, and put on a sport coat, Angie knew it was pain medication and the news that Doug's injuries were restricted to C-7 low-cervical nerves that had temporarily boosted his spirits. With luck Doug might be able to breathe on his own and recover movement of his arms and shoulders. Angie had no such positive hopes for Zack's prospects to succeed with his plan to confront S.A.

"What else am I supposed to do?" Zack shot back.

"What about that professor of yours? The one who's been leaving messages on your phone..."

"Doc Sandberg can't do anything."

That only exasperated Angie even more. "And what if another one of Chandler's goons comes after you?"

Zack did not flinch. "Then you'll tell Detective Maulden what we found at the house. Maybe something happening to me will finally get his attention."

"For Chrissakes, Zack. This's nuts!"

"Tell that to Nicole, Sandy, and Doug," Zack snapped.

Angie shook his head in utter bewilderment. "She means that much to you?" The question struck a chord in Zack. It was time to be honest. Angie deserved that much. "There's a whole lot of stuff I haven't told you."

Angie reacted to the shift in Zack's tone. "I'm not going anywhere."

Zack finally unburdened himself. The confession was filled with disbelief, sadness, and relief all at once. "I've been seeing Nicole," he began slowly. "Since she died. Seeing her a lot."

"Okay. You had trouble letting go..." Angie replied, misunderstanding what Zack was telling him.

"No, I mean I've been *seeing* her. She's still in my life."

Angie had no idea what to say. Given the traumatizing episode involving the nonexistent priest, Zack was in worse shape than he thought. It was time to act. "Then going in there's the last thing you're gonna do," he decreed, starting the engine.

But when he threw the car into gear Zack grabbed him by the arm. "I know it sounds wacked, but I have to finish this." He paused to look at his mentor. "I'm her only hope."

"And I'm starting to think that I might be yours," he shot back, removing Zack's hand and reaching for the gear shift. "No way am I letting you go in there."

Zack glanced at a several television executives and their crew approaching a uniformed police officer at the receiving door, then back at Angie with defiance. "I'm confronting that asshole, Angie. No way's he getting away with this."

Before Angie could react to the alarming reference to *confrontation*, Zack was out of the car and scurrying past parked vehicles. Angie cursed and jumped out to stop him, but in his thrift shop sport coat and slacks Zack had already smoothly blended in with the television group as they were admitted to the hotel.

Angie arrived at the door moments later and addressed the officer. "Excuse me, my friend just went inside and it's important that I talk to him," he opened.

The policeman reacted blankly. "Are you on the list?"

Angie knew this was pointless. "No. But I really need to talk to him. It's an emergency." He held out his Willis Ambulance identification.

"Then call 911. Nobody gets in without being on the list."

Angie cursed under his breath. He now fully understood that Zack lied about reporting Chandler to hotel security. The kid was going after the senator.

In the ballroom, which Zack knew from an online hotel map was near the receiving dock, Ron Chandler was at the microphone. "I'm always asked how I feel about the polls," he told them. "Before tonight I never knew how to answer. But now I do and the word *euphoric* comes to mind."

Everyone cheered. Chandler was a politician who could effortlessly touch the hearts of everyday citizens. People knew that the simplicity of his message and personal style were born of humble beginnings. Chandler had worked hard for everything that he had achieved. There were no handouts, no family connections, and absolutely no special privileges to help him along the way. A blue-collar guy with working class dreams, when Chandler talked about personal struggles he spoke from experience. Ron Chandler understood.

"But let me be frank," he continued, "I'm also concerned..." The mood in the room sobered. "I'm concerned that we risk becoming complacent in this campaign, that we'll take for granted that our neighbors will support our vision for America."

Chandler scanned the room. He was in command. He owned them. "Complacency is our enemy and we must stamp it out before it takes root," he concluded. "Because the moment any of us believes that victory is ours... then I guarantee that is the moment when we've lost."

Zack stood three floors beneath the main hotel lobby, in the carpeted corridor of the California level where Chandler's voice echoed with what felt to him like garish persistence, *"This candidacy is about more than winning office. It's about reaching out to our neighbors and friends with ideas for better schools, better health care, and a better economy for everyone. A better future that we can all share."*

"A better future..." Zack repeated under his breath. *Sure, you disingenuous prick, like Nicole's future? And Sandy's and Doug's?!*

He was not sure what to do next. The sight of uniformed officers checking the credentials of people filing into the rally was an obstacle to be reckoned with. He would have to improvise.

Zack turned and approached the domed foyer outside the ballroom in the hopes of finding an alternate way in. It was empty except for a folding table covered with Chandler campaign brochures and buttons. Zack affixed a Chandler campaign button to his jacket and smiled with deliberate nonchalance at two inattentive security men while continuing towards the restrooms signs at the end of the corridor. Doing his best to conceal his halting stride, he slowed and examined the swirling patterns in the carpet. His perverse observation was that the images resembled giant sperm laid out end to end, which made him wonder if that is what the designer intended. Or maybe Zack had just flunked the Century Plaza Rorschach Test.

Alone inside the spacious men's room, he splashed cool water into his deadened cheeks and treasured the invigorating wetness. As he trapped more of the flow in his palms, he slurped some down before burrowing his whole face in the remainder. The open tap was running colder now, and as he savored the feeling of one handful after another on his skin, he was taken back to sweltering summer days as a child when a cannon ball dive into somebody's swimming pool was as good as life got.

At long last he lifted his head to examine the reflection staring back at him. The carefree student he used to be was gone, though he certainly looked better than he did in the hallway mirror at Nicole's house. How he longed for the impulsive fun he used to be famous for! Sadly, those pinball tournaments at the student union and old film marathons at the NuArt Theater on Santa Monica Boulevard were ancient history. None of those activities really meant much to him at the time, but after the ordeals of the past few weeks the simple freedom to goof off had unforeseen significance.

Zack reached for a towel and the coarseness of the paper was a disagreeable surprise. What had been the embrace of restorative liquid was negated by something akin to sandpaper scraping his skin. He marveled at the lack of civility shown by the janitorial staff.

Then someone spoke. "You never give up, do you."

Startled, he turned to face Nicole who was behind him. "Nicole..."

"I was afraid that I would never see you again," she observed.

He stared at her before speaking. "I know. I... was, too."

"But here I am... you brought me back."

Obviously, he had. Yet despite what he now understood about his tenuous grasp on reality, she looked so vulnerable. *So lonely and sad.* "I guess I did," he admitted as his throat tightened. "But I know you aren't really here."

She sat on the counter to face him. "Don't you think we've come too far for talk like that?"

"I know the truth, Nicole. I'm having a breakdown," he said. "If seeing you again wasn't messed up enough, what happened with Father Solano proves it." He forced himself to continue. "I never thought I'd say this... never in a million years... but I can't do this anymore. You and me."

Her face flushed. "Are you sure?"

"I'm not in any shape to be sure of anything. But yeah."

"Zack, I don't want to leave you," she pleaded.

"It's not what I want, either."

A rush of panic came over her. "Then why are you saying

this?!"

"Look at me," he came back. "Look what this's doing to me. Having you, not having you, and now these revelations of what's really going on. It's gone way too far. It's killing me."

Her eyes filled with tears as the end to their relationship loomed. It was inevitable and she knew it. Her sorrow began to give way to gratitude. "Do you have any idea how lucky I have been to have you for a friend?"

"There's nothing I wouldn't do for you. And your baby."

"I can't believe what you've gone through already." Touching his cheek, her fingers traced a scratch on his skin. "I'm so sorry about Sandy."

He couldn't let himself go there, back to the horror of her murder or the unsolved disposition of her remains. "I'll tell you one thing," he divulged. "She wanted to get the bottom of this as much as me..."

Zack trailed at the reference and she noted his change of mood. "What is it?"

He didn't want to say it. "I know I'm delusional, but I have to ask anyway... will you tell me about him?"

She was straightforward. "We're both from Ohio and we met at a campaign rally in Chicago when he was first thinking of running."

"The guy's married," he objected. "How could you fall for somebody like that?!"

"Sometimes things happen that we don't plan," she reminded him. "Like us."

Zack stroked the skin of her hand as if to memorize the feel of her. She had been seduced by a craven politician who will stop at nothing to get what he wants. He could hardly blame her for that. "I want you to know that I'm still going to clear your name."

She touched his face one more time. "I love you, Zack."

"And I love you," he assured her as they drew into one last kiss.

Outside the Century Plaza, Angie was pacing. He was upset that he became entangled in this, no matter how condemning the evidence was against Chandler. He had somehow confused affection for his protégé with being supportive, letting empathy bring him this far. He should have physically restrained Zack if necessary and he felt like an idiot for not doing it.

He tried texting Zack one more time, pleading with him to walk away from this. When no reply came, he left a heartfelt voice message. "Zack, listen to me.... there's some stuff I gotta say," he began softly. "When we went looking for Father Solano, I was really hoping that he'd be able to help. The fact is, even though I'm not what anybody'd call a spiritual guy, I believe in God. I don't go to church or anything, but I do pray. But instead of asking for good things to happen to me, I pray for other people. I keep thinking that a prayer from me might be just the push they need to get over the top... towards wherever it is they're supposed to go." He paused to find the right words. This was more difficult than he had imagined. "Anyway, I just wanna say that I'm out here by my car praying for you right now. Praying that you'll listen to me and give this up."

Angie took a moment to gather himself after ending the call. Then he Googled the West Los Angeles Police and decisively punched in their number. "Detective Maulden, please," he said as the call went through. "It's an emergency."

When his cell phone rang, Brad Maulden was at home immersed in the files that Zack and Sandy gave him. From what he could understand of Zack's medical notations, and what he could confirm with online searches, they were pretty convincing. So was the conspicuous timing of the pathologist's death by drowning.

Maulden regretted not being more receptive to the young couple. A good cop would have never discounted a lead simply because a story had run in *The National Enquirer*, he told himself. But he had more time to consider it now and he was giving it more than a cursory glance.

Ignoring the ringing phone, he circled an explanation of subacute bacterial endocarditis in a dog-eared department reference book. The ringing stopped, only to resume as the caller persisted. "Maulden," he answered at last.

"Lieutenant, I'm a friend of Zack Raskin's," Angie announced.

"The med student who came to you about Nicole Branson. He said you've got her files."

Maulden sat up straight. This might be his chance to correct his previous error in judgment.

Zack took the escalator from the ballroom to the plaza level one floor beneath the lobby and spotted a pair of policemen at the door. Making a nimble turn, he followed a sign leading down a zigzagging corridor to a bank of courtesy telephones. Once again Chandler's voice boomed from the ballroom above, as if taunting him to continue.

As he rounded a corner he saw a policeman pick up a house phone, leaving a nearby service door unattended. Zack slipped through and found himself in a long hallway lined with stainless steel carts, stacks of tables, and props used for hotel events. Hobbling past small groups of white-capped food handlers, he could hear excited cheers from the ballroom reverberating off the austere tile and concrete passageway. The jubilant voices were in marked contrast to the rage that was building inside him. The fluorescent glow in the hall reminded him of a hospital basement corridor that usually leads to the morgue.

The morgue... Nicole...Sandy... God knows how many others... and possibly soon to come, Zack Raskin. He did his best to push such thoughts from his mind.

Picking up his pace, he defied the burning that had returned to his leg. He kept moving, his singular purpose never leaving his thoughts. Turning one corner after another in the lengthy passage, Chandler's voice on the ballroom public address system grew steadily louder. It made his flesh crawl.

Zack tried several doors, but they were locked. His frustration and fear were expanding fast. He knew that any moment someone from the security detail might see him and ask to see his pass.

Then an entrance ahead opened, one with a sign reading:

SOUTH GALLERY - BALLROOM CONTROL CENTER
SOUND AND LIGHTING DEPARTMENT
AUTHORIZED PERSONNEL ONLY

A hotel staffer passed through the door and hurried off. Zack grabbed it before it closed and entered. He was making progress! The narrow hall where he now found himself could be his ticket to Chandler.

As he approached the control room, Zack's heart skipped when he noticed a security camera on the ceiling. Thinking fast, he lifted a clipboard from its hook on a wall and pretended to study it. Then with his face turned away from the camera, he continued on.

At the end of the hall was a door marked *ELECTRICAL ROOM*. Assuming that a hundred security experts were watching, Zack ambled forward with the same deliberate casualness that got him past the police earlier. Anecdotes that he heard as an EMT at crime scenes reminded him that people often overlook someone who looks like he belongs, even in a heightened security situation.

Chandler's speech was louder now, with each political promise echoing with escalations more annoying than those before. Zack wondered how anyone could stand it, until he appreciated that what he was hearing was such a distorted jumble that it was probably his imagination at work again. He could no longer count on his instincts.

Reaching for the door handle, he gave it a tug. Fortunately, it moved in his grasp and it swung open. Stepping out of the camera's view, he turned the lock behind him.

Onstage, candidate Chandler was on a roll. "There's so much that we have to fix in this world... I'd be lying if I said I had all the answers. All I can promise are my best judgments and efforts. But first we have to win our primaries. And to do it we can't depend on what the polls tell us."

Zack flinched at the words, which closed in on him like thick fog. Especially, *"All I can promise are my best judgments and efforts."* Yeah, he grumbled to himself, like Chandler's other efforts at eliminating people.

He climbed a service ladder and imagined the senator's words floating in the air like giant quotes from tomorrow's media accounts of the speech, multiplying and mutating one lie at a time. The images only made him more determined to push on.

Completing his ascent, he reached a catwalk in the ballroom ceiling. He moved carefully and peered through small openings to the rally below.

"We have to get out there, roll up our sleeves, and knock on doors," Chandler was saying. *"We have to pick up those phones and call. I know the work is hard, because every day I watch my most tireless supporter in action. I'd like to bring her out right now. Please welcome my darling wife, Helen."*

Zack was directly above the stage now, gaping through banks of Klieg lights as people shrieked with joy. He saw Helen Chandler wave energetically as she made her entrance. She was attractive and refined, and his jaw tightened when her husband hugged her in a grand display of affection.

At the same time, a few feet behind the candidate Ted Gimble inspected the ballroom with a practiced eye, glancing briefly into the lighting grid. Zack barely saw him in time before pulling himself away from the opening. *Shit!*

Not only had Zack nearly been seen, but he recognized one of Nicole's security men—the driver of the Dodge van. *The man standing with Senator Chandler was one of the killers!* If there was any doubt about the senator's involvement in all this, then the sight of Gimble at his side sealed it.

Zack steadied his breathing. S.A. thought his thugs had done their job, but he was wrong. They had failed to stop Zack Raskin and he took comfort in the edge that the knowledge gave him. Knowledge was power, after all, and he had learned far more than Chandler ever anticipated! He smiled grimly at how anxious the senator must be right now, beneath the mask of exuberance that he wore for his political sycophants.

The pep band played again and Zack stole another look at the stage. Chandler and his wife were waving to the audience, pointing to individuals they recognized, basking in the moment. They were the picture of a happily married team dedicated to making the world a better place.

Yet there was no telling how many other women Chandler had screwed on the side and how many of them might have suffered untimely deaths. Images flickered through Zack's mind of Chandler's deadly fixers surreptitiously making his indiscretions disappear, thereby keeping his path to power unimpeded. As Helen Chandler turned her adoring gaze to her husband, Zack wondered if she had any suspicions about her spouse's philandering. *If she only knew what a duplicitous piece of shit he was.*

Backstage, the young man descending a ladder was concealed among curtains and ropes. Even if somebody did look in his direction, he would be indistinguishable from the staging crew that moved through the area as Seifert's team of roadies had at the concert.

At the base of his climb Zack slipped into the thick folds of a theatrical drape and watched a group of people approach. He zeroed in on Senator Chandler among them. Soon Chandler and his aides were only feet away and the anxiety that Zack felt was considerable. There he was, the man who betrayed Nicole and their baby! The asshole who bore responsibility for so much misery and death. Zack wondered how anyone could maintain such a calm demeanor in the wake of that. But then as he watched the candidate deal with questions from his handlers, he gathered that narcissists like Chandler live to be the center of their universe. He knew from his psych classes that the distance between common self-absorption and being a full-blown sociopath is less than people think—and to someone like Ron Chandler the things required to attain his desired status probably seem trivial.

Imagine, human life being trivial. Maybe it's easier to order a death than having to do the deed with your own hands.

Zack waited until he saw Chandler leave through a rear door. This was his chance. The son of a bitch was alone. When the aides hurried off to attend to tasks their boss had assigned, Zack slid unobserved through the same door.

The backstage hallway where Zack found himself was bustling with activity. An army of hotel workers rolled stacks of tables and chairs into readiness outside the ballroom's artist green rooms in preparation for a breakfast that would take place the following morning, while staff members handled business on their phones and iPads.

He located the senator among rows of folded banquet tables that were lined up like a squadron of bombers on an aircraft carrier, wings in the air. Zack had to move. Wincing with pain as he demanded too much of his leg, he found more of Angie's magic meds in his pocket and swallowed them.

Noticing that Chandler was still unaccompanied by anyone, Zack moved as expeditiously as he dared without drawing attention to himself, zigzagging through tables and workers as he narrowed the gap separating him from the senator. Each step was accompanied by an interminable repression of time.

How long was this taking, anyway?

Someone was bound to see him any second. And if not, then surely Chandler would sense the man following him.

Zack was nearly upon him now. He could see the wrinkles that should have been pressed from the candidate's suit before the rally. Beneath the fabric he could make out the muscles of Chandler's athletic build, which meant he was probably capable of defending himself.

Zack had not thought about that, about their confrontation becoming physical. But there was no turning back. He had to see this through even if it meant a fight. Then he flashed to his confrontation in the alley and wondered if he could be pushed to such extremes twice.

As he passed a campaign worker begging someone on the phone to correct a booking for Chandler on *Charlie Rose*, he could not believe that no one had stopped him. Pulling alongside his target, Zack's heart seemed to misfire as he reached into his jacket and palmed a hypodermic syringe filled with clear liquid.

When Chandler turned to acknowledge the young man who

appeared beside him, Zack made his move. Removing the protective plastic cap from the needle, he shoved Chandler into an open cargo elevator and jammed the weapon against his throat. "I wouldn't move if I were you, Senator," he warned.

"Don't hurt me..!" he implored

"Then don't make me. You don't want what's in this hypo, believe me."

Chandler didn't need convincing. Yet as startled as he was he never flinched, a behavior that Zack noted as a potential threat to his plan. Using his free hand to push the down button, Zack's whole body filled with contempt as the doors closed and he finally faced his prisoner. The only sounds that could be heard were Chandler's taut, raspy breathing, and the distant whine of elevator machinery.

BACKGROUND ITEM:

LAPD Radio Dispatch Transcript, May 12

All units... be on the lookout for 187 suspect, Zack Raskin. Male Caucasian, blonde hair, age twenty six, six feet-one hundred seventy pounds. Wanted for questioning in three homicides. Los Feliz area residents reported possible 10-66 suspect matching Raskin's description in the area. Approach with caution.

Chapter Nineteen

Angie did not know how long he waited outside the loading dock, only that it seemed like forever. His guilt over not stopping Zack was getting to him. Upon seeing an approaching LAPD squad car, he scrambled to flag it down. "Detective Maulden?"

Brad Maulden nodded soberly as he stepped from the passenger seat, leaving a uniformed officer behind. "I appreciate you calling me, Giambalvo."

"I still can't believe I let him con me," Angie cursed.

But the detective already knew the story. He had heard everything on the phone. "The good news is nobody's reported anything yet," Maulden advised. But the words were barely spoken when he swept his analysis across the rear of the tall building, only to be struck by the prospect of a crime unfolding behind one of the hundreds of windows. Zack was motivated by hatred and no small amount of irrationality, factors that did not bode well.

Angie had the same thought. "Where do we start?" "Your guess is as good as mine."

Inside the cargo elevator Zack had not told Chandler what this was about. Staring at him, he tried to come to terms with being in the presence of the man responsible for so many wrongs. *How could Nicole have ever given herself to a piece of scum like this?*

But Ron Chandler was a politician, Zack remembered. An ambitious political animal. Any decent qualities that he may have possessed had probably long since been subverted by the corrupting influence of power and public adulation, like the movie stars and sports heroes Zack encountered in whom the warm celebrity spotlight incubated nothing but distended egos.

Chandler was unable to take the silence. He had to know why this was happening. He had only been vaguely aware of the irrational letters his office received from society's disenfranchised periphery, those troubled loners who blamed their leaders for everything from imaginary poisons in the water supply to the cancellation of favorite TV programs.

Whatever the grievances of the young man holding him hostage, Chandler thought, his desperation was clear. "Please... tell me what you want..."

Zack continued his glare. "Put your mind to it, S.A."

The senator's eyes flickered.

"You... knew Nicole?"

"I sure did." Zack's thumb quivered at the memory, threatening to push the syringe plunger into the barrel, sending its contents spurting into his neck.

Chandler's mind raced. *What to say? What to do?* Somehow this man knew about the affair. "I... didn't think anyone knew my nickname... besides Nicole," he stammered.

"Maybe the name Zack Raskin rings a bell."

"I'm afraid not," Chandler admitted, desperately wishing he could get a grasp on the situation. Was this a fanatical devotee of Nicole's? A confidant? Whoever Zack was, Chandler knew that his only chance was to keep talking. "I don't remember the name..." he continued, "... but if you were a friend of hers she must have mentioned you."

Zack leaned in hard and the movement cut Chandler off in mid-sentence. "I'm not buying the fucking bullshit. Your goons've been trying to kill me for days!"

The elevator came to a jolting halt and through his confusion Chandler doubted that he had much longer to live. He was at this madman's mercy, if there was any mercy to be had. And he doubted there was.

In the ballroom, a state assemblywoman was doing her best to whip the party faithful into a lather with the usual campaign rhetoric: Senator Chandler's opponents had lost touch with the people, she insisted. They were slaves to special interests, they had inferior records on the issues, and she was certain that nobody could come close to the senator's integrity and family values.

Ted Gimble turned a deaf ear to the blathering and approached Helen Chandler as she was finishing an interview with an attentive male reporter in the Santa Monica Room next to the ballroom.

"There's no question that my husband is the only candidate speaking to women and senior citizens in this election," she was saying. "They know that his economic plan is geared to them and not to the privileged officers of corporations and unions. We've had enough of the elite class running roughshod over the public and when he's elected president, Ron Chandler is going to do something about it."

Gimble whispered in her ear, "We have a problem."

Mrs. Chandler did not miss a beat, turning to the reporter who had listened to every word with such attentiveness. "I'm terribly sorry, David, but there's a phone call I have to take. Do you have enough for your story?"

The reporter smiled and unconsciously adjusted his tie before gushing his assurance that he had more than enough. Helen shook his hand and used his first name once more before exiting with Gimble.

The reporter let out a long contented sigh as he watched her go. *She had called him David.* After all, greatness is one of those qualities that feels almost as gratifying to be near as it does to actually possess.

"What is it?" Helen snarled at Gimble in stark contrast to the conduct she showed the reporter.

"LAPD found Gunter," he reported. "Beaten to death."

The candidate's wife paused for a moment to smile at a group of well-wishers passing on the backstage stairs before responding to the revelation. "Jesus Christ!"

"There's no way to connect him to you, don't worry."

Helen turned to face him. She was as cold as a marble statue. "What went wrong?"

"Raskin," he told her, waiting for the eruption he knew was coming.

"You're telling me *he* killed your man?! A fucking student?"

But that is exactly what Gimble was telling her. "I guess he's tougher than we thought," he gauged impassively, down-playing his embarrassment.

"You guess?!"

"It gets worse. Hotel security says they think a ringer slipped through forty-five minutes ago. With the media."

Helen yanked him into the receiving dock office, which was unoccupied. "I warned you about bungling this."

"It's a rough business, Mrs. Chandler."

"It certainly is," she replied, giving no ground. "It makes me think there were good reasons you were canned from Langley."

He ignored her reference to his departure from the Central Intelligence Agency over his use of enhanced interrogation techniques even Congress did not know about. "Raskin's a wildcard. Spontaneous personality, extremely bright, trained to function under pressure..."

"He's a kid, for Godsakes," she interjected.

"We can't discount anything," he corrected. "His father was a decorated veteran. He obviously acquired some skills."

"Fine, fine," she cut in. "I get the picture."

"One more thing. He spent the night with Branson at the Greek," he added sharply. "The night before she died."

Helen Chandler smiled grimly. "So she was fucking him, too? This's unbelievable!"

"How do you want to handle this?"

Glancing at the media vehicles outside, her political accommodationist instincts clicked in. "Raskin knew to come here," she reasoned. "Gunter must have talked."

"He'd never do that," Gimble assured her. "He was a pro."

"Then the girl told him. Whatever. He knows about Ron, which means Raskin probably blames him for everything."

"What do you want me to do?" Gimble asked.

"Pass a tip to the police. Raskin's been threatening the senator for months but we kept it quiet. Then find that son of a bitch and throw him off the fucking roof."

Down the hall from the receiving dock, Angie was checking

doors near the cargo elevator. Something that he overheard backstage was gnawing at him: there was disarray among campaign workers over Senator Chandler's whereabouts. He had not returned from a trip to the restroom, they were saying. A buzz of concern was beginning to spread.

Detective Maulden approached from the opposite end of the passageway. "Any sign of him?" Angie asked hopefully.

Maulden shook his head. "Or Chandler, either."

NEWS ITEM:

KFI-AM TalkRadio Transcript, May 12

Well folks, it looks like we've got another whack-job running loose on our streets. Remember that medical student who ignited a firestorm of controversy when he challenged the medical examiner's findings in the death of Nicole Branson? His name is Zack Raskin. Well, an anonymous tip has now linked Raskin to threats against Senator Ron Chandler, who's holding a campaign rally in Los Angeles tonight. The police have also confirmed that a bullet-riddled car registered to Raskin was found in Griffith Park last night... near the bodies of three murder victims in the area.

An all-points bulletin has been issued for this guy, so if you happen to know where Zack Raskin can be found, the LAPD would love to hear from you.

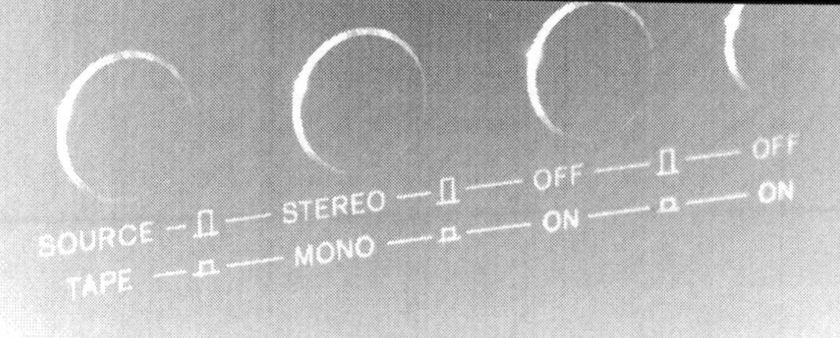

Chapter Twenty

The elevator opened to a subterranean maintenance tunnel. Zack motioned to Chandler, "The ride ends here, Senator."

Chandler hesitated, ever mindful of the syringe at his throat. "Please, I'm begging you... don't hurt me."

"That's almost funny, coming from you," Zack remarked with dripping irony.

"You've got to believe me," Chandler pleaded, "I never sent anyone after you."

"Oh, no. I've just been having a shitty run of bad luck."

Zack shoved the needle closer and its micro-sharp point pricked the senator's skin. "I wouldn't know!" Chandler cried out before lowering his voice. "Can't we talk about this? I might be able to help you."

"And what about my friends, can you help them, too? They're already dead or close to it," Zack grilled. "Isn't it remarkable how nice people keep getting hurt while you cover your miserable ass?!"

Zack nudged him from the elevator. Chandler faltered as they stepped into the dimly lit tube lined with conduit, telephone wiring, fiber optic cable, and water pipes. The air was stale and heavy with a faint petroleum smell.

"What are you talking about?" the senator implored. "Who lost their lives?"

Before answering Zack glanced around to confirm that there were no security cameras in the vicinity. "You probably didn't even blink when Nicole died."

"It broke my heart!" Chandler answered. Then, reading Zack's mistrust he went even further. "Honestly, Mister Raskin... Zack. I loved her."

"You sure had a sick way of showing it."

"My God, why are you doing this?!" Chandler demanded. "If you were a friend of hers you'd know I'm telling the truth!"

"I thought politicians were better actors than that."

"I'm not acting! Why won't you believe me?!"

Zack moved closer, barely able to restrain his rage. "Because you were so moved to hear she was pregnant that you fucking dumped her." Chandler's jaw dropped and his face paled. "... Pregnant?"

An African-American ex-marine with combat experience, Commander Scott Daniels was an impressive SWAT officer. He knew the rules and lived by them; never asking anything of his men that he could not, and would not, do himself. Daniels was known around the LAPD for dogged adherence to his entrenched and undiluted value system.

A young patrolman entered the ground floor hotel security office with Helen Chandler and Ted Gimble, heading straight for Daniels, who was setting up his command post. "There's no sign of Senator Chandler anywhere, Commander."

Helen broke in with an emotional plea. "You've got to find him! Please... Raskin is capable of anything. I tried to warn Ronnie about him when he first came around."

Commander Daniels nodded his terse appraisal before addressing the group of police and hotel security people who were assembled at the door. "I want employees and guests gathered in the California Showroom and secured for screening," Daniels ordered pointing to a large framed hotel floor plan on the wall. "Then sweep every inch of this property. We don't know who else is involved or what they may have planned," he added. "And somebody get me a rundown on this guy, Zack Raskin. He's fixated on Senator Chandler. Do I make myself clear?"

The officers scattered. As Helen flopped into a leather chair, Daniels sat beside her. "Mrs. Chandler, it might be best if you waited in the lobby."

"I understand," she responded in a practiced show of strength. "Thank you for being here, Commander. As you know, we won't have Secret Service protection until after the convention. I know my husband is in good hands with you."

"Thank you, Ma'am."

As Gimble escorted her out, Helen's smug satisfaction

remained hidden behind a practiced mask of wifely devotion.

Backstage in the Los Angeles Ballroom, Angie and Detective Maulden entered to find police ushering people from the area in a methodical fashion. Maulden showed his badge to a female officer. "What's the situation?"

"Some lunatic took Senator Chandler hostage," came the reply.

Angie swallowed. Zack had lost it.

"Who's in charge?" Maulden asked.

"SWAT's on it, sir," she added. "Commander Daniels." Without further discussion she moved off to take up her position at a nearby door.

Angie traded sour looks with Maulden. With a SWAT operation unfolding, their chances of preventing something terrible from happening were rapidly deteriorating.

Zack pushed Chandler as they continued through the tunnel, the syringe still poised. "Keep moving or you'll be history before you could ask for a recount."

Chandler once again tried to reason with him. "Please, I know you're upset, but you have to believe me... Nicole never told me about the baby."

"Come off it, Ron. It's over," Zack snapped back. "The cover-up, the killings..."

"I don't know anything about those!"

Zack shoved him hard. "Sandy Phillips." Chandler reacted vacantly and Zack couldn't believe it. "You didn't even know her fucking name?!"

"I don't know anything about her," his prisoner replied.

"Griffith Park... ring any bells?" Chandler could only shake his head. "What about Dennie Seifert? Nicole's road manager. He took a bullet between the eyes."

"Oh, my God..." Chandler came back. "You can't think I'd have anything to do with that!"

Zack grabbed him by his lapel and spun him around. "I saw one of your thugs on stage with you, Senator. I saw him myself."

Chandler's mind reeled. "On stage...?" He paused as the image came to him. "Ted Gimble... he's not a thug... he's just..."

"... The one who does your dirty work," Zack finished sharply, "so you can stand here pretending to have no idea what I've been through."

Chandler stared. He had no idea who Zack was or what he had been through.

A police technician studied multi-screen images of fifty cameras on three large monitors in the hotel security office. The displays presented simultaneous surveillance views of the Century Plaza's primary corridors, stairwells, service areas, exits, grounds, and parking facilities. Police teams could be seen as they cautiously advanced through the complex.

Commander Daniels approached the technician, a prim female officer. "Let me see playback of the loading dock."

"Yes, sir," she replied as she typed commands into her computer keyboard. "We've got two angles."

The picture in one of the monitors abruptly changed from a composite image of the parking garage to a grainy accelerated-motion view of the backstage hallway door leading to the loading dock. The exaggerated scurrying of people in and out of the door as if in a sequence from an old Keystone Cops movie, an effect that might have seemed comical if so much was not at stake.

A digital time-of-day display in the corner of the video frame changed so fast that it would have been impossible for an untrained civilian to follow it. But the officer knew precisely what she was looking for. With the push of a button, the playback reverted to normal speed, revealing Zack slipping into the television crew as it passed the policeman outside.

Daniels scrutinized the screen. "Again."

Without further instruction, she typed a few more commands and re-played the image of Zack, this time in slow motion.

Daniels reached for the keyboard spacebar and pressed it to freeze the image. This was not the crack-crazed perp he usually encountered these days, a disgruntled employee, or a head case who was unwisely released from a mental hospital. And it certainly was not the foreign terrorist he originally feared it might be. This guy was different. Daniels knew that if he could figure out what made him tick he might be able to save the senator's life.

He turned to the officer. "What's the other one?"

"Backstage hall, wide-angle," she reported while typing commands into the computer.

Daniels pulled up a chair as images of the hotel kitchen vanished from an adjacent monitor to reveal a downward shot of Chandler moving away from camera through the stagehands and rows of folded tables and chairs.

"That's Senator Chandler," the technician informed him, pointing to the screen. Moments later, Zack could be seen entering the lower portion of the frame. "That's your man following him... there," she added.

Daniels watched, riveted, as Zack closed in on Chandler, periodically glancing over his shoulder. "This's unbelievable," he muttered.

"It gets better, sir."

Daniels sipped the remainder of his can of Sprite, too involved with the unfolding soundless drama to care that it had lost its carbonation. On the screen just inches from his face a young man was mouthing something to a candidate for President of The United States and then with a single body check he was shoving him out of frame.

"My God, we got the grab?!" Daniels exclaimed. "Where does that put them?"

"Cargo elevator," she surmised. "Runs top to bottom."

Just then Craig Komado, the chief of security at the Century Plaza, approached Daniels as he consulted a hotel map. His anxiety over what was taking place in his hotel was evident. "Commander, there's a Detective Maulden from Westside Division to see you. He's got a Mister Giambalvo with him, a friend of Raskin's."

Daniels perked at the news. "Send them in."

Komado motioned to a security guard and Maulden soon appeared with Angie, who carried a stack of files under his arm. Daniels met them as they entered.

"What have you got for me, Detective?" he asked while extending his hand.

Maulden shook Daniel's hand before motioning towards Angie. "This's Angelo Giambalvo, Zack Raskin's partner at Willis Ambulance. He knows why Raskin's doing this and I can vouch for the fact that the kid isn't the nutbag you think he is."

"He abducted a United States Senator," Daniels countered. "I just watched the playback."

Maulden nodded. It was only a few hours ago that he, too, failed to listen to the story. "Raskin came to me yesterday with these files and they explain a lot."

Angie handed the stack to Daniels. "I can fill in the rest," he said as Daniels looked at him. "Somebody's trying to stop Zack from investigating the death of a friend. It's gotten pretty hairy for him and he's doing what he can to survive."

"And of course the best way to do that is by assaulting a presidential candidate," Daniels added sharply.

Angie tried to clarify his point. "He's scared, Commander. People have lost their lives as a result of this. His reasoning's all mixed up."

Daniels was not moved. "They also tell me there are three homicides tied to him."

Maulden joined in to reinforce their tempering characterization. "He's a good kid. Outstanding medical student, no priors."

The Commander pointed to the video images that so graphically incriminated Zack. "It's a little late for that, don't you think?"

In a service alcove at the end of the tunnel, Zack pulled Chandler to a halt. "Stop here." Chandler had learned to obey his captor's commands and he stood in place, awaiting the next installment of his unfolding fate.

Making certain that the syringe remained firmly pressed against the senator's throat, Zack reached into his pocket for a pair of pliers. "Don't move," he warned as he used his free hand to break the lock on a metal control box.

"What are you doing?" Chandler asked nervously.

Zack handed him a tag that had been attached to the box. "Buying time," he answered.

Chandler glanced at the tag:

VIDEO SECURITY SYSTEM
Property of Century Plaza Hotel
Do Not Tamper With Under Penalty Of Law

Zack used a utility knife to cut the coaxial cables inside the box before shoving Chandler forward. "Keep moving, Ron."

"I'm not getting anything," the officer complained as she adjusted the controls one more time. "Video's gone."

"Everywhere?"

"Yes, sir."

Commander Daniels stared at the blank monitors and barked an order to one of his men. "Send a team to check it out. And notify all units that we're flying blind."

Then Daniels turned his attention back to Angie and Detective Maulden. "While we're waiting, gentlemen, why don't you give me the headlines on Raskin?"

"Can I at least ask where you're taking me?" Chandler asked

as Zack guided him up a stairwell.

"Someplace we can talk," Zack answered.

"I've already told you, I thought Gimble was legitimate... he's former CIA. He was thoroughly vetted."

Before Zack could refute the statement, he heard a clattering of distant footsteps and shoved Chandler against the wall. The syringe remained tightly in place as he whispered, "One word and you're gone... I've already killed one man, understand?"

Chandler nodded fearfully and the two men remained still as a SWAT team entered the stairwell from an upper floor. Their combat boots descended the metal stairs with staccato precision and Zack held his breath as the footsteps vibrated closer and closer. He guessed that there were five men, though it was impossible to tell. Nor could he even be sure where they were.

Was it one floor away? Three?

He'd know soon enough. The question was what to do if SWAT burst upon them. Dropping the syringe and giving up made the most sense, though that would mean never hearing a detailed confession from Chandler. On the other hand, continuing to hold Chandler hostage would probably get him killed.

But then as quickly as the footsteps had entered Zack's metal and concrete shelter, they departed one floor above. Zack and Chandler jointly sighed in relief. Neither was prepared for what might have happened in a stairwell confrontation.

"Let's go," Zack whispered. "Not a sound." They proceeded upward, past the floor the SWAT team was searching. Zack paused to listen for any trace of danger.

Chandler decided to try establishing some sort of rapport. "The police are everywhere, you won't escape... I can help you."

"I'm not sure I want to escape," Zack came back.

Chandler swallowed hard as his apprehension intensified. "You're going to kill me, aren't you."

Zack thought a moment before answering. "That depends on whether or not you tell me the truth."

By the time Angie and Lieutenant Maulden finished telling

Commander Daniels Zack's story they had omitted nothing. Everything they knew about him spilled out as if his life depended on it, which it did. From his affair with Nicole to the partnership with Sandy Phillips and the fake autopsy report, from *The National Enquirer* headline to the attempts on his life, and from the attack on Doug McKay to the deaths of Sandy, Dennie Seifert, Park Ranger Darvell Sims, Gunter Strauss, and Doctors Takahashi and Glasner, Daniels listened to it all. Angie was beginning to think they had found a sympathetic audience.

But it was the allegation of Nicole's pregnancy with Ron Chandler's child that dashed any such hope. "Mrs. Chandler says Raskin's been making threats on the senator's life for months," Daniels declared.

"That's not true," Angie shot back.

"Why would she lie?"

"I didn't say she lied. She's mistaken."

"Her security man backs it up."

"Then they must have him mixed up with somebody else," Angie argued. "Zack didn't even know about Chandler and Nicole until a few hours ago."

"That's right," added Detective Maulden. "Nothing that I came across in Raskin's background indicates any association with the senator.

Daniels dug out a copy of *The Enquirer* from the file and grimaced. "This tabloid shit doesn't exactly bolster his credibility."

"That's what I thought, too," Maulden divulged, hoping to use his police credentials to build a bridge. "But I was wrong."

"About a lot of things," Daniels came back. "Mrs. Chandler mentioned Raskin by name."

Angie was emphatic. "Commander, look, I was with the guy when he learned about Chandler's relationship with Nicole. We made that discovery together. No way was Zack threatening him."

Just then, the video technician called out from her control station. "Commander, we're back on-line."

Daniels rushed over to the monitors and was soon joined by Angie and Maulden. "The video feed was sabotaged in the maintenance tunnel," she reported.

The screens were once again filled with images of hotel sectors. "And what do you know..." Daniels muttered after a long silence, "There they are."

Angie and Maulden inched forward and saw what Daniels was referring to: Zack and Chandler could be seen entering a storage room crammed with mountains of furniture and hotel equipment. Daniels picked up a radio handset. "Command to all units. Raskin is holding Senator Chandler in a storeroom," he said before pausing to check a note pad. "Code 100. Tango Nineteenth floor, south end. Suspect is armed and dangerous."

The sonorous intonations of a man who sounded like an airline pilot came back in clipped response. "Roger that. Teams are moving into position."

Daniels manipulated a joystick that zoomed in on Zack. The scene looked ominous, indeed—a disheveled man holding a syringe at Chandler's neck. Even more troubling to Angie and Maulden were the pictures on the adjacent monitors, where SWAT units could be seen converging on the location:

Fire teams moved across the tower roof...

Pairs of officers advanced vigilantly down hallways...

Squads moved up stairwells...

A trio of men rappelled from an upper window along the exterior tower wall...

Angie turned away from the images. There was nothing more that he could do. He had called Detective Maulden and pleaded with Commander Daniels. He had begged Zack not to do this. The one thing he could not do was stand by and watch as the police tactical response progressed.

It was almost over.

NEWS ITEM:

KNX NewsRadio Transcript, May 13

There's a major Sig-Alert underway in Century City in this early morning hour, encompassing Beverly Glen Boulevard and Avenue of the Americas to the east and west, as well as Santa Monica Boulevard and Pico to the north and south. LAPD is keeping all traffic, including pedestrians, out of the area. Though details are sketchy, sources at the Century Plaza Hotel report that a deranged man has taken Senator Ron Chandler hostage. SWAT teams are said to be conducting a manhunt throughout the hotel complex.

Rush hour promises to be a difficult time for anyone trying to get to work in that area.

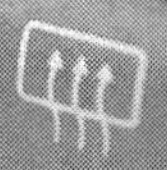

Chapter Twenty-One

If anyone at the Hyatt Regency Century Plaza Hotel had paid attention they would have seen a magnificent sunrise that morning. A series of brush fires north of the city had provided enough airborne smoke and ash to create a truly dazzling display of colors across the horizon. It was the stuff of great postcards.

Of course, nobody at the hotel or in the swarm of television and law enforcement helicopters overhead was interested in sunrises or postcard opportunities. As daylight arrived in Los Angeles the whole country was focused on a distraught medical student who continued to hold Ron Chandler captive in a storage room for reasons the senator professed not to understand.

"Zack, please listen to me..." he prefaced in another attempt to break through. "I meant what I said... I didn't know Ted Gimble was dirty. And Nicole never told me about the baby."

Zack glared back. "Why wouldn't she tell you?"

"I don't know, maybe she wanted to spare me something she didn't think I could handle."

"And you sure as hell couldn't."

"I'm being honest with you."

"You wouldn't know honesty if you choked on it."

Chandler considered what to say next. The crisis was not going well, but at least they were talking. "She and I agreed to end the relationship for the good of the campaign..." He trailed as Zack cynically rolled his eyes. "She believed in me," he finally argued. "More than I believed in myself. She said the country needed me but what she never understood was how much I needed her."

Chandler paused as a wave of regret filling him. Zack studied him warily. He was morbidly intrigued by how far a soulless man would go to save himself. "Go on..."

Chandler's eyes glistened. "Saying good-bye was the worst thing I've ever been through. I would've spent my life with her if I could have, if she would've let me." He wiped away a tear. "If you knew her like I did then you'd know what I'm talking about."

Zack reacted and Chandler read it immediately. He had seen

it in himself many times, just as Glen Conway had when Zack came to see him. "You do know what I'm talking about," he observed. "You loved Nicole, too."

Zack did not answer. He was unprepared for a sympathetic Ron Chandler. Since the moment he learned of the pregnancy every cell inside him had been geared towards hating this man.

What was he supposed to do now?

The exchange was interrupted when a phone rang in the storage room.

Commander Daniels and Detective Maulden were watching a security monitor as Zack ushered the senator to the service phone on the wall by the elevator. Zack did not know the surveillance camera mounted among the matrix of exposed ceiling pipes was operational.

Angie was pacing in the background as he watched his friend pick up the phone. Daniels spoke first. "Zack, don't hang up. This is Scott Daniels of the LAPD. We have to talk."

Zack was not sure how they found him, but he was not surprised. "I already tried talking to you guys."

Daniels glanced at Maulden. "You talked to Detective Maulden, but you never talked to me."

"How'd you know about Maulden?"

"He's here with me. So's your friend, Angelo Giambalvo. They're worried about you, Zack."

"Did they tell you what this's all about?"

"Yes, they did. But I'd rather hear it from you."

Zack glanced out the window and caught a glimpse of a SWAT sharpshooter in the condo tower next door. "Shit!" he blurted as he slammed the phone down.

Daniels cursed, never taking his concentration from the screen. Maulden shoved the files across the console at him. "Maybe this'd be a good time for you to catch up on your reading, Commander."

Daniels was not listening, however. He was absorbed by the striking image on one of the other monitors, that of a SWAT team attaching plastique explosives to the outside hinges of the storage room door. One way or another he was going to get Senator Chandler out of there.

Zack closed the drapes with his free hand while the syringe remained poised to strike his captive with the other. But the needle was no longer a weapon intended for Chandler. It was nothing more than a relic of assumptions-past. Zack's mind was spinning, searching for equilibrium in the information he never anticipated.

S.A. was not guilty!

Chandler was a man, like Zack, who fell in love with Nicole Branson. Yet so much of Zack's ability to outlast his ordeal had been predicated on the idea of revenge. One revelation and conclusion had been systematically built upon another, and now the truth was collapsing that structure. Exhaustion and grief added to his bewilderment. From seeing people who were not there to faulty deductive reasoning, Zack could no longer count on himself to distinguish what was accurate and what was not.

It scared the hell out of him.

"All right, I believe you," he eventually said. Withdrawing the syringe from Chandler's throat and pocketing it, he began to pace.

The tension withdrew from the senator's body. "Thank you," he muttered simply.

"Save it," Zack added. "If she found something to love about you, the least I can do is trust her judgment."

"I understand," Chandler offered, still uncertain about what might happen to him.

Zack shut off the lights, plunging the two men into gloomy isolation as he studied Chandler in the slivers of morning sunlight that leaked through openings in the drapes. "The question is who wants you elected enough to kill for it? Gimble didn't think this up by himself. The CIA?"

Chandler had been consumed by that very point. "I'm one of their biggest critics on Capitol Hill. I can't imagine who'd do such a thing." And he meant it. Ron Chandler respected the law and the obligations of public office. He was one of a dying breed of politicians, some said, who actually still believed in duty and honor.

Chandler had also believed in the sanctity of marriage, which made his relationship with Nicole every bit as troubling for him as it was wonderful. Loving her was the only time he had ever crossed the line of respectability. And while another man might have rationalized his actions with the bitter truth of his toxic relationship with Helen, it was not in him to do so without guilt. That was not who he was.

"Names, Senator. I need names," Zack reiterated, bringing Chandler back to the subject. "Somebody went to a lot of trouble to wipe the slate clean. They descended on Nicole the moment she collapsed and bought off a pathologist to fake the autopsy. That wasn't easy. Then they sent thugs to bury anybody who might know the truth about the baby. Who has that kind of clout?"

Chandler tried to conjure up an image of his database, which held a substantial list of names. "I can't think of anyone."

"Don't you owe her more than that?"

"I'm trying..."

"Try harder," Zack pressed. "What about your friends in Washington?"

"There's nobody," Chandler admitted. "If anything a lot of people there would love to see me fail."

"I can't believe that."

The candidate looked at him sadly. "I'm not the only one who wants to be President."

Angie fidgeted in the security office. Commander Daniels was absorbed with the strategic placement of his men for a rescue action, so he had still not read the files that Maulden and Angie had given him. That meant his comprehension of Zack's motives was woefully incomplete.

Angie and Maulden agreed that for Zack to have any hope of making it through this, Daniels would first have to grasp the conspiracy he was up against. He would have to relate to the fragile mental state of a desperate young man he knew nothing about. Only then could he see Zack as a victim of a crime, rather than the perpetrator of one.

Maulden was on the phone with LAPD headquarters in an effort to find someone who might designate him as principal negotiator. Angie and Maulden believed that if anyone could diffuse the crisis with Zack, it was one of them. Unfortunately, the abduction of a United States Senator and presidential candidate was a hot-button issue. Any number of Los Angeles police careers might hinge on the outcome of this situation, so Maulden was unable to find an administrator willing to push aside a decorated SWAT commander for a journeyman detective.

Then at the height of Maulden's frustration the female officer called out from the console. "Commander, the window's opening!"

Maulden saw Daniels rotate towards the monitor where Zack could be seen pacing in the darkened storage room, moving away from Chandler, his guard lowered.

"That's what we've been waiting for!" Daniels barked. He gripped his radio and spoke the words that Angie and Maulden had been dreading, "Command to extraction teams... breach and clear!"

Angie and Maulden were horrified. But the protestations they unleashed were lost in the commotion that flowed from Daniels' order. Police and hotel security people rushed from the room while a cluster of others squeezed around the monitors. Angie and Maulden could only watch as the door to the storage room was blown from its frame by a controlled explosion and SWAT teams rushed into the smoke-filled opening with their weapons at the ready.

It was nothing less than a miracle that Zack made it out of the chaos unscathed. In the simultaneous events following the explosion, two decisions that he previously made resulted in his astounding evacuation. The first came when he saw the sharpshooter on the condominium tower and closed the drapes. His newly honed instinct for survival had conditioned him for the possibility of a police assault and he wisely decided that his only chance would be to kill the lights, thereby shifting the probabilities in his favor.

The second critical decision came earlier, when he left the doors to the cargo elevator open. During the SWAT assault, he used the cover of darkness to dive into the elevator. Even the precise weapons fire of experts failed to stop him. The elevator doors closed before anyone could stop him.

The one hitch in events that did occur was not his fault: a bullet intended for Zack found its way to Senator Chandler and tore through his shoulder.

In the disorder of the blitz Angie and Maulden had no way of knowing what was going on. Angie flew into Commander Daniels' face. "What the hell are you morons doing!"

Daniels never took his eyes off the monitors as he gruffly called to a subordinate, "Somebody get this guy out of here."

Three stocky policemen responded, pulling Angie off his feet as they headed for the exit. Maulden was quick to intervene with Daniels. "We could have ended this peacefully. You didn't have to jump the gun."

The video of the storage room returned to the security monitors as the lights were switched on. Daniels assessed the situation before turning to Maulden. "Chandler's breathing, isn't he?"

Inside the elevator, Zack's heart pounded and his head ached. His body trembled as he wrestled with what just happened. Chandler had been shot; he heard the senator yell as the elevator doors closed. But somehow Zack was still alive.

He glanced at the digital indicator counting the floors as the car descended, *Nineteen... Eighteen... Seventeen.* Sooner or later he would reach bottom and the police waiting below would not take any chances. He could almost see their fingers twitching on the triggers of their weapons in anticipation of his arrival. Or they would stop the elevator and trap him between floors, guaranteeing his capture.

Truth be known, part of him did not mind. He so badly wanted this to be over that practically any ending would be welcome. And with Chandler's innocence now known to him, the investigation was in real jeopardy. The killers were still at large.

Soon Zack regained his purpose. He could not let them get away with it. *But where the hell was Nicole when he needed her? He needed answers! Then he remembered that she could not help him. She did not exist. And she was gone from his life.*

Zack needed time. He was running out of floors. Guiding his hand to the elevator controls, he pushed *Emergency Stop* and brought the car to a halt between the eighth and ninth floors. Then glancing at the ceiling panel designed for emergency use, he knew there was only one way out. A moment later he pushed himself up from a metal handrail and forced himself through the hatch.

Rising into an uneasy stance against the car's vertical guide rail, Zack found the elevator shaft dark, dank, and dirty. His stomach churned anxiously. One false move meant plunging eight floors down. Having once helped handle the body bag of a man who took a similar plunge, he was petrified.

Gripping tightly onto the greasy metal sling that connected the car to the building's hoist cables, he looked at the thick lines belonging to another elevator across the shaft and swallowed at what he had to do, which was attempt a vertical slide for life. As he tore the sleeves from his sport coat to wrap his hands, he reassured himself that he had been doing things that he was unqualified for since this nightmare began. But now here was something that he was actually trained for. Everyone at Willis Ambulance Service had to practice rappelling and slides in case they were ever called to a crumbling high-rise building after an earthquake or found themselves trapped in one. Thank God, Mrs. Willis believed in preparing for every eventuality.

Those hoist cables in the darkness would be his salvation, if he could jump that far. He stretched his stiffening legs. Somewhere overhead the sound of SWAT teams opening elevator doors on adjacent floors resounded.

It was time. Dropping into a low squat, he concentrated on the cables dangling several yards away. His muscles twitched in anticipation of what was about to be required of them. "Here goes nothing," he muttered.

Springing up and out, Zack launched himself with every bit of strength in him. A fraction of a second later he narrowly seized one of the lines with his left hand. The momentum of his leap was greater than he anticipated and it was all he could do to grab on with his other hand. Hanging precariously in the open shaft, Zack winced at the realization that he nearly overshot his goal. *Fuck!*

Then, after doing what he could to gather himself, he began his long, slow descent into the void.

Senator Chandler struggled to concentrate as his gunshot wound sapped his ability to think. He had no recollection of being rescued, yet now he was outside on what seemed to be a loading dock being put into an ambulance.

"Helen..." he whispered in a weak voice that frightened him. *Damn it, couldn't he even speak anymore?!*

"I'm here, darling," she comforted. "They're taking you to the hospital."

She nodded to the paramedics to proceed. Chandler grasped her hand with urgency. He was drifting in and out. "... Don't let them... hurt him."

"Nobody's going to hurt you. Don't worry," she replied, impatiently hoping the paramedics would get moving.

"No!" he protested. "Don't... hurt Raskin."

Helen shifted so the paramedics and others nearby wouldn't hear. "I said don't worry about it."

Chandler's mouth was chalky. Panic-stricken at his inability to communicate, he summoned everything he could to speak. "Raskin is innocent... someone... killing people." A paramedic passed by and Chandler shouted out to him, "You must stop... it!"

The paramedic was waved off by Helen, who glared at her husband. "Goddamn it, Ron. You'll ruin everything."

"What...?"

"The police will handle Raskin. I made sure of it."

"But you can't..."

"He's a threat to the campaign," she said tersely. "To us."

Chandler struggled to focus, but even through his fading faculties he understood at long last. "It's... you?"

She blinked innocently. "Why darling, I don't know what you're talking about."

"You're... behind this..." he wept. "Nicole..."

Helen stared bitterly. "Did you think I'd let that whore destroy my plans?" She turned his head to face hers. "I've worked too hard for that."

Chandler was aghast. "My God, Helen..." And then he passed out.

Climbing from the ambulance, she explained to the paramedics that she was needed in the search for the madman who kidnapped her husband. As they pulled away from the loading dock, she stood alone, satisfied that things were working out quite well.

But not as well as she assumed.

Hiding in the recesses of a service door to the nearby elevator shaft, Zack had heard everything. He was wearing the LAPD windbreaker of a policeman whose unconscious body he stashed in a laundry bin, and although he had not wanted to hurt a cop, it was unavoidable. Fortunately, he was able to sneak up on the unsuspecting rookie and subdue him with a carefully applied carotid chokehold. A roll of masking tape that he found would keep the officer from calling out when he regained consciousness.

The sickening information that he overheard on the loading dock was still sinking in as Helen headed for the entrance. Zack did his best to quell his hatred as she passed the door. Opening it, he grabbed her before she could see who he was. Her scream for help was muffled beneath the greasy fabric of his wrapped hand. Glancing over his shoulder, he confirmed that no one had seen a thing.

Zack could hardly contain his fury as he shoved Helen Chandler into a corner of the noisy elevator equipment room. He felt like his heart had burst and discharged a tidal wave of venom into his throat. But here he was, staring into the face of the person who was accountable for everything. She had admitted it. She was the mastermind of Nicole's, Sandy's, and Doug's fates, among so many others.

Helen Chandler's face was contorted with unbridled disdain. "What are you going to do, kill me, too?"

"You know better than that," he countered, still adjusting to the dispassionate way she had explained herself to her husband.

Helen's leer narrowed. "The police know all about psychotics like you..."

"Do they?"

"... Fixated on men of power because you'll never achieve anything on your own."

"Stuff it, lady," he snapped. "I heard everything you said out there. And soon everybody else will, too."

"The hell they will." She lunged at him with a vicious flurry of kicks and screams.

Zack slugged her hard across the jaw and she crumpled to the concrete floor. The feeling of his fist connecting with her was amazingly satisfying. So was the sight of blood spurting from her thin, cruel mouth.

He nudged her with his foot to confirm that she was out cold. "That was for Sandy and Doug, you bitch," he vented. But he did not have time to gloat. It would not be long before the security staff came looking for her. Using her expensive designer scarf as a gag, he slung her over his shoulder in the fireman's carry that he used so many times as an EMT.

Then he headed straight for the stairs to the hotel sub-basement.

NEWS ITEM:

CNN SITUATION ROOM TRANSCRIPT, May 13

WOLF BLITZER (INTERVIEWER):

Dr. Habib, sources on scene have now confirmed that Senator Chandler was rescued by the Los Angeles Police just moments ago. But his kidnapper is still on the loose. Is there anything that can be done to prevent such acts from taking place in the future?

DR. OMAR HABIB (TERRORISM EXPERT):

Unfortunately, no, Wolf. While a combination of informants, infiltration, and surveillance can often contain terrorist organizations from achieving their goals, there is little that can be done when the culprit is a disenfranchised loner, as Mister Raskin seems to be. Individuals with extreme views and violent tendencies are nearly impossible to monitor in a free society.

BLITZER:

That isn't very comforting, professor.

HABIB:

It's reality. Thank God the LAPD was successful in this particular intervention.

POLICE LINE - DO NO

CHAPTER TWENTY-TWO

Commander Daniels was not a happy man. One of his men had wounded Senator Chandler while the kidnapper managed to escape. Now the senator's wife was missing and the media was going ballistic over one unsubstantiated rumor after another. Although SWAT teams were combing all rooms and various meeting spaces in the hotel, the only two things that Daniels could be sure of were that Raskin was still in the building and it would not be long before every politician in the city showed up to pronounce his misgivings about the police action that allowed such a travesty to take place.

For some unknown reason, nothing about Mrs. Chandler or Zack Raskin had yet shown up on the video system.

Zack carried Helen Chandler deeper into the complex, moving carefully to avoid security cameras. The facility had been cleared, so the long tiled corridors and immense service areas were unearthly in their emptiness. Like a ghost town where the hurried departure of its inhabitants left so many tasks unfinished, it was as if workers mysteriously vanished where they stood or sat. Mindful of SWAT teams that were surely searching for him, Zack kept to the shadows as he moved past storage cages filled with shelves of cleaning solutions, paper goods, and cartons of tiny shampoo bottles awaiting their call to duty.

Eventually, he arrived in the laundry department, where a silent row of twenty-foot high washing machines reminded him of over-sized comedy props from the old movie *Honey, I Shrunk The Kids.*

As he entered the unoccupied hotel kitchen, he snatched a handful of saltine crackers from a counter and shoved them into his police windbreaker. The reflection of an approaching SWAT unit in a hallway collision-avoidance mirror alerted him in time to slip out another exit. The door to the physical plant stairway clicked shut seconds before the police arrived.

The basement where Zack and his hostage were deposited was an environment quite different from the elegant facilities that hotel patrons normally see. Here rows of giant turbines roared with deafening power. A network of overhead catwalks linked the myriad ventilator pipes and machines with control valves and maintenance panels.

In the security office, Angie and Detective Maulden returned to study the monitors for any sign of Zack. Commander Daniels was on the penthouse floor with one of his teams and his video technician was preoccupied with a phone call, giving Zack's allies their only opportunity to get ahead of the manhunt.

It was an opportunity that they appreciated. Maulden could well anticipate the conclusion of the unfolding events and Zack's chances were slim. He knew that SWAT's need to redeem itself after wounding Chandler and the subsequent disappearance of his wife meant that little regard would be given to taking the suspect alive. Bagging Zack Raskin at this point would look good in anyone's record.

Angie and Maulden hoped that if they could locate him first then they might be able to take the preemptive measures needed to save him. Whatever those were.

Angie sipped from a bottle of water. His corneas burned from staring at too many television pictures, but his dedication to watching them paid off when he flinched at something in the corner of one of the monitors. Not sure what he was seeing at first, he leaned in for a closer look and verified that the tiny image in the background of the frame was Zack advancing through the hotel sub-basement. And it was Helen Chandler he was carrying over his shoulder.

Despite his elation, Angie was careful to avoid alerting security people moving through the room. Casually taking another sip of water, he signaled Maulden with a tap on the arm. Maulden turned to see Angie nod towards the screen—and what he saw made him smile. *Found him!*

Maulden slowly withdrew from the monitor while Angie

made certain to knock his water bottle onto the video controller. The spilling liquid shorted everything out with a furious electrical sputter. The technician's anger at Angie's carelessness was made clear as he was promptly banished from the room.

But the objective had been accomplished. As Angie joined Maulden in the hallway they shared a grim smile of victory. The LAPD would not be seeing Zack on their security monitors anytime soon.

Maulden led the way as he and Angie stepped onto the escalator. While it was an indirect route to the sub-basement, it was one that would avoid an untimely encounter with Commander Daniels.

Maulden's cell phone rang and he answered with a brusque, "Maulden." He listened briefly, nodding soberly. "Thanks for the heads-up. I appreciate it." Then the detective turned to Angie for their first conversation since finding Zack on the monitor. "We found Sandy Phillips, in a dumpster."

"Zack's gonna want to know about this," Angie concluded.

Maulden held his look. "Are you sure?"

"What do you mean?"

"This could really send him over the edge. Forget what we told Daniels, your boy's pretty far gone."

"He'll listen to me," Angie asserted.

"What if he won't? People can only take so much stress. They think things they'd never ordinarily think and they do things they'd never do."

"I never thought it would get that far," Angie told him with rising fear.

"Do we have a Plan B?" Maulden asked. Angie thought about that, frantically trying to come up with something. Then it dawned on him. "Yeah! There's a professor at UCLA... what's her name...?" His mind floundered, frustrating him. "Damn it, I know this... he talked to her about Nicole. Doc... what the hell is it... Doc..." His voice trailed before the name precipitously came to him. "Sandberg! Doc Sandberg!"

Maulden was already hitting an auto-dial number on his phone. "I need a ten-twenty on one Doctor Sandberg," he informed a subordinate. "UCLA Medical School professor, female, first name unknown. I need her at the Century Plaza immediately."

After propping Helen Chandler against a structural pillar, Zack was tying her hands and feet with masking tape when her eyes fluttered open. Her confusion was immediately superseded by total fury, though the scarf in her mouth prevented her from making much noise.

"Well, Mrs. Chandler," Zack began. "Here we are. I wonder what Nicole would want me to do with you." He examined her reaction to the name. "She was kind and caring and full of love, you know. And she sure as hell didn't deserve what you did to her. Neither did my friends Sandy or Doug. But you, you miserable piece of shit..." he paused, taking the syringe from his pocket, "... you deserve anything that happens."

Her eyes widened as she concentrated on the hypodermic, tracking the sharp needle waving inches from her face. Obscenities spewed from beneath her gag.

"What's that? You got something to say?"

He removed the scarf, unleashing an explosion of outrage. "You goddamned punk! Who do you think you are! You're out of your mind if you expect to get away with this!"

"I already have," he pointed out.

"They'll find you."

He shrugged. "The question is will they find you?"

Suddenly, the equipment around them stopped and the lights went off as the room plummeted into inky silence.

"What's happening...?" she asked anxiously.

A moment later a patchwork of emergency lights in the space went on. As his eyes adjusted to the subdued surroundings, he put it together. "The police shut off the power. Guess they think it limits my options," he reasoned before turning to her. "But it doesn't."

Helen tried not to look as terrified as she was. "What are you going to do?"

"I was thinking about shooting you up with a pentobarbital

sodium injection," he answered, savoring the description. "Barbiturates depress the sensory cortex and they do a real job on your ability to move. An overdose would stop your heart almost immediately... but a small dose would just paralyze you like you paralyzed my roommate. And then I could just toss you in the incinerator." He pointed across the floor. "It's right over there."

She glanced at the metal door. "You wouldn't dare...!" she seethed.

"Or I could just deposit you right now. That sounds like justice to me," he continued, grabbing her arm and dragging her across the cement.

Helen screamed, "Please, don't! No!"

Zack paused. "Why shouldn't I? After all you've done."

"I did what I had to do."

He could hardly believe his ears. "You had to kill people and throw Doug off a balcony? You fucking bitch..." Resuming his grasp, he dragged her a few more feet when she managed to wrestle her arm free.

"Let me go!!!!!" she yelled. "You insignificant nobody! Who are you to interfere with my destiny!"

The reference stopped him cold. "*Your* destiny."

Helen was unaccustomed to anyone having more control than her, but due to her current circumstances she was compelled to calm down. "Ron Chandler is the most important man on Capitol Hill," she disclosed. "In a few months he'll be in the Oval Office."

"That's his destiny, not yours."

Her smirk was bitter. "Don't make me laugh."

"I won't, believe me."

"I've done everything for him," she went on. "He's a product I'm selling, that's all."

"Nicole got in the way, is that it?" he concluded.

"My husband knocked up his mistress and I cleaned up the mess."

It was all Zack could do not to inject her right then and there. But he had come too far to end this without answers. "How'd you pull it off?"

"I'm good at my job," she gloated.

"Tell me or we're done." He held the syringe up for emphasis.

She eyed the needle with fear, but despite the obvious jeopardy savored what she was about to tell him. "I knew she was pregnant. That was easy. My people were in place to make sure she never delivered."

"You were going to kill her?!" he sputtered.

A stony smile appeared at the edges of her mouth as the next sentence formed. "Mother Nature did it for me." She saw the ire rising in Zack and relished it. "My husband got a second chance."

Zack bit his lip. "What about Sandy and Doug?" he asked, tasting blood.

"Who?" she asked indifferently.

His hand quaked as he clutched the syringe. He had already killed once. Would a second offense make him feel worse? Certainly there was a case to be made for equity. This woman brought nothing to the world but misery and death. To her Sandy and Doug were collateral damage and they did not even have names.

Zack relived the sensation of bludgeoning his assailant in the alley and considered how much more simple the press of a calibrated plunger would be. Helen Chandler's circulatory system would do the rest.

Then it would all be over but his capture, which was a certainty anyway. Unless SWAT blew him away first. If they did arrest him the worst that would probably happen would be life in a psychiatric facility, which meant the onerous sedation prescribed to the criminally insane. Zack reflected on the concept of induced tranquility, of perpetual escape from the torture of knowing what happened to his friends.

Frankly, it sounded appealing.

The Century Plaza Hotel is located just a few minutes from Linda Sandberg's Santa Monica home, which is where she was when the police called. Within twenty minutes she was being briefed by one of Maulden's men in a squad car speeding along Wilshire Boulevard through Westwood and Beverly Hills. Upon arriving she was met by Detective Maulden, who escorted her to the lower stairs where Angie was waiting. The trio then descended through the sequence of sub-basements.

Soon Angie and Maulden were moving with the professor through twisting walkways that reminded Angie of the catacombs in Rome. But that was an image associated with death and he tried to force such thoughts from his mind. He looked for inspiration from his hero, Steve McQueen, but for the first time in his life he was unable to even remember what McQueen looked like.

"Zack, it's Angie..." he called into the dimly lit recesses of the power plant. "I know you're down here."

"He's going to kill me!" Helen's voice shot back from an unseen location.

"Is that right, kid?" Angie asked apprehensively. "Are you gonna kill her?"

"She doesn't deserve to live after what she's done." echoed Zack's answer from the maze. "She's behind everything."

"HE'S INSANE!" came Helen's cry before she was again muffled with her scarf. "Shoot him!"

Angie looked at Maulden. *What the hell has Zack talked himself into?* "We've got to let the police handle it now," he called out to Zack. "What you're thinking's a mistake."

This time Maulden spoke up. "Zack, it's Detective Maulden. Angie's right. The pieces are coming together. I just got word that we found your friend Sandy... and we know you aren't responsible for any of this."

Zack collapsed against the pillar at hearing the news. He struggled to deal with his overwhelming emotions.

When no reply came from Zack, Angie broke in. "That's one less thing to worry about, Zack. Think about it... they found Sandy."

Maulden put more authority into his voice. "The system will deal with Helen Chandler. Zack." Still there was no response. "I read the files. You were right about everything. All we have to do now is get the word out."

"It's too late," came the hesitant answer. "Nobody'd listen."

"I'll make sure they do," Maulden committed. "We can turn this around if you'll trust us."

"Zack..." Angie added. "There's somebody else with us, too."

Doc Sandberg called out. "Zack... it's Linda Sandberg. We understand what you've been through. We can tell the world about what Helen Chandler has done."

The sound of Sandberg's voice was a surprise to Zack and so was his reaction to it. He started to cry. A flood of emotions poured out of his exhausted and confused mind. *Doc Sandberg was there... and Angie! His teachers. Why had he entangled them in this?*

Sandberg continued, "Please listen to me, Zack. You are a good man. Everyone knows that. A good man with a big heart. That's why you want to become a doctor, isn't it?" Her calming words got his attention and his feelings subsided a little. She added, "Do you remember The Oath of Hippocrates that we talked about in class? *I will prescribe regimen for the good of my patients according to my ability and my judgment and never do harm to anyone.* I believe those words mean something to you, despite what's happened. I have faith in you and so do these men who brought me here."

Angie's voice boomed out. "Come on, kid. What do you say? Will you let us take care of this mess?"

The wait seemed longer than it actually was. But after a few minutes Angie, Maulden, and Doc Sandberg saw a figure step cautiously from behind a boiler with Helen Chandler. Zack was still weighing the situation, but they could tell that the desperation inside him was dissipating.

Helen snarled a profanity from beneath her gag but Angie showed little interest as he swept Zack into a hug. "Way to go, kid," he whispered.

"Thanks," was all Zack could say.

Then as Angie put his arms around his protégé, Maulden noticed something in the corner of his eye—the image of a gun reflected on the side of stainless steel pipe: *Ted Gimble was on the catwalk preparing to shoot!*

Bellowing, "Look out!" the detective simultaneously spun towards the catwalk and squeezed off five rounds from his 45mm semi-automatic. In the same instant, Angie tackled Zack to the floor. But as it turned out, he need not have bothered.

Four of Maulden's slugs struck Gimble in the chest, sending

him hurtling from the platform to the equipment below. A violent blast of steam erupted from broken pipes beneath Gimble's body, signaling the grim punctuation to Zack's terrible odyssey.

Having heard the gunshots, Commander Daniels and his SWAT team rushed onto the scene moments later.

Maulden shouted, "CODE FOUR! CODE FOUR!" in a booming voice, providing procedural assurance that the situation was in-hand. Daniels quickly assessed the situation and then waved his men off.

Angie and Doc Sandberg were helping Zack to his feet when Daniels approached. "Mister Raskin," he began, "Senator Chandler called from the hospital and told us everything. Are you all right, sir?"

Zack reacted evenly. "I'll let you know when it's over."

"What are you talking about? It is over," Angie assured him.

"No, it isn't. Not yet," was his puzzling reply.

Having returned to the Los Angeles Ballroom of the hotel later that evening, a weakened Ron Chandler was in the middle of the toughest public appearance of his career. Reporters from every newspaper, magazine, wire service, broadcast outlet, and national network packed the room. Chandler was, after all, a media darling.

Flanked by police, senior aides, and physicians, the senator shifted uncomfortably in the sling that he wore. His mood was lower than the traveling press corps had ever seen. "Ambition in politics has a way of consuming people who don't have strength of character," he told them. "They sometimes convince themselves that the pursuit of power overrides the necessity for simple human decency... let alone law abiding behavior. As a result they are often driven to commit truly appalling acts. Sadly, my wife Helen has turned out to be one of those people."

Zack listened from the entrance, unseen by Chandler or the media. He was surprised that the senator's revelation of his wife's culpability did not have the same impact on him that it was having on the audience. But then, Zack had lived it. These folks were merely getting their initial taste.

When the buzz of disbelief among the crowd subsided, Chandler continued slowly, his voice wavering, "I am disheartened beyond words to tell you that as a result of what took place here last night and today, I have learned the details of Helen's victimization of innocent people in her deluded quest for my political success."

Zack headed for the lobby and as he reached the exit he caught a glimpse of Angie and Detective Maulden watching him from across the room. They nodded and Angie followed with a supportive thumbs-up, but while Zack appreciated the gesture he was beyond responding. He was numb inside and out.

The last words that he heard were as difficult for him as they seemed to be for Senator Chandler to say. "*With the help of members of my personal security team, Nicole Branson became Helen's first victim...*" Chandler stopped as his emotions got the best of him. Nobody moved. Nobody made a sound. Finally, he was able to complete his admission, "...because she discovered that Nicole loved me as much as I loved her..."

Emerging from the hotel Zack drew in the cool night air. Yet, while it was the first unencumbered breath that he had been able to take in a long time, there was little comfort in it. Just as there was almost none of the satisfaction that he thought he would feel upon clearing Nicole's name. Her fate remained unchanged. She was still gone and he was still alone. Those were two outcomes that he was unprepared for.

He walked up the incline of the circular drive to the Avenue of the Stars without thought. The act of motion felt better than standing still and anything that brought relief to his diminished state was welcome.

Then he stopped short—standing beside the majestic fountain in the traffic island was Nicole, looking exactly as she did when he first talked to her at the Greek Theatre. Radiant in that miraculous shimmering silver dress with a plunging halter neckline. However, he was startled by the uneasiness that overwhelmed him. He had sacrificed everything for her, pushing himself beyond his limitations, and thrusting himself into an intensely troubling personal realm.

Yes, he had done it all. But at what cost? Sandy was brutally murdered. And Zack had savagely taken a life with his own hands. There would be no forgetting that, or the image of Doug McKay lying helplessly in the hospital. They were all indelibly carved into his soul with a dull scalpel, graphic traumas that would permanently define who Zack Raskin is and what he feels. He could never be the same and he knew it. All the therapy in the world would barely make a dent in what was wrong with him.

Blinking those thoughts away, he wondered why Nicole – or at least the memory of her—had been so patient with him. She had endured so much, including finally being banished from his mind, and yet here she stood. Waiting for him.

He could not resist. Zack found himself inexorably drawn to her as he approached on the grassy median. "You did it, Zack," she offered timidly. "I can never thank you enough."

He could only nod in response. The feelings stirring inside him made conversation difficult. "You think Chandler's telling the truth?" he finally mumbled.

"Yes, I do."

He tried to determine if he believed that. Ultimately, despite everything that he previously assumed about the senator, he concluded that he did. As much as Zack did not want to believe it, the look of devastation on Chandler's face when he learned of the pregnancy was genuine. But the nuances of such details were fast falling away from Zack's concerns. The truth was all he cared about was he was somehow with Nicole again. He was lost once more in those glorious green eyes, transported to a place where suffering and distress dissolved into pure serenity. And it felt so good.

"God, I'd give anything if you could really be here," he confessed.

She moved closer and her body pressed against his. "How do you know I'm not?"

"You're only in my mind."

"I'm also in your heart, aren't I?"

"You know you are," he answered simply.

"Then what's the problem?"

Zack searched for a way to phrase it, to soften the truth. "Ron Chandler," he said, looking at the hotel. "You're in his heart, too."

She reached out to turn his face to hers and her soft hand felt warm on his skin. "Whatever I had with Ron ended. It was nothing compared to what I have with you."

The scent of her perfume enveloped him, as if directed to do so. "But you were going to have his baby," he countered.

"That was before I met you," she stated honestly. "You are an extraordinary man, Zack. I'm not worthy of what you've done for me, all that you've sacrificed," she added, folding her hands around his neck. "But I'd like to be."

"You're more than worthy," he assured her. "But seeing people who aren't there isn't exactly normal, you know?"

"All I know for certain is that many people spend their lives looking for what you and I have, and most of them never find it." Her affection for him was unambiguous and it seemed to touch the core of his being. "Doesn't that make hanging on to our relationship the right thing to do?"

He did not answer right away. As much as he wanted to, as much as he relished the idea of saying the words, he could not allow himself to succumb. "What happens if I say yes?" he tentatively asked. "One minute you're here and then... and then you're gone. It's been ripping me apart."

Her face flushed slightly as a gentle coastal breeze tousled her hair. Her voice was earnest and soothing. "You were there for me and I promise you that I will be here for you from now on. For as long as you want me... and in every way that you need me."

He wiped away a tear that trickled down her cheek. *If only that could really be true!* "What if I said I wanted you forever?" he asked.

She kissed his hand, never releasing her gaze from his. "Forever sounds nice."

Of course, forever was unattainable. Staying with her was not possible, yet here she was offering it to him. To stay with her meant being in the only realm where she can exist, where passion can only flourish without the limitations of reality.

Yet somewhere within the swirl of conflicting thoughts and emotions Zack understood that he had arrived at the crossroads his ordeal had been approaching all along—to reject Nicole once and for all or remain with her in her world.

A world that only existed in his mind. His expended, ravaged, aberrational mind.

Where this seemed to be heading was disquieting and Zack struggled to retrieve what might be left of his rational cognizance, but he could not. Because as inconceivable as her proposal was, it was also tempting.

Zack studied the innocence on her face as his dilemma reverberated inside him. Most people would call him deranged for even thinking about staying with Nicole. Certainly the psychology professors at UCLA would and he knew they would be right. After all, who would ever knowingly live in a state of non-reality? *Nobody in his right mind would ever consider such an act... right? Reality is not an option, it is mandatory.* At best, people who inhabit alternate dream worlds are considered eccentric. The deeper the dream, the less tolerated the person who dreams it. At the heartbreaking end of the spectrum looms madness.

Those who submit to non-reality are deemed *clinically insane*. And yet that was the choice being proposed to him now by the woman who made him feel as he had never felt before, to whom he had grown so attached that the rest of his life no longer had much meaning.

Sensing his quandary, she studied him hopefully. "You can always send me away if you don't feel the same."

Zack again looked into her eyes, which seemed larger than before. And even more innocent and loving. As if drawn into a reassuring hypnotic state something passed between them, something truly momentous. "That's not likely."

Nicole pulled him closer and shared with him what he hoped would be the first of a lifetime of warm, romantic kisses. Where they would inhabit an existence of uncompromising pleasure, where their love would be the essence of their lives, where he would wake up each morning to find her beside him, where he would never be alone. Where the stresses and sadness of the world would not, could not, intrude.

Finally, Zack made his decision.

He kissed her again, more fervently than ever. And when they separated, it was clear there would be no leaving her. Not now, not ever. At long last he knew that, it was time to turn the page. "I love you, Nicole."

"And I love you more than I can describe," she replied.

Then, taking his hand in hers they walked across the Avenue of the Stars towards the sparkling canyon of Century City office towers and wherever providence might choose to take them.

Zack and Nicole were together. That's all that mattered.

THE END

Epilogue

NEWS ITEM:

Entertainment Tonight News Transcript, June 15

Veteran record producer Elliot Kefler has announced the signing of a development deal with Ron Howard's Imagine Entertainment for an upcoming movie based on the life of singer Nicole Branson. Kefler reported that while the screenplay will touch on Nicole's brief infatuation with Senator Ron Chandler, the story will focus primarily on Kefler's own previously undisclosed lengthy romantic relationship with her.

"She was the one true love of my life," the producer declared at an emotional Beverly Hills Hotel press conference. "And I know I was the love of hers."

Entertainment Tonight has learned that luscious Jennifer Lawrence is being touted for the role of Nicole, with screen legend Matt Damon portraying her lover, mentor, and soul mate, music industry legend Elliot Kefler.

Other Books by Tom Blomquist

EYE OF THE STORM:
Directing for Film, Television & Emerging Media
Written by Maria Viera, Ph.D. & Tom Blomquist
Kendall Hunt Publishers
www.kendallhunt.com

Made in the USA
Middletown, DE
03 May 2018